Exeter House Publishing was founded in 2024 to bring attention to literary voices outside the mainstream. Beneath our feet a wealth of treasures lies buried, waiting to be discovered.

Courage shall be the harder
Heart the keener
Spirit the greater

ALEXANDER ADAMS is a British artist, poet, and critic whose work spans visual art, poetry, and cultural commentary. His art is held in public collections including the Victoria & Albert Museum and the National Museum of Wales. As a writer, he contributes to *The Critic*, *Apollo*, and *Print Quarterly*, and is the author of several books of poetry and essays exploring art, politics, and censorship. In 2018, he received the Francis Bacon MB Art Foundation Artist Scholarship. He lives and works in the north of England.

The Naked Spur

Alexander Adams

EXETER HOUSE
PUBLISHING

Published by Exeter House Publishing

© Alexander Adams, 2025

Used under license to Exeter House Publishing

All rights are reserved. No part of this publication may be reproduced, stored in a retrieval system, or transmitted in any form or by any means, electronic, mechanical, photocopying, recording, or otherwise, without prior permission of Exeter House Publishing. Enquiries concerning reproduction outside the scope of the above should be directed to Exeter House Publishing.

FIRST EDITION

A catalogue record for this book is available from the National Library of Australia

ISBN 978-1-923104-93-8 Paperback
ISBN 978-1-923104-94-5 E-book

Exeter House Publishing has no responsibility for the persistence or accuracy of URLs for external or third-party Internet websites referred to in this publication and does not guarantee that any content on such websites is, or will remain, accurate or appropriate.

This is a work of fiction. Although some of the places and institutions mentioned exist, none of the characters are based on actual individuals, living or dead. Any resemblance is purely coincidental.

CONTENTS

I   3
II   157

The Naked Spur

I

(1)

The key did not fit the lock. A. held the key ring in his hand and tried the same key. Again, it did not turn the lock. He tried a second key. That did not fit.

"They're putting the squeeze on us. No two ways about it."

A black man wearing a baggy sweatshirt was descending the stairs. There was plaster on his hands.

"Take a look at the poster."

A. looked over his shoulder and saw a laminated poster tied to the gate. He stepped over to read it.

"We're sitting tenants but that don't mean a fuck to them."

A. could hear the sound of hands being scrubbed under running water as he read.

"Those bastards would burn us out if they could. They still might."

A. walked from the gate to the administration office. On the gate was the same laminated poster and under it a photocopied flyer. The door was open.

"Yes, I know. Here's your key. Sign here."

The woman at the desk held a key out over a register with signatures. She brushed her hair behind an ear.

Against her other ear was a telephone.

"We're setting up a committee to fight this," she whispered to A. as he signed the paper. "The first meeting's tonight. I hope you can come." Then in a louder voice she said, "Yes, the business manager or the- Yes, I'll hold."

Back at the door, the man was drying his hands on his sweatshirt.

"Resist?" He nodded to flyer pasted to the toilet door. "No way. I'm fucking beat. I've got a van coming tomorrow."

"You have somewhere to go?"

"A mate of mine is a photographer. He's got a space in Hackney. He said he'll store my stuff for a bit."

"You're not going to this meeting?"

"Nah. Fuck that. Committees about committees. I wish them all the best but they're no match for the owners. Those Jew landlords'll just change the locks again and again. They're going to wear us down. Grind us to powder, man. They know there's people sleeping in these units but they changed the locks anyway. Place could have burnt down and we'd be toast. Changing the locks while there's people asleep. That's sick. How can you fight that? This place is finished. No committee'll save it."

He started up the stairs.

"Good luck, man."

"Yeah. Good luck."

The new key opened the lock. A. closed the door, paused then walked back to Limehouse station.

THE NAKED SPUR

(2)

The sycamore trees on Grays Inn Road had shed their leaves. They lay on the pavements and at the kerbs where passing traffic stirred them.

An array of filing cabinets was being set out on the pavement by a man. The cabinets were in many colours, labels on the sides partly peeled away. A boy carried out a pair of tall lamps. The man gestured him back inside the shop. On a chair, a fat man was reading a newspaper.

A. stopped walking and opened a card drawer. The fat man looked up.

"I do you a deal."

A. looked over at him.

"Fifteen pounds. Antique."

"I only have five."

The fat man grunted and returned to his newspaper.

A. walked away heading north, leaving the drawer open behind him. At the corner he turned right into Clerkenwell Road. He passed a pub with a green facade; a board outside read "Strippers every day. New girls at 2pm. Free entry." Further on were an art material shop and a hardware store. He reached a newsagents and entered it.

He looked at magazines on the top shelf. He picked a couple, leafed through them, replaced them. On the cover of a magazine called Sex Direct was a woman wearing jewellery and make-up, kneeling on a bed. A circular inset showed a woman lifting off her T-shirt. There was a graphic strip blanking over her eyes. Text read "Local contacts. Meet me inside!"

A. carried the magazine to the counter and paid for it. He put it in his bag before leaving the shop.

Clerkenwell Road to Hatton Garden. Two Indian men rested against a car, both concentrating on their mobile-phone screens. Orthodox Jews carrying suitcases walked in synchronised step. A security van pulled up outside a jewellers.

A. emerged on Holborn and crossed over the street. He entered a door next to a fast-food restaurant, went through another door and reached a small lobby. A guard at the desk gave him a nod. Waiting for the lift, he checked his watch.

At the fifth floor he exited the lift and used an electronic pass to unlock a door. The room he was in had a cluster of mismatching desks with computers, chairs with stained upholstery pushed underneath. A. opened a drawer and put his bag in. He walked back to the lift lobby and walked through a galley kitchen to reach a toilet. He locked the cubicle door behind him and buckled over the toilet bowl, vomiting until nothing more came up. He pulled a length of paper from the toilet roll and wiped the bowl rim before flushing away the wad of tissue.

Outside, the lobby was empty.

(3)

The couple was arguing on the street.

A. leant on the windowsill in the office. The air conditioning from the grill unsettled his shirt front.

The couple was standing on the corner of Grays Inn Road and Holborn. The woman was wearing a

THE NAKED SPUR

dress and high heels. The man had baggy clothes and a baseball cap. He was shrugging, arms wide. She was shaking, jabbing a finger at him. As they walked by, passersby were turning their heads to watch. The man was shaking his head, face averted. The woman was shouting. No sound passed through the double-glazing. The woman bent towards him. The man approached her, jutted his face to hers. Then he took a step back and gestured her away.

At the clothing shop, a pair of sales assistants loitered at the entrance. People at the bus stop were watching.

The woman walked a few steps, shouted at the man and turned to cup her face in her hands. Her head shook and sides jerked convulsively. The man was shouting at her, waving an arm. A woman stopped by the crying woman and spoke to her. The crying woman wiped her eyes, shook her head and wrapped her arms around herself. Again she shook her head and the second woman continued on her way.

The man was closer to her, still talking, gesturing less. Her face was lowered. She did not reply. He approached and put his face into her field of vision. He offered her an open hand. He put a hand on her shoulder and she twisted away. He talked some more. When he put his hand on her shoulder a second time, she did not withdraw. Talking, he drew her closer. He held her head to kiss her. She tried to move away, then went passive. He moved his left hand from her head to the small of her back, his right cupped her breast. Her arms hung by her sides. The man smiled and whispered into her ear.

The sales assistants went inside.

With his left hand, the man steered the woman along the pavement. When he kissed her again, she touched his sides. The man guided the woman round the corner and out of sight up Grays Inn Road.

(4)

At lunchtime, A. left the office and walked north up Grays Inn Road on the east side pavement.

There was a dead man lying on the asphalt by a bus stop. His profile was a white cut-out against the black. His coat was spread under him. A briefcase stood upright on the pavement. A semi-circle of bystanders was looking at him. On the corner, people queuing at the bank ATM craned their heads. None left the queue to view close up. A girl with curly hair was talking into a mobile phone, leaning out to look at the corpse.

At the junction with Clerkenwell Road, A. turned right. He stopped outside a black-fronted shop with "T.N. Lawrence & Son" written on the fascia. Inside the shop, he browsed racks of oil paint tubes before selecting two brushes and paying for them at the counter.

By the time he reached the bus stop, an ambulance was pulling away from the onlookers, siren and lights off.

(5)

A. sat on the bed, leaning on the headboard. There was a sketchbook on his lap, a magazine open beside him. He looked at the magazine and drew a square in pencil in the sketchbook and filled it with an outline of a man

THE NAKED SPUR

on a sofa. Next was a nude woman bending over, seen from the rear. Below the photograph was a box of text giving her age, location and sexual preferences and a reference number to quote in order to contact her via the magazine. A woman was wearing net stockings and panties with a slit in them; the fold of her post-partum belly sagged over the waistband of her panties. A woman lying on her front on a bed, propped herself on her elbows and smiled over her shoulder. A woman on her side on grass pulled up a buttock to show her anus; a packet of cigarettes lay on the turf beside. A woman in a red, rubber basque posed by a chimney breast; the mantelpiece over the gas fire had a collection of ornamental elephants. A girl with bared breasts slumped in a chair, smoking, cigarette in hand. A man in bathing trunks sat on a kitchen stool; through French windows palm trees were visible. Two photographs: a woman with a striped top, naked from the waist down, bent over a camping-area picnic table; in a second photograph a portly man wearing flip-flops stood nude by that table. In both photographs the faces had been removed. A man with a grey beard rolled up his T-shirt under his chin to show a pale stomach and exposed genitals; the doorframe around him bowed convex with lens distortion. An Asian woman on a sheet-covered seat splayed her fingers in a triangle of pubic hair, her teeth bright between her lips. Image of a smiling face above cleavage, cropped above mouth and below midriff. A woman seen in profile lifting her blouse in a living room with floral wallpaper and closed curtains; her eyes were blanked by a stripe. A limp penis gripped by a hand, one testicle riding over the waistband of underpants. A Fillipina in a bathing costume sitting on a carpet. Close-up of the side of a woman's belly and hip speckled with droplets, tuft of pubic hair visible; behind was a grid of wet tiles. Passport-booth photograph of a man wearing chequered shirt and sunglasses. A muscular male torso. View of a woman lying with open legs on a white rug, beyond her a collection of video cassettes and a compact dictionary; a dormant television screen flared with camera flash. A woman with long blonde hair brushed over her face was sitting on a washing machine, legs spread. In a mirror, a man photographed himself, flash reflection covering his upper body and head. A woman on a road verge opened a long raincoat to reveal her pierced and tattooed figure. A plump woman stood on a hotel balcony, skin red next to white stucco. A slim man with an erection stood in front of a cloth backdrop, camera lead in hand, head cropped from the picture. A woman lay on a duvet, face and jewellery scribbled over in ballpoint. A brunette wearing underwear was next to a car, the registration plate blanked out. A black woman pulled aside her underwear; she was seated on a leather sofa. Blurred shot of male genitals tied with a cord. An old woman in a silk slip, objects on a bedside table obliterated with black pen marks. Woman in a lace nightie lifted up to her hips sat on a stool; her head was thrown back in the act of laughter, eyes blanked out. A slender woman glistening wet stood erect in a hallway, hands clasped over her vagina. A brunette sitting on stairs cupping her breasts. A man was at the far end of a room by a built-in wardrobe, penis stiff, face covered

THE NAKED SPUR

by a white oval. A woman was standing by a brick wall, wearing an elasticated bowtie and pinafore, nothing else. A woman with peroxide-bleached hair with one foot on the bumper of a Porsche. A black woman on her knees, upright, back straight, arms extended by her sides. A hairy belly over a tiny, shrivelled penis. A fat man with crossed arms, by him a kitchen door, edge of the picture frame cropping out his head. A glistening hand gripping a breast, unfocused, camera flash putting highlights on the knuckles and fingernails.

(6)

Sun was shining through the skylight of the studio. The pitched skylight covered one third of the studio. It made sharp forms on the concrete floor and cast T-shape shadows from screws on the walls. It lit blank canvases resting on the floor, showing the linen grain. On a sheet of glass were some brushes, a couple of paint tubes, a plastic tub with clear liquid, another tub with brushes. There were tangled rags, newspapers brown and brittle, spattered with diluted paint, two white chairs and an easel. Against a wall was a stack of canvases, some in polythene, others in bubble wrap.

The door opened and A. walked in. He was wearing boots and jeans. He dropped his bag and took off his coat, pulling a sweatshirt he took from the floor over the one he already wore. His breath made bright clouds in the sunlight.

He dusted the glass sheet with a rag. Then he sat down and squeezed on to the sheet two lines of paint: one white, one black. Between these, A. dripped oil from a bottle. He reached over, picked up a square canvas and hung it from a screw at his seated eye height. From his bag he took a magazine and a bulldog clip. He flipped the pages for several minutes, turning them back and forth until he paused to fold round the pages and clip them in place. He propped the magazine on the chair nearby.

Then he began to paint.

A. diluted paint with oil and the liquid in the tub. Referring to the page, A. sketched out forms on the canvas. At first they were rough, imprecise and constantly corrected. Forms became more solid: a figure, a door, a handle. Outlines began to fill.

He charged his brush with medium grey and blocked in inside edges of the figure. A. used a rag to clean an area. He painted with the brush in his right hand, occasionally exchanging it for one in his left hand. He mixed a paler grey with a third brush, others in his left hand. More oil was dripped on the glass. He tucked brushes under his left thigh between leg and seat, reaching for them without looking, eyes fixed on the painting. He mixed a darker grey to the consistency of mustard and applied it in short horizontal dabs. He did not move as he painted, he reaching down to mix paint and changing brushes without altering his posture.

There were the sounds of hammering, footsteps, doors shutting, a radio turned up loud. Someone was operating an electric drill. A toilet was flushed. A heavy object was carried down stairs by two people. Sunlight shapes crossed the floor.

A. cleaned a brush in the tub and dried it with a scrap

THE NAKED SPUR

of cloth. He flexed his shoulders and looked between magazine and canvas, breathing on his cupped hands. Then he mixed a black on the palette, wiped the excess from his brush and added to the painting. Then white, medium grey, light grey, then white again.

Later, A. went to the door and switched on fluorescent tubes. Above the skylight was a building dark against an indigo sky, windows lit. In the glass was a reflection of him looking up.

The painting was finished. On the canvas was an image of a woman standing with hands pressed on a closed door, back turned. Her hair was long and dark. She was naked except for a thong.

A. scraped the glass with a palette knife and rubbed it clear with a cloth damp with turpentine. He washed the used brushes in turpentine, flicking excess liquid on to newspapers. He picked up a cake of coal-tar soap and carried it with the brushes out of the studio. The corridor was unlit. A. hit a switch and lights came on. He walked left to a turn in the corridor and reached a metal sink next to a fire exit. He washed the brushes, rinsed them in running water, washed his hands then turned off the tap. He leant over and spat into the sink. In his saliva was a flower of red. He washed it away.

In the studio, he put the brushes in a jar and took off his top sweatshirt. He pulled on his coat, switched off the lights and locked the studio door behind him. He went right and reached a door. Through the door was a space leading to a staircase, a toilet and a gate. The gate opened on to a courtyard. Another gate opened on to the street. A. passed a mini-cab depot and crossed the highway at the traffic lights. He entered Narrow Street and walked east. At the canal lock, there was a view of the Thames in the gap between converted wharf-side warehouses. The lights of Lavender Wharf flickered on the river. Past a convenience store, which cast light over the pavement from a plate-glass window, the view was gone. The street began to widen. A. walked by "The Grapes" and "The Booty", each issuing noise and smell of beer and tobacco smoke.

At the end of Narrow Street, A. crossed a junction. At the underpass A. approached a spiral staircase to Westferry Circus. As he reached it, a burly man emerged, zipping his flies. Following a few paces behind him was a young woman hitching up a pair of knickers with one hand; her skirt was rucked up around her waist. In her other hand was a mobile phone into which she was talking in Russian. Her high heels struck an irregular staccato on the stone stairs.

As A. rounded Westferry Circus and moved away from Canary Wharf Tower, he descended a ramp to Westferry Road. As he continued, walking south, office blocks were replaced by brick houses and terraces. Carrier bags snagged bus stops, polystyrene food containers were locked in frozen puddles.

A. entered a mews of brick houses and unlocked a front door. He kicked off his boots and climbed the unlit stairs. Nearby a television was on. A. went to a kitchen and made a mug of tea and a sandwich and took them upstairs.

The room he entered had a double bed, chest of drawers, wardrobe, writing bureau, kitchen chair and armchair. The armchair was worn green velvet, braiding coming loose, material peppered by moth holes. The furniture and floor were covered with books and papers. The carpet was green, walls dark red, ceiling white.

A. lay on the bed, eyes closed. Then he sat up to eat.

(7)

A lorry filled with gravel was waiting at the gate to the concrete yard. Wind blew grit into A.'s eyes. He blinked away the particles. On the gate a laminated letter had been tied. One word had been scratched across the plastic.

A. keyed a code into the lock and pushed open the gate. Rain had washed plaster dust into spaces between cobbles. Droplets on the brickwork winked in the sun.

A bill had been put under A.'s door. He pushed it aside with a foot and laid aside his coat and bag. He approached three square paintings on the right-hand side wall. He brought his face close to one and touched part with a fingertip. It came away dry but the other two canvases were wet. He added the dry painting to a small stack of other square paintings, from which he brushed leaf litter and a dead spider, laying over the canvases a sheet of plastic. Out of his bag he took two Sunday newspapers and removed half of the sections, which he added to the stack of papers in one corner. The remainder he returned to his bag.

A. tuned the radio to football commentary. He worked on a canvas of a woman stripping in a hallway. After a few hours he left the studio. Occasionally, he drank from a bottle of water.

On the street, he turned left along Cable Street and then took the first right up a side street under the train tracks. To the left was a yard with a high fence. It was stacked high with wooden pallets, the ends were sprayed different colours; hanks of cellophane dangled from them. At Commercial Road, he turned right and entered a kebab shop.

He ordered food and rested his arms on the chest-high counter, watching passing traffic. A fat man with tattoos came in and bought a double portion of chips. A girl in a tracksuit bought a burger. A Pakistani youth came in for a can of drink. As the man went to fetch it, the youth tapped a coin on the countertop.

Outside, a woman bundled in clothes waited at the bus stop.

A. paid for his order and took his food to the studio. When he finished, he tied the tray up in a plastic bag and put it in the sack of rubbish.

He returned to painting and continued after it was dark, working under the fluorescent tubes. He pulled the cuffs of his sweatshirt over his hands. That evening the radio signal fluctuated, voices rising and sinking on a swell of static.

(8)

Harry Dent entered the gallery with two cardboard cups. The wind that came through the open doorway upset a pile of receipts, which A. bent to retrieve. They were from framers and removals companies.

"How much do I owe you?"

THE NAKED SPUR

"Don't worry about it."

Dent handed A. a cup and put his on the only clear space on his desk.

Across the square a window-cleaner was working outside a café. The wind was turning over dry leaves.

"No sales then."

"Sorry."

A. heard fingers on a keyboard.

"If it's any consolation, it frustrates me as much as it does you."

A. walked around the gallery, drinking coffee. One canvas showed the exterior of a warehouse in afternoon light. Another showed a brilliant sunset, only clouds and sky showing. A third was of ice skaters blurred against a white ground.

"That one's sold," said Dent. "The buyer gave me a deposit yesterday. He's coming to collect it this afternoon."

Another painting in the same style was on the wall. It had a red dot next to it.

"His work seems to sell."

"It's great. His work sells itself. His sales make up about a third of my entire turnover and his prices are going up all the time. It's a dream. There have been a couple of articles about his work. That always helps, of course. Have you met him?"

A. shook his head.

"It's amazing. He's almost blind. He has this eye condition. It's degenerative and there's nothing that can be done about it. He's only my age. He'll be completely blind in a few years."

(9)

A. stepped from the pavement into a whitewashed two-storey building off Whitechapel. Through a set of glass doors, he passed an array of easels and shelves of box frames. He climbed a set of metal stairs. He turned right into a space filled with racks of canvas on rollers. The canvases were cotton duck and linen, both primed and unprimed, in different widths and weights. Labels gave the weights per square metre and prices by the metre length. On a table below were a measuring stick and a heavy pair of scissors. On the facing wall were shelves with bundles of canvas bound with adhesive tape. After searching for a minute, A. picked off a shelf a bundle of linen and put it under an arm.

Under a skylight were racks of wooden bars, chamfered and mitred at the ends. On the floor was a bucket of thin wooden wedges. On one side were shelves with tubs, on the other partitions with folios in different sizes and makes, graded by size.

A. picked a one-litre tub marked "Roberson's Primer" then walked to the racks of wooden bars. He emptied the rack marked "16" in pen.

In the next room customers queued at a cash till. A girl with reddish hair cut in a bob was restocking shelves of sketchpads. She waved to A. He waved back. Down one aisle a woman with a walking stick was watching an assistant roll sheets of paper. Once the sheets were rolled in brown paper, the assistant wrote on the outside the price. In another aisle, two Japanese girls were examining pots of acrylic paint.

THE NAKED SPUR

On the PA system "Gimme Shelter" by The Rolling Stones was playing. Outside, a muezzin was chanting the call to prayer.

A. took hog-hair brushes in two sizes from a display and carried his selection to the counter. A slim girl was working the cash till. The queue was four-people long. A. looked over the magazines by the till: Art Monthly, Artists' Newsletter, Modern Painters, Art Review. On the cover of Art International the third item listed was "The Death of Collecting: Art Consumption after Aesthetics, by Nelson Nicobar". The queue moved along. A. did not touch the magazines.

On the way out, A. stopped at a pin board close to the entrance. There were invitation cards to private views, posters for exhibitions and art competitions, handwritten notes offering accommodation, studio shares, used art equipment, painting holidays, van hire and nude models. At the reception desk sat a short girl wearing a hijab, head bowed over a book.

A. tore a stub with a telephone number from a sheet offering van hire. Putting the stub in a pocket, A. lifted the bag on to a shoulder and left the shop.

In the courtyard of Cable Street Studios were two Orthodox Jews in long, black coats and wide-brim hats. Ringlets hung by their ears. One had a clipboard. The other had a camera and was photographing parts of the buildings. He swung an arm to indicate an expanse of brickwork. The other wrote something on the paper fixed to his clipboard.

At the administration office, there was a face at the window.

In the passage was cardboard packaging flattened, a collection of aerosol cans and a sponge roller hard with emulsion.

In his studio, A. put down the bag and stretched. He went to the stereo and switched on football commentary. Out of the bag he took some wooden bars and assembled six square stretchers from them. There were two bars left unused. He tapped the frames with a hammer, then, measuring diagonally, adjusted each until he put them aside.

A. took out the bundle of linen from the bag and laid it out. He put the stretcher frames on it and cut the material around them with a pair of scissors, making each square bigger than the stretchers by an inch and a half on every side.

One stretcher on a square of linen, A. folded over a side of cloth and tacked it to the stretcher. He did the same on the bar the opposite side, then the two other sides, placing the tacks in the centres of each side. Then he put two tacks in one of the sides, each equidistant from the centre tack. Then he repeated the procedure on the opposite bar. Once the canvas was fixed over the stretcher, A. tapped the bars on the inside hitting them outwards. The linen became tight. It yielded under A.'s touch then sprang back. The material reverberated to a tap.

He worked until all six canvases were stretched.

A. turned up the volume of the radio. He loosened his shoulders and neck.

He poured some primer into an empty tub and added water. When this was mixed, he painted the front of each canvas with the solution, hanging each from a screw in the walls as it was completed.

A. sat and ate a chocolate bar. There were black-wing gulls and smoke in the white sky, pigeons perched on the wall outside. A distant rumble came then a puff of dust rose. He picked up used newspaper sheets from the floor and bundled them into a black sack. To those he added empty paint tubes, plastic lids, a broken glass jar, strips of tape matted with dust, a paintbrush, its bristles worn to a stump.

A. pressed his palm against the canvas he had first hung up, then examined the heel of his hand. It was clean. Taking the canvases from the wall in the order they had gone up, A. painted them with neat primer from the tub he had opened, then replaced them on their screws. A. left the studio and rinsed the brush under the tap in the corridor. When the brush was clean, he spat into the sink and looked at it. He twisted the tap on then off and went back to the studio.

It was almost dark. He did not switch on the lights.

In the studio, A. dropped his brush on a stack of folded newspapers. He switched off the radio and locked the door after him on his way out.

(10)

Off Manchester Road was Island Gardens, a small park next to the Thames. The traffic noise and sound of road works diminished here. Beyond a confectionary kiosk was a brick rotunda with a glass dome. Facing A. as he entered the building was the black casing of a lift shaft. The dome above surged with leaf shadow. A. descended a flight of metal stairs which spiralled around the lift shaft. They led to the lower exit of the lift and a narrow, circular tunnel. The floor was flagged with stone which was dark with condensation. The wall was covered with glazed tiles which were cream colour. Along the tunnel apex ran tubing between lights and security cameras.

A. walked the tunnel. A man wheeling his bicycle. A woman with two children, the children's shouts echoing.

Stairs at the other end led up to a second rotunda. At the exit, Italian teenagers were photographing each other. A. passed the Cutty Sark and "Goddard's" and went up Creek Road. Two seagulls were fighting over something black with grit in a polystyrene tray. At Creek Bridge he crossed the road. Beside the concrete works there were two barges tethered on Deptford Creek, both heaped high with sand.

At the corner of Copperas Street there was a closed tyre warehouse. Against the wire-mesh gates piles of tyres pressed outwards. The building's windows were smashed. Pocked bollards showed rust pits. A mattress was slumped over an external staircase.

The road was uneven; large puddles spanned its width. Loose chippings lay on the road surface and pavement. The street was flanked by boundaries of timber held by concrete posts. Visible over them were crushed cars, a bus chassis, scaffolding, wooden pallets. A crane with grabber was motionless. The asphalt was black with sump oil. Puddles had rainbow petrol glazes. A fire sent smoke and wood ash into the air.

A van was parked two wheels on the kerb. In both cab

seats men slept, heads back, mouths agape.

Where Copperas Street joined Creekside, A. made a left turn. To his right were houses, then four-storey blocks of flats built in brick; to his left were more yards: a recycling centre, a tool-hire yard, warehouses. A train viaduct cut Creekside. When he reached an entrance between grey walls, he turned off the street. Across a yard, he entered a two-storey building and took stairs to the top floor.

A. knocked on a double door. It was opened by a man with sandy hair. There was paint on his trouser cuffs, shoes and hands. He smiled.

"Hi, Adam."

"Hi, A. How are you? Come in."

The studio was hot. On the walls were abstract paintings, rectangles of strong colour on a white background. There were open tins and tubs half full of paint on the floor. The colours were custard yellow, pumpkin orange, dark green. In a corner was a panel standing on one side in a pool of cerulean.

A. took off his jacket, placed it over a chair.

"This one first."

The two men carried a panel across the studio, tacky dabs of paint stuck newspaper sheets to their shoes. They laid the board flat on four upturned tins on the floor. On his knees, Hartley adjusted the position of the tins. Hartley put out some tins and they put out a second panel as big as the first.

Hartley led A. to half a dozen large wooden crates. The crates were cross-braced and held together with nails and screws. The edges were worn and dirty. On the sides were labels in different languages: German, French, Portuguese.

Hartley patted one.

"Down there." He nodded towards the floor.

They put the crate on its back. Hartley levered off the cover to reveal a painting screwed into the crate with mirror plates. Hartley used an electric screwdriver to unscrew the panel and they lifted it to the wall where they hung it on two nails. They brought over a scarlet-and-black painting, which Hartley fixed into the crate.

With a grunt they righted the crate on its side. They took a few breaths.

"Are you painting much?" Hartley was pulling labels off the top edge.

"A bit."

Hartley rested an arm on the crate.

"And the studio?"

A. shrugged, hands in pockets.

"Pretty soon there'll be no studios left. You heard Delta Studios folded? A month or two ago. All the places are getting closed down, done up, sold off."

"Your old studio?"

"The waiting list for those places is two years. More. And the artists' committee has to approve your application before your name goes on the list."

They walked to the wall. Hartley looked along the surface of a primed panel. He ran his palm over it.

"This place is good but expensive. You pay business rates here. Studios run by charities are exempt but this is an industrial unit."

Hartley studied the white panel, hands on hips.

THE NAKED SPUR

"What can you do?"

Rolls of used masking tape had been loosely coiled. Paint on the edges was pink, mauve, ultramarine. They had been arranged in a row on a plank.

They sat for a while. Hartley smoked. A. wiped paint out of the treads of his soles with a scrap of shirt cloth.

"Are you around next week?" Hartley asked A.

"Yes."

"Some new panels are being delivered."

"I'll give you a hand."

"Call me."

"Sure."

On his way to the stairs, A. passed a shaven-headed man. He was leaning out of a window, smoking. He was saying into a mobile phone: "I don't care. Give me a reason to care. You don't think I'm serious. I'm serious. This is no game."

(11)

A. washed the last paint from his hands and went to his room. As he was closing the curtains, he paused. A couple was crossing the courtyard. The girl was wearing a blue-and-white scarf, a letter "Q" visible on it. Her hair was cut in a bob. The man was wearing a hood. They passed out of sight. There was a pause then a door shut. The man walked away alone.

A. closed the curtains.

(12)

The woman in the magazine photograph was in late

middle age. Her hair was cut short. She was naked. Her lower arms, face and upper chest were sunburned. The rest of her body was untanned. There was an arc indicating where a round-neck top had covered her lower chest. Her hands were on her hips, head tilted back, cocked to one side. She was smiling slightly.

A. was crouching forward, reaching for a tube of paint on the floor. He squeezed out some white and mixed a light grey. He applied it to the thigh of the figure. The figure was complete. The background was bare primer except for a few watery marks in one corner.

There was a cough. A. stopped painting, waited. After a while he extended his brush to the canvas. There was another cough, a shuffled step. A. froze. He waited.

A. rose to his feet. With deliberate steps he moved to the door. There he put his ear to the door. After a minute he unlocked the door with keys that were in the lock. Pause. Silence. He opened the door. The corridor was deserted, dark. Remaining where he stood, he switched off his studio light. No light came from under any door along the corridor. The door at the end of the corridor leading to the courtyard showed an unbroken line of light underneath.

A. waited. Nothing changed. He switched on the studio light and locked his door. Somewhere there was a footstep. A. sat. He opened his hands and looked at them. The palms were wet.

(13)

"I walked in on him sitting in my living room having a wank."

THE NAKED SPUR

Dent rolled his eyes.

"I said, what are you doing. And he replied, cool as you like, that he was checking his foreskin. Well, I'm sorry, I am a man too and I know you don't do it by tugging it up and down. I don't care what he says; he was stark naked, sitting on my sofa tossing himself off. Sex is one thing but you've to have boundaries. Have a bit of decorum for pity's sake! So I gave him his marching orders."

"This was the Syrian?"

A. was stooping to examine a stack of framed paintings on the gallery floor.

"Did I tell you about him? No, he went ages ago. I couldn't take it any more. He was a terrible moaner. He never stopped complaining. Non-stop it was. He was twenty-five, no, twenty-six. He had nothing to complain about. He was unattached, no financial worries. I was picking up the tab when we went clubbing. I said, for Christ's sake, at your age I was working all hours. I didn't know what I wanted from life."

Dent swung an arm.

"I said, appreciate what you've got and be grateful. Not that he should be grateful for me, but for his life in general. Life could be a lot worse."

A. stood up.

"What did he say?"

Dent spread his hands.

"Oh, he looked at me as if I'd gone mad. He didn't seem to understand at all." He gave a laugh. "I know how to pick them. So, it's me and Bruno again."

The Chinese Crested Dog, between framed canvases

27

on the floor, turned its head.

"I'm sure it will work out."

"I'm sure it will. Listen, I'm not having any luck with your work at the moment. No takers at all, I'm afraid. Nibbles but no bites. I think we should have some new stuff from you."

A. pressed together his lips.

"There is something. There's some in the old style and a new series."

"Good, then I'll come by. Cable Street Studios, isn't it? I can come by on Saturday before I open the gallery. Is ten o'clock okay for you?"

(14)

The girl with reddish hair was rolling paper on a wide table. She wrapped each roll with brown paper, secured it with tape from a dispenser and wrote on the outside. When she finished each roll, she ticked an item on the list beside her.

"Hi, A. How are you?"

"Hey, Eleanor. Not interrupting, am I?"

"I'm finishing this order. No problem."

"How's your art going?"

"Fine, when I'm in the studio. The teaching takes it out of me. Don't get me wrong, it's satisfying. More satisfying than this place."

She cut a sheet of wrapping paper, sliding the parted blades of the scissors through it.

"I got back my pictures. Finally."

"Yes?"

"Yeah. I had words with Gareth. I said to him, that's

no way to treat paintings, just pushing them into the store with no wrapping. The floor is dirty and one sharp corner or loose staple—"

She shivered.

"He's been in the business long enough. It's shocking. I saw one of Angela's paintings in a corner and it had a tear in the front. I asked one of the assistants what happened and she mumbled something about the courier having an accident. I didn't believe her for a second. My paintings would be safer being driven around the country and unloaded every day for a year than they would be supposedly safe in Gareth's store for one month. My God. Angela is Gareth's darling now Saatchi's bought her stuff. Imagine if he treats his star that way, what he's doing to our stuff. I promised myself I had to say something to him the next I saw him."

"What did he say?"

"Oh, he acted as though I didn't know what I was talking about. I felt like he was going to pat me on the head, and say, there, there, dear. Silly girlie."

"Old-school style."

"Old everything. I think you were right splitting from the gallery."

She sighed and tossed the pen on the table.

"I said, Gareth, this isn't good enough. I found a couple of staples stuck in the side of a canvas of mine in the store. The edges are getting all scuffed and dirty. You're asking a lot of money for these paintings, and not getting it, and buyers can see you slinging the paintings about like, well, like you don't give a flying damn about them. Or rather he's getting his assistants to do the slinging, he's not in a position to do it. And then you're asking people to pay top dollar for them. In future, when my work comes off the walls, it comes back the studio where I know it's safe."

"What did he say?"

Eleanor closed her eyes and pouted her lips.

"He said one of the assistants was doing it. But the only reason they treat paintings that way is because they've seen him do it. I've seen him do it. He acts as if paintings were framed, like he was still in a time when you could just stick paintings on the floor and it didn't damage the pictures. Practically everything is shown unframed now. That's why the canvas edges are so important. Well, when he started dealing I think everything had gilt frames and glass and he hasn't caught up."

Eleanor gathered the rolls and put them into a box and taped the list to the outside.

"His eyesight's going too. I don't think he sees the scratches."

She swept a hand over the table.

"And then he goes on about the latest visit by Charles Saatchi. Like I care. He hasn't sold anything of mine to Saatchi."

Eleanor leaned over the table and said in a quieter voice, "Did he ask you if you'd be willing to cut your price by a third to sell to him?"

"To Saatchi?"

"Yes."

"No. He asked you?"

"Yes. I said I'd think about it."

She frowned.

"It's not very fair giving a rich collector a big discount and a little old lady who spends her life's savings is charged full price. Not that I think an old lady would be buying my work."

"The little old lady hasn't got a giant gallery in St Johns Wood in which to exhibit your pictures to the public."

"It helps an artist's profile," Eleanor conceded. "But he's buying with big discounts, showing the work, promoting it, then selling it at auction. He's getting a discount at one end and a mark-up at the other. How is that fair?"

A girl with an asymmetrical hairstyle and nose piercings approached up to the counter and ordered half a dozen sheets of black paper.

When she had gone, Eleanor said, "As soon as I get an offer I'm off."

"From Gareth's gallery?"

"From there and here. They're such jerks. I had so many problems rearranging my shifts when my teaching days changed. Like I'd rather be here than teaching."

She snorted.

"I don't think the artists here are going to last much longer. Goran's getting in more his Croatian cousins. They're such chauvinists."

"Keep your options open," she said, weighing the scissors in her hand. "I am."

(15)

"I can't take them."

Dent was standing with his arms folded. He was looking at four square paintings of figures undressed and half undressed.

"Don't get me wrong, I like them. You've got something but…"

He shrugged and turned his hands palm up.

"It's not something I could have in the gallery. Nude paintings are difficult to sell. People assume they sell, artists assume they sell, but really it's a tricky proposition. I hardly ever have nudes at the gallery. Purely on business terms, I've found them bad deals. Hard to shift. You get collectors coming back a week later saying their wife won't have it in the house and can they have their money back please. Or a new partner has a problem with an old painting and the owner wants to trade it in for something else which leaves me with a nude that I have trouble selling. Corporate collectors won't touch nudes. Specialist galleries deal nudes. I don't. Or rather, I can't, for practical reasons. Like I say, there's some good stuff here but..."

A. sat down.

"And that's the stuff that you've been working on since February?"

"There is some other work." A. indicated canvases leaning on a second wall.

Dent paused.

"I like these better. I could take some of these."

Dent chose four paintings and A. wrapped them in plastic.

Dent said, "Don't get too dry in your handling." He pointed to the square paintings. "They're a bit detailed.

I like it when your style is more fluid."

"You don't want to buy one of the square paintings for yourself? I have some with men."

"Not at the moment. I'm not adding to my collection. I have more stuff than I can hang in my flat."

Dent picked up the wrapped canvases.

"It's good stuff. It just isn't right for the gallery. It's nothing personal."

"Just business."

"Just business."

A. went with him to the courtyard where Dent put the pictures in his car.

"Call round in a month. Make it two. We'll see how these go down."

A. returned to the studio and looked at his watch. He took out his keys and left the studio.

(16)

When the traffic lights changed to red, A. crossed Holborn under the dragon of the Corporation of London. He turned left at Hatton Garden.

It was noon. Newspaper sellers were at their pitches. Figures carrying paper bags and cardboard cups filled the pavements. Outside a sandwich shop, a line of people waited. Where a large puddle had formed, traffic splashed the pavement. A couple of young women paused at the limit of the splash zone, watching the oncoming traffic.

A. crossed the railway bridge on Clerkenwell Road and halted at a doorway. There were brass nameplates at the entrance.

3. TLD Accountants
2. Nicole Giapetti Art Projects
1. Thamesplus + Recruitment Ltd (staff only)
G. Thamesplus + Recruitment Ltd

A man in a white raincoat cycled by, coat tails flapping behind. A. entered the building and climbed the stairs.

The gallery had white walls. Its floorboards were painted with grey vinyl gloss. Ceiling-mounted halogen lamps warmed the room. At a desk near the entrance a woman with a Roman nose and gold jewellery was looking at a computer monitor.

A. looked at photographs displayed in the gallery. They were not framed. They were attached to the walls by double-sided tape. The photographs were of puddles, balls of chewing gum and screws lying on work surfaces. A. almost stepped on a length of thread which was fixed to the ceiling by a drawing pin. A label on the nearby wall gave the title of the work.

The woman looked at A. then returned to her computer.

After circling the room again, A. approached the desk. The woman said "Hello". From his bag, A. withdrew a plastic sheet holding 35mm mounted slides.

"Oh, you're an artist."

"Yes," said A. unfolding a photocopied page.

"Let me see."

"You don't have to look at them now. I have a self-addressed envelope here."

"No. I can tell you now."

She glanced at the page and held up the sheet of slides to the light. A. went to stand facing a photograph.

She sighed.

"They're a little…obvious."

A. said nothing.

"And you don't have a gallery."

"No."

She put the slides and page on the desk.

"Well, I'm sure there is a place for your art but I'm not sure there is anything I can do with it."

A. collected the slides.

"You can keep the photocopied information."

"No, thank you."

A. put the page and slides into his bag.

"Good luck with the show."

"Yes. Goodbye," she said, looking at her screen.

A. walked west along Clerkenwell Road and bought two contact magazines on the way back to the office.

(17)

A. walked west down Holborn, jacket and bag over one shoulder. His sleeves were rolled up. He squinted his eyes against the low sun. A cycle courier squeezed a bottle of liquid into his mouth, sweat running from his temples, before he upended the bottle over his head. A beggar was sitting by the statue facing across Holborn to the entrance to Chancery Lane. His dog was lapping water from a plastic tray in the shade at the statue's base. A road-surfacing crew worked bare chested, raking steaming macadam. Behind a road-roller, one worker walked bent over, pouring a rivulet of tar from a can along a join.

On the pavement, people sat at tables. Men with suit

jackets slung over shoulders drank beer outside pubs. At Holborn underground station, people waited by the newsstand kiosk to be served. Women were buying fruit from a barrow down Kingsway. A short man was arguing with a member of station staff. A pock-faced hawker was selling a used travel card to a teenager at the station entrance. A man folding a coat over his arm stole a glimpse at a tanned girl wearing a crop top waiting at the street railings. The newspaper vendor was calling out over the babble.

On High Holborn a line of people queuing for an ATM ignored a sleeping tramp on compacted sheets of cardboard. The wall around the tramp's pitch was scuffed dark with grease. Scaffolding had accumulated litter around its wooden bases. Passengers walked from a parked bus to one with engine idling, shepherded by a Sikh driver. Shade. A. took the turning into Drury Lane.

There were fewer people here. The street was narrow, high buildings casting shadows. Taxis headed north. A huddle of schoolchildren at a junction was studying an item one of them held. A. entered a doorway on the right side of Drury Lane and descended a steep flight of wooden steps. The basement was small and lined with canvas rolls on wall-mounted spindles. When the assistant greeted A., A. indicated a wrapped roll under a counter. The assistant pulled out a roll of polythene sheeting. A. paid for it in cash. As he waited for the receipt, he bundled his jacket into his bag and put it on his back. He carried the roll up the stairs. In the shaded street, A. lifted the roll on to a shoulder and walked down to Aldwych.

A. followed Strand until it became Fleet Street. He skirted the television crews outside the High Court. He headed east with the sun at his back. Ludgate Circus, then the slope up Ludgate Hill. A. wiped his brow with the back of an arm. The offices of Ludgate Hill parted around the bulk of St Paul's Cathedral. In St Paul's Churchyard, where tourists photographed and pigeons strutted, A. shifted the load to his other shoulder. Paternoster Square was hidden by a wall of hoardings. He walked the north path around the Cathedral, then up Cheapside. Offices were emptying. People flowed eastward. The takeaway-sandwich bars were closed, blinds down. Men with blue shirts, gelled hair and slip-on, square-toed shoes were drinking cans of lager and walking east. A diminutive Indian woman with a red bindi on her forehead was stacking pallets into a wheeled cage at the supermarket entrance. A woman in a suit was eating fruit salad from a transparent box with a plastic fork.

A. took steps down to Bank station. He made his way down to platform nine, where he stood the roll on its end between his feet. Women in summer dresses and men in shirtsleeves read novels and newspapers. A frowning girl with a ponytail was writing notes in the margins of spiral-bound manual. Seated on a bench, a large black woman in a garment with a pattern of peacock feathers was reading a Bible. A young couple embraced, kissing.

When the Docklands Light Railway train arrived, A. did not take a seat but stood close to the doors, resting his hands on the top of the roll. The dark tunnel punctuated by lights rose into afternoon sunshine. The tracks ran parallel to Cable Street. There were women in burqas with pushchairs. An old man with a walking-frame watched the train pass. Children wearing helmets roller-skated along the pavement, waving to the train passengers.

At the second stop, A. alighted at Limehouse station and walked to the studio. Brief darkness and sound of water dripping in the narrow passage beneath the railway bridge. There was a dead pigeon crushed to feathery pulp at the kerb.

In the studio-building courtyard, a couple of women in work clothes were sitting against a sunlit wall, smoking. There was dried paint on their shoes.

The windowless passage to A.'s studio was cool. As A. handled the roll, reaching for his keys, it slipped in his wet hands. A wave of hot air emanated from the studio when A. opened the door. A layer of dust lifted from the floor as the roll of plastic hit it. A. checked a square painting on the wall, examining it close, then at an oblique angle. Then he took off his bag, picked up the cake of soap and went to the basin in the corridor and washed his face and hands. There was a small oval of darkness on the back of his shirt. He took the soap back to the studio, picked up his bag and left.

When he arrived at Limehouse station, a train was pulling into the platform. A. emerged from the coolness of Island Gardens station and walked along Manchester Road. Outside the remnants of the former Island Gardens station, children on bicycles were throwing pebbles at a hoarding.

(18)

There was a knock at the studio door. A. set down his brush and pulled on a T-shirt over his bare chest.

The man at the door was wearing a shirt and a pair of jeans with holes cut in them. His trainers were luminous green.

"I'm Andy."

He outstretched a hand which A. shook.

"I have studio two-eleven."

He pointed over A.'s shoulder through the window to the building above.

"Wow. Hey, can I take a look at the work?"

A. stood aside and Andy walked in and began to look at the square paintings. They were arranged in a grid formation on the wall which faced the building through the window. He leaned close to a picture.

"These are oil paintings. From where my studio is I can see in. I thought they were photographs. They look photographic. You use photographs? Wow. But these are from photographs, right? I've been doing something similar. With photographs. I'm a photographer. Where do you get your images from?"

A. pointed to an open magazine.

"These images are so good. They're like my photographs. You should see them. You'd like them. Do you have a gallery? Do you exhibit?"

A. was looking at the man's trainers.

"Don't they work well? Laid out like this, I mean. I think the grid does something. It really does something.

Makes them more serious. No, I mean, not that they're not serious. It's just, the pattern—"

Andy put his hands in his back pockets.

"Isn't it a coincidence that we're doing the same thing? The images. And if I hadn't looked through the window I wouldn't have seen your work. You don't show at the open studio days, do you? You should. I had a lot of interest the last time. It gets people through the door. I sold a couple of works too. And you get visitors to sign a book and you can add them to your mailing list. We share names and addresses. I never knew you were here before. You don't have your name on the door."

He was looking at the paintings.

"When I saw through the window, from where I was looking, I thought they were photos. From a distance they look photographic. With the black and white. It's deliberate, though, isn't it?"

Andy nodded his head.

"Yeah. Wow. Really."

He moved to the door.

"You should come up. I think you'd be interested. Andy. I'm in two-eleven. My name's on the door. If I'm not in leave a note. Everyone in the corridor knows me. Jamil is in almost every day except for Mondays. You know Jamil? Well, you can leave a note for me with him. Really, you should come up. I think you'd like my photos. We're on similar lines. What great paintings."

After the door was closed, A. began to take down the paintings.

THE NAKED SPUR

(19)

A. pushed open the gate and walked up the concrete path. He rang the doorbell. He stepped back and looked down the street. Both sides of the road were lined with parked cars. A. rang the doorbell again. After five minutes he walked to the gate and faced the house. Then he stepped out to the pavement and walked down an alley.

It led to a wide street thick with traffic which was flanked with semi-detached houses. The alley was next to a parade of shops consisting of a Chinese takeaway restaurant, a hair salon and a newsagent.

A. sat in the shade on a low wall and wiped his brow with the back of a forearm. The wall was in disrepair. Bricks had fallen on to a patch of grass. A. checked his watch.

There was a cat on a wall. It was white with a black patch on one side of its face. It miaowed at A. Then it approached A. with an unsteady gait. It had three legs. He stroked the cat and undid two shirt buttons.

A couple of children in school uniform walked along the pavement eating ice creams. A. wiped his brow again. The cat was sitting beside him on the wall.

A. reached down and picked up a brick. He rubbed a finger in the depression, blew into it and placed the brick depression up on the grass. He walked into the newsagents and came out with a carton of milk. He opened it and poured some into the hollow in the brick. The cat hopped down from the wall, sniffed the milk then began to lap it. A. watched it drink and drank some of the milk from the carton spout.

An aeroplane flew overhead. A. checked his watch and looked back down the alley. He pulled his shirt free of his waistband.

A. refilled the depression in the brick twice then the cat came to him. He stroked it and it purred. Then it hopped back on to the wall and disappeared round the corner. A. was finishing the milk as a red saloon car passed the far end of the alley. He crumpled the carton and dropped it into a litter bin as he walked back to the front of the house where the red car had parked.

(20)

The two figures climbed to the second floor. Hartley pushed the door and held it open for A. The room was not full but noisy. A woman with a Roman nose stood next to a younger woman who was handing out glasses of wine. The older woman was dressed in black. Her hands were pressed together in front of her. A big man with dyed hair was standing next to her, speaking into one ear. She was facing forward, nodding every so often. On the wall behind her the words "Feminine Intuition: 5 New Artists" had been applied.

The woman in black smiled in the men's direction.

A woman in a trouser-suit entered, carrying a bouquet. People gathered for a group photograph. Hartley went to talk with the woman in black. A. picked up a press release and looked at the art. A young girl in a summer dress was standing under a photograph with arms folded, scowling at people.

Hartley returned with a glass of wine.

"Well?" asked A.

THE NAKED SPUR

Hartley looked around the walls and shrugged.

They caught a bus to Hoxton.

A large building with a stone facade stood at the corner of the street. On the first floor they entered a bar with dark decor. Damien Cole was sitting in a leather armchair by one window. He introduced Hartley and A. to his mother and sister Ella.

"A., you remember Dave Gibb from college, the year below us?"

A man with fair hair shook A.'s hand.

"Nelson's written a review of Dave's exhibition for the new issue. Dave's got a show coming up this summer in where was it? Holland?"

"Luxembourg. I was trying to talk Nelson into going over there to review that too."

"He said no?" said Damien.

"It's a bit further than Shoreditch. He said he doesn't get expenses."

Nelson Nicobar had arrived and was talking the man behind the bar.

"Do you still make art, A.?" Dave Gibb asked A.

"Yes."

"Where's your studio?"

"Cable Street."

"Hasn't that closed down? I heard it was closing down. A friend of mine has a space there and he says the place is on the skids, threatening letters from the landlord and stuff. All the good places are going."

They drank in silence for a moment.

"Have you been in any shows?" Dave Gibb asked A. "You know Nelson curates? Ask him over to your studio, maybe he'll put you in a show he's putting together for Max Piaggi."

A. did not reply.

"Have you been in any shows lately?"

"No."

"Who's your dealer?"

"Harry Dent."

"Right. Isn't he on Hoxton Square?"

"No. He has a gallery near the river."

"Oh. I haven't heard of him. The gallery isn't in the listings, is it? I guess it doesn't matter as long as he sells. Is he okay about you taking part in curated shows?"

"That isn't a problem."

"You should have a chat with Chris Kaminsky. You know he's got a gallery on Rivington Street now? He's a nice guy. I've shown with him."

"He wrote a piece for the current issue," said Damien. "Have you seen a copy? I asked for the copies to be put by the entrance."

Damien moved his head to look across the room. He produced a magazine from behind his armchair. "Have mine," he said, giving it to A.

On the cover was a photograph of a woman lying on a bed, fully clothed, eyes shut.

"Everyone's been wondering whether she'll come tonight," said Ella. "Is she coming tonight, Damien?"

"I don't know. She's been invited but, well..."

"I don't know how you got her for the magazine. She's quite big now."

"I think she just liked the idea. I guess we just got lucky. I don't know if she'll turn up tonight."

THE NAKED SPUR

A. flicked through the pages, Hartley at his shoulder.

"Agnetha's coming later," said Damien. "Did you know she had a baby? She's still writing though, I think. I sent Piers an invitation."

"Do you think he'll turn up?" asked Hartley.

"Well, Piers is Piers. You never can tell with him."

Damien and Hartley went to talk to Nelson Nicobar on the other side of the room. Ella and her mother talked. Dave Gibb and A. sat next to each other in silence. When footsteps came from the staircase, people turned to look.

(21)

Knocking on a door. A. stopped painting. The person in the neighbouring space answered the door.

"Sarah."

"Hello, Martin. I've just come around to tell you about the committee meeting next week. It's on Friday, at the usual time."

"About this bill I got. I don't know what to do with it."

"Bills keep going out but that account has been suspended. If you write a cheque it can't be deposited."

"I know. I got my cheque back. It was disconcerting."

"At the moment no rent is being collected. We're talking to the estate managers about opening a trust account. We'll cover that at the meeting."

"I haven't paid rent for three months. I feel like a squatter. This can't carry on. If they ask for a lump sum to cover the period I'll have to go to my savings."

"We're all in the same boat, Martin. That's why we

have to stick together. You'll be at the meeting then? Do you know about…"

Her voice dropped.

"No, I've never spoken to him. I wouldn't know. You could try him."

She replied sotto voce.

"Okay, Sarah. See you…"

"Friday."

"Friday, that's right."

The door closed. There were five light footsteps, a pause, then footsteps diminishing until the passage door banged open then shut.

(22)

The locker door rattled when A. opened it. The lock had a slot for coin deposit. The sticker on the inside of the door showed "£1". In the lock was a one-pound coin. A. put it in his pocket.

The museum attendant at the cloakroom desk was reading a paperback. A. moved along the wall of lockers. In open doors he found two more coins. He deposited his bag and went into the museum. An hour later, when he collected his bag, he found a coin in the door next to the locker he had used.

(23)

A. crossed the studio courtyard and went through an arch. On the left was a metal door. A. knocked on it, waited, looked at a row of windows with grills. After a second knock, the door opened and a Japanese woman's

THE NAKED SPUR

face appeared in a crack between door and jamb. The face disappeared, leaving the door ajar.

A. entered a corridor with a long skylight its length. The Japanese woman was gone. A door lock clicked shut. A. tapped on a door. A woman with reddish hair answered.

"Come in."

The studio was full of paintings, rolls of paper and materials. The floor was lined with cotton duck. A. took a seat and Eleanor crouched on the floor. She was wearing socks. There was a sheet of paper and a mirror. Looking at the reflection, she drew a face in charcoal.

"This is for the Paris show," she said, not looking up.

The shelves were full of CDs. Light came from a fluorescent tube and a line of windows high on one wall opening on to the corridor. There was a sheet at the windows. Paintings on the walls showed a woman with reddish hair in a variety of poses and costumes: in a singlet, crouching on the floor, sucking a lollipop, pursing lips.

"I don't know how much longer we can last."

A curving line unspooled beneath her stick.

"We're all getting notices under our doors. You too? If they change the locks again and I have a van coming to collect work for a show that day, I don't know what I would do."

She sat back on her haunches, head cocked.

"I know a couple of places. There's a room I can use. It's closer to the gallery. It's not the same as a dedicated studio though."

She looked her face in the mirror, then at the drawing. She half closed her eyes.

"What will you do?" she asked A.

"I don't know."

"Do you have anywhere to go?"

"No."

She moved closer to the mirror, eyelids lowered, mouth pouted.

"It could happen any day."

She sat back and laughed, turning to A.

"I don't know what I must look like. Isn't it ridiculous?"

She put her charcoal on the floor and dusted her hands on her trousers.

"It could be any day now. Each day I arrive, I get knotted up inside, thinking that today the combination won't open the lock."

She got to her feet and walked to a cardboard box.

"I'm packing in the job at the store. Everyone's leaving. We haven't had a pay rise in two years. They're terrible about holidays and sick days. All the best people have gone. Lucinda went. I'm going next month. I have some teaching, a few pictures have sold. The only reason I stayed on was the staff discount on materials. But not even that is enough. There's a place near Finsbury Park that's better."

With a hand she was turning over the contents of the box.

"The management is letting the best staff leave. All the artists are going. A person used to be able to go in and ask about this or that material and the staff could reply, I use this or have you tried this. Now they're hiring local girls."

Eleanor tipped the box. Lipsticks in different colours tumbled on to the floor.

"They all live at home so none of them needs much money. They don't need to pay for travel. None of them are artists."

She spread the lipsticks out. She picked up one, uncapped it and held it up. She twisted the red tip out of its sheath.

"Compliant."

She settled over the mirror and applied lipstick.

"Do you know what I mean?" she asked, pressing her lips against each other.

On the paper she drew in the mouth of the face in lipstick. When she finished, sat back on her haunches and capped the lipstick, a faint smile on her lips.

(24)

In "The Engineer's Arms", two men were sitting at a table, drinks before them. One man had shaved hair and glasses. He was wearing white trainers and a leather jacket with red shoulder patches. The other man had a blue shirt. The pair stood to greet A. as he entered the pub.

"Hi, Mack. Hi, Simon."

They shook hands. Two white men at the bar were looking at them. One bent to the other and said something that provoked laughter.

A.: "You've got a tan."

Mack: "I got back from a shoot in Texas. It was so bastard hot. We only went out of the air-conditioned trailers when we had to. No, really, not what you're thinking. Not in the least glamorous. No one looks glamorous when they're sunburnt, wearing a floppy hat and sweating like a rapist."

A. ordered a half pint of bitter. The woman at the bar gave him a short measure, serving him with a wineglass and charging him for more.

When A. got back to the table, Mack looked at the glass and said, "What the fuck is that?"

"East End hospitality. Drink up and let's get out."

It was getting dark. By the minicab office two old Bengalis with hennaed beards were in conversation. The studio gate was unlocked. A. led Mack and Terry to his studio and switched on the light.

"You've been busy," said Simon.

A. unstacked canvases, propping them upright.

Simon said, "Mack has been thinking of buying his girlfriend a present. It's her birthday next month."

"Yes. How much for the little canvases? Okay, really I was looking for something that's…a bit less expensive."

"Cheap."

"Ideally, yes. Very cheap. So cheap it might cost less than a card or in fact not cost anything at all."

"You're a real prince among men," said Simon. "I hope your girlfriend appreciates you."

Mack looked closely at a painting.

"I like this thing you've got going on with the amateur nude photos. The square paintings are a series? From magazines?"

Mack picked up a painting of male genitals. He tipped it toward A.

"Someone I know?"

Simon: "How much are you asking for these?"

A.: "Six hundred and fifty pounds."

Mack: "Each?"

"Each."

"Okay." Mack paused. "How many have you sold?"

"None."

"Do you think there's a connection between the two facts?"

"If you go into the Dent Gallery, everything this size is the same price or more expensive."

"I suppose. I don't go to many galleries. That's good money though."

"If it sells."

"If it sells."

"And the gallery takes commission out of that. Twenty-five percent? A third?"

"Fifty."

Simon whistled. Mack raised an eyebrow.

"That's the racket to be in," said Simon. "How much do the materials cost you?"

"About fifteen pounds for each of these canvases."

"Plus the cost of your time."

A. nodded, shrugging.

"So you make a decent return on your money. If it sells," Simon said.

"A picture's only worth what people are willing to pay for it," responded Mack.

"But on the other hand, if A.'s paintings aren't selling that doesn't mean they're worth nothing, Mack."

"Ah, you've spotted where my devious logic was taking us."

"To a freebie."

"To a freebie. How long do these paintings take to make?" Mack asked A., eyes on a painting of a lying woman smiling towards the picture plane.

"It depends. One session, two sessions, three sometimes. Half a day to maybe two days to paint each."

"But you're not painting every day," said Simon. "You've got office work."

"I paint every weekend and two or three evenings during the week."

"So you could paint two or three of these per week. And you set your own pace, not like the rest of us," said Simon. "But where would a person hang one, if he bought one? They're not really paintings you'd put in the living room."

"I don't agree," said Mack. "I know guys who'd put this stuff on their walls. They might take them down when their parents came to visit, but the rest of the time their friends would be cool about the pictures."

"Maybe," said Simon. "But I think you'd have a few female friends who'd have a hard time facing that across the dining table."

Simon tipped his trainer towards a painting of a vagina close up.

"Even I have, right now. I don't know how Ilse would feel staring at that every day."

"Get her to give A. a photo and he'll do one of her," said Mack.

Simon pursed his lips.

"I don't think either of us would want to stare at her

vagina every time we ate breakfast."

Mack laughed.

"Point taken. But it's a question of degree. The right painting for the right person in the right room would work. Like the bedroom, for example. Possibly under a bed. Taken out for special occasions. With one person present."

"Show us more," Simon said to A.

A. brought out more canvases and hung them from the screws in the wall.

The men left without buying. When they had gone, A. restacked the paintings and walked to the train station.

(25)

A. exited the lift and walked to the reception desk. One of the guards brought out a clipboard. A. took a security pass out of his suit-jacket pocket and put it on the clipboard. A. signed the sheet, opened the glass door and stepped on to the street where he turned left.

(26)

In the mews a girl was walking towards A. She was in jeans and a T-shirt with the slogan "You can look but you can't touch". On her feet were open-toed pumps with stack heels.

"Hello, Theresa."

"Hi. How are you?"

"Fine. Painting. You know."

Theresa had started to walk away when A. called out

to her. She stopped and turned to him.

(27)

"The most expensive one? You're sure? No, I don't mean there's anything wrong; it's just I've never sold one since I've been here. I'll have to ask Goran if we've got one in stock. Hold on."

The woman at the counter picked up the telephone and pressed one key. In the distance a telephone was ringing.

"Goran? Have we got the biggest Mabef easel in storage?"

The woman gave A. a smile and sat with the handset pressed to her ear. A. looked at the counter. It was littered with lists, ring binders and invoice books. On the notice board behind the till was a flyer for a public talk at the Mall Galleries by Edward Lucie-Smith, David Lee and Nelson Nicobar. The two of them waited in silence.

There was a shout from the far end of the room. A man in a white T-shirt was raising a thumb towards them.

The woman put the sale through the till. Goran led A. through to the storage space and they lifted a large box on to a trolley and wheeled it into the forecourt. Two men and the woman from the till were smoking, sitting in the sunlight on tubs.

"No chance," said one of the men. "That's not going anywhere. We're on our lunch. We're almost out of diesel and all the garages are empty. Fuel strike."

"Big purchase, one stop," said Goran.

THE NAKED SPUR

The second man hawked and spat. The woman grimaced and averted her face.

"It isn't far," said A.

The first man squinted at A.

"Where?"

"Cable Street Studios."

The first man sighed.

"Now?" he asked.

"Please."

The second man sighed.

"You get rest of your hour after you get back," said Goran.

The first man said, "Okay."

They loaded the box on to the van. The first man and A. drove down Commercial Road past long queues of vehicles, engines switched off, waiting outside garages. A man was putting out a handwritten sign saying "SOLD OUT" on a gas canister on the garage forecourt. A driver in a red Ford was leaning out of his window and shouting at the man.

They unloaded the easel and wheeled it into A.'s studio.

"Eleanor's just round the corner, isn't she? I've done deliveries for her," said the man, as A. initialled a receipt for him.

He tucked the receipt into a pocket.

"You're lucky. An hour later and we'd have been immobilised. We're not going anywhere until they get the fuel moving again. You were the last."

He rubbed a cheek.

"This country's fucked, mate."

(28)

"I'll do it, just don't tell anyone."

Theresa was stirring hot chocolate with a spoon. Outside the café a cycle courier was entering the Barbican. At the table next to Theresa and A., a boy was writing a text message on his mobile phone.

"You're not going to put my name on it or anything like that?"

"Along with your phone number? No. Everything is untitled."

"You mustn't tell anyone. Don't tell my parents. I'm not even going to tell my boyfriend. He'll kill me. He'll stop me for sure."

She spooned the cream under the surface.

"Seven pounds fifty an hour? That new job must pay well. That's what you get for working evenings, I suppose. I could use the money. I've got university next month. I need to save. I was meant to get an office job this summer but I didn't want to. My boss wanted me to come back to the place I used to work last summer."

"You didn't want to?"

"He was touching me up. I mean, not even subtly, just, you know." She pressed her hands over the front of her breasts. "He's old enough to be my father. Anyway, it was so boring just filing and answering the telephone. I'm a bright girl, you know?"

She lifted hot chocolate to her lips with a spoon.

"It's not going to be too cold, is it? It's almost autumn. I walk around the house with no clothes but there's carpet and stuff. I mean, I walk around like that when there's no one home. I'm not weird or anything."

The boy stood up and went to the counter before leaving.

She paused, licking the cream from her lips.

"So, what do you look for in a model? I mean, I'm not classic model material. Regardless of prettiness, one way or another, I mean, I've not got the type of figure you'd expect from a nude model. Well, I guess there was Rubens in the whatever-century-he-lived-in."

"Someone I can spend hours with each day."

"Oh, so you're hiring me for my conversational talent." Theresa's eyes sparkled. She leant over the table towards A. "Ah ha. But won't my complete and thorough nakedness distract your intellect?"

A. smiled.

"So, if I like it, how long would you want me?"

"Until you go. Next week, is it?"

"Next weekend. My father's driving me up on Saturday. I'll need to finish my packing on Friday. So, all of next week except for Friday I am free. And we can start tomorrow? I better go to the gym tonight and exercise. I'm okay about how I look but I want to look my best for posterity. I don't know. Can you slim me on the canvas? Or…My God," she said, gazing into the distance. "I can't believe I've just agreed to take off all my clothes in front of you. It's only because I trust you that I'm doing this. I'd never do it in front of a stranger. Unless…"

"You've taken your clothes off and had sex with men you know less well than me."

Theresa sucked her spoon.

"I guess. Since you put it like that."

She smiled and dipped the spoon into the chocolate. "I'll have to cut down on this if I'm going to keep up my career as a nude model."

She sighed and raised the cup to her lips. The door opened and a couple with a child in a pushchair took seats on the other side of the café.

"This time tomorrow... It'll be in black and white, won't it? I don't want you to paint me in colour. Will you paint me or just draw me? How are you going to paint me? Do I get any breaks? I don't have to stand still for two hours or anything like that, do I? Can I have a comfortable pose? Sitting? Lying? Asleep? You won't be too strict with me? I mean, this is my first time."

She smiled and lowered her head, catching the last of the froth in the spoon.

"Do you want me to...?"

"What?"

"Nothing."

A. looked at his watch.

"I have to get to the office. I'll walk you to the station."

They walked from the café to Shakespeare Tower.

"I want to stop in there," Theresa pointed to a sheet music shop.

They kissed on the cheeks and parted. At the revolving doors, he looked back. Theresa had gone.

(29)

Theresa was waiting at the gate when A. got there. They walked up to Mudchute station. The sun was hot,

THE NAKED SPUR

burning dew off privet hedges.

"No, I'm not nervous. Well, a little. It's odd. Does everyone feel the same way the first time?"

A team of workmen were pollarding linden trees on Marsh Wall.

"I was thinking about this all last night. I wondered what it would be like. So, no one will see me? Do I look okay?"

They bought tickets from a machine on the platform, boarding the second train that arrived. They did not talk on the journey until they alighted at Limehouse station.

On the other side of Butchers Row, she asked, "You won't be rude about my figure, will you?"

"Why would I do that?"

"Oh, I don't know. I don't know what you are used to, with models." She drew her handbag closer to her.

They crossed the threshold into Cable Street Studios. A woman was loading plinths into the back of a car.

"And if I change my mind, you won't shout at me or force me, will you?"

The woman at the car watched them pass.

"You can have your money back. If I don't take off my pants, can I do it at a reduced rate? I don't mind showing my boobs, I show them when I go on holiday on the beach, but…"

A. keyed in the code into the gate lock.

"All or nothing but I won't force you."

Theresa sighed. A. unlocked the passage door and pressed the light switch. In the studio, A. locked the door and left the keys in the lock.

"That's so no one walks in on us."

"Would they?"

"No. It's just so you won't feel they might."

Theresa looked up at the skylight, then the walls. She moved to the square paintings hanging up.

"I'm not going to be in one of these, am I? These are the ones from photographs you told me about, aren't they? They're quite full-on, aren't they? Not in a bad way. That looks familiar." She was facing a painting of a squatting woman, breasts bared.

"In what way?"

"Well, you know. The way breasts hang. They do that. It's just right."

She rested her handbag on a chair and clasped her hands in front of her.

"So."

A. took off his jacket and took a roll of used cotton duck which he unrolled with the painted side to the floor.

"So you don't get dirty."

"Should I…."

"Go down to your pants."

Theresa took off her clothes while A. moved a chair and picked up a sketchbook and pencil. They did two poses, A. drawing quickly.

"Now the rest."

She looked at him.

"Now?"

She paused then with a deep breath took off her pants and put them on the clothes draped on the chair.

THE NAKED SPUR

(30)

"No."

"Why?"

"It's personal."

Theresa was lying on her back with one leg raised. A. was seated at her feet with a large sketchbook.

"You're completely naked, letting me draw you and you won't tell me."

She laughed. A. carried on drawing.

"What do you usually talk about with models?"

"It varies."

"Do you always ask questions like that?"

"A lot of models write it on their cards."

"Cards?"

"Cards they put up on notice boards."

"My God, I wouldn't put that on a card. It's nobody's business but mine."

Gulls were circling glyphs visible through the skylight.

"It's odd. I didn't know what to expect but I didn't think it would be like this."

"What did you expect?"

"Oh, divan chairs, swathes of drapery, palms, oriental embroidery, parrots in grand cages."

"A view of the Riviera?"

"Don't tell me, at your summer residence, right?"

She scratched her knee and returned to her position. An electric drill sounded.

"How much would you pay for photographs?"

"I hadn't thought about it."

"I'm not saying I'd do it but if I were to, how much

would you pay?"

"I'll have a think."

Pause.

"Thirty-six double C," Theresa said and laughed.

(31)

A. brushed the dust from Theresa's back using a bundled bed sheet.

"I can do tomorrow. If you want me."

"All week if possible."

"Great."

She stepped into her pants.

"It wasn't so bad. It wasn't what I expected. When you said, now the rest, I thought, well, might as well and took them off before I could change my mind. The funny thing is, I felt more exposed and naked when I had my pants on. Afterwards I felt better. More normal. I just forgot I had no clothes on."

She drew in her stomach to do the waist button of her jeans.

"Don't tell anyone about this though."

(32)

"I told my boyfriend last night."

Theresa was lying on a length of canvas, stomach down. She was leafing through a contact magazine.

"I wasn't going to tell him but it just sort of happened. You know how it is."

A. sharpened his pencil.

"So, I told him and I thought he was going to explode. Well, I don't know. Maybe I wanted to see his expression. Anyway, we talked about it and I said there was nothing going on between us, you and me, I mean, and he relaxed a bit. He asked me how much I was getting paid and then he said, well, if you want to make more than that I have a friend who makes porno films and he'll pay you more."

Theresa frowned.

"That's not a very nice thing to suggest to your girl-friend, is it?"

She sighed.

"Maybe I like his unpredictability. He wrote off his Mercedes last month and he didn't care. It's amazing. Imagine that. I suppose he's got enough money. He's a drug dealer. Anyway, he's banned from driving. He'd been driving me around for a week before he tells me though. Maybe he isn't banned though. Maybe he's just trying to impress me. It's difficult to tell, isn't it?"

She paused.

"He drives wildly enough for me to believe him. My God. I told him to slow down or I'd get out and walk. He stopped the car, reached over and opened my door."

Pause.

"Anyway, he took the hint and drove a bit slower after that. He only skipped a couple of red lights."

She flipped closed the magazine and sat up. The grain of the canvas had left stippling over her stomach and breasts. She rubbed a patterned elbow.

"I'd like you standing."

"Like this?"

She stood up against a wall.

"Hands on the stretchers."

She raised her arms into a crucifix position between two large stretchers. A. picked up a sketchpad.

"I told all my girlfriends. We went for a pizza in Stratford. They were, I don't know, shocked and impressed. Impressed that I would do something like that. They said, out of all of us, it could only be you, Theresa, who would do something like that. It's funny, I made this promise not to tell and then I ended up talking about it all night. In the end they had to say stop talking about it, Theresa. You know, Theresa the nude model, blah blah. Well, so much for my promise."

She altered her balance slightly. A wheeled cart crossed cobblestones, rattling.

"None of them would do it. I mean, I asked because you might want a model while I'm at university. They're all Indian. You'd like them. They've got large breasts. You like large breasts, don't you? I think they're pretty conservative or maybe their families are. Either way, they won't do it, so you'll have to look elsewhere. I know I'll be hard to replace."

She laughed. A. made an erasure and redrew a line.

"It's strange. I've spent more time with you with no clothes on than with clothes on. Sometimes I forget that I'm nude. I just find it so normal. I don't notice any more. You'll have to stop me if I wander out of that door like this. I get up in the morning and I have to remind myself that I have to put some clothes on to get to work where I take them off."

"It's sad when you cover yourself with clothes. It's like the sun going behind a cloud."

THE NAKED SPUR

Theresa smiled.

"That's very sweet." She paused. "That's nicer than anything my boyfriend's ever said to me."

A. carried on sketching.

"Are you warm enough?"

"Yes. Well, not warm but enough. Women have one more layer of fat than men. Perhaps I've got more than that. I don't know. You're a better judge of that than I am. You've been looking at me long enough. It's rude to stare."

The corner of her mouth rose.

"I suppose this is meant to be rude, taking your clothes off and being looked at, but it doesn't feel very sexy. I mean, it's nice but it's not really like anything else, is it?"

Later: "Can I move my arms?"

"Have a break."

She stepped away from her position, flexed her arms.

"My shoulders are stiff. Could you…"

She turned her left shoulder to A. who massaged it. Theresa had her head inclined to one side and had her eyes closed. A. massaged the right shoulder.

"Sometimes I don't remember… It's like…"

Theresa's eyes were shut. A smile crossed her lips.

(33)

"Sometimes I feel like glass."

Theresa was on her back. Her breasts flattened, making short crescent creases inward from her armpits towards her collarbones. She was gazing at the skylight.

"Sometimes I feel as transparent as glass, as though people are looking through me or maybe just looking at their own reflections. When they look at me, I wonder who they're seeing."

She paused.

"After sex, sometimes I look back at the bed and see my outline in the sheets where I was lying and I think, my God, that was me. That was me getting fucked. All there is now is a shape in the sheets. Then I pull the sheet tight and the shape disappears. Maybe everyone thinks things like this but no one talks about it."

After a moment, she gave a laugh.

"I don't know why I'm telling you this. We should have an intellectual conversation about art or music or something."

She rolled her head to look at A.

"I'm a bright girl, you know?"

(34)

Theresa had her eyes shut. The light was subdued. She was standing with a hand on one hip. A. was seated, looking at eye level towards her.

"I haven't heard that before. Is he any relative of yours? I'm sure the tutors at university would know him," she said, when the CD had finished playing.

She watched his eyes and the movement of his pencil over the paper. When someone walked down the corridor she did not glance to the door. A. erased then reworked a dense triangle at the centre of his page. He stopped, looked forwards, resumed drawing.

After a minute, Theresa said, "I can shave it off, you know."

A. paused.

THE NAKED SPUR

"That. I can shave it off, if it's causing you problems."

"Would you do that if I asked?"

She studied the painting of an unclothed man.

"Yes, I suppose. My boyfriend might wonder about it though. He might think that I've gone all kinky. Or maybe that you'd gone all kinky. I could do it tonight if you want. But as you've already started, you'd have to re-do your drawing without the curly stuff."

He continued drawing.

"You wouldn't believe…"

She stopped.

"Never mind." Pause. "He said- Well. The things he's asked other girls to do. I don't know which is worse, what he asked them to do or the fact he told me about it afterwards. I wonder what he'll say about me in the future. I'll bet he's saying it already to his friends. They're as bad as he is, apparently."

She sighed.

"He's a bit of a wanker, really."

Theresa took a break and stretched. A. reached below his chair for the eraser and caught a sleeve on a stretcher bar. The bar fell, its tip sinking deep into a package wrapped in brown paper on the floor. The wood made a purring sound as it ripped the package.

"Oh," said Theresa.

A. lifted the package and pulled scuffed wrapping away from the tear. Inside was a canvas with a triangular puncture.

"Was it important?" asked Theresa, at A.'s elbow.

A. paused.

"No."

(35)

A. set a blank canvas on the easel. He drew Theresa's outline on the canvas in pencil, correcting from observation. When they took a break, Theresa looked at the drawing. She did not express an opinion. When the drawing was finished, A. called her to look at it. She was wearing trousers and shoes and held her bra and T-shirt when she walked over to see the picture. When she was dressed, A. took out his wallet and counted a number of banknotes and handed them to her. They walked out to the courtyard. It was raining lightly. They hugged, then Theresa went to the front gate and A. returned to the studio where her perfume was in the air.

(36)

Butchers Row was a mass of traffic at an excavation. Workmen were laying pipes in a pit. Sand stuck to the hot tarmac. A. walked up to Limehouse station and caught a Docklands Light Railway train to Bank and changed for the Central line. On a platform seat, a girl with lank hair and sores by her mouth was sniffing glue from a plastic bag. A. took the underground to Tottenham Court Road station and flowed with the crowd up to the hot, bright air of day.

(37)

A. stood outside a bookshop on Brewer Street. The window was of large photographic books on ethnography, burlesque performers, motorcycles. Above was a graphic transfer: "EXTENDED OPENING

HOURS".

A. entered. On one wall was a large sign which read "Erotic Section Downstairs. 100s of Titles". An arrow pointed to a flight of stairs.

At the bottom of the stairs was a case. Behind the glass was a selection of items. There were vibrators and dildos of varying designs, sizes and colours. A range of dildos in transparent plastic, green, red, yellow, blue, stood in a row. Beside jars of lubricant and tubes of gel was an uninflated pneumatic doll. A vacuum pump was propped against a box on which was printed "MR ERECTOR: Una bomba que transforma un pene mediocre en uno de gigante" with several diagrams labelled in Dutch. At the bottom of the cabinet were a life-size rubber fist and a plastic replica of a lower leg and foot. Around the case edge was a line of illuminated fairy lights.

The room had a low ceiling and was brightly lit. There were racks of videos and DVDs. On the walls were shelves of magazines. At the sales counter a member of staff played a video for a customer who was reading a video-cassette box. The man was frowning. Another assistant was totalling a purchase on the cash till for an elderly man in a tweed suit.

A. scanned rows of magazines. Each shelf had a laminated card taped to its leading edge. After making two circuits of the room, A. approached the counter.

"Have you got any contact magazines?"

"No. We don't stock that stuff. Try the newsagents instead."

"You don't have any contact magazines? No amateur magazines?"

"No, it's only specialist stuff we take. Nothing like that here."

A. visited three more sex shops in Brewer Street and found no contact magazines.

He walked up to Oxford Street, turned east and walked up to Centrepoint. High Holborn, Holborn, Holborn Circus, Holborn Viaduct. Newgate Street, St Paul's Cathedral, St. Martin's-le-Grand, Gresham Street and an eight-storey office building. Over the door was written "CLEMENT HOUSE".

(38)

"Malaysia Telecom Systems Inc. is a prominent operator with a track record of working with SI providers in Singapore (since 1998) and Indonesia (since 2000) as well as diversifying core networking interests on a shared framework basis."

A. pencilled in a hyphen between "shared" and "framework", putting a small cross in the margin. He looked up from the pages on the reading stand. Visible from the window were the gilded orbs of Monument. Gresham Street was in shadow. Outside "The City Tup" men in shirtsleeves were drinking from pint glasses. Below the window, traffic lights changed in unison to red. A lone cyclist halted at the junction. A red pillar box was being emptied by a man in a blue shirt, the van hazard lights blinking. Crane jibs were motionless, pointing westward. The City towers were bright in the sunlight. Flags of St George and the Corporation fluttered in westerly wind.

The drawstrings of the window blinds shifted in the

THE NAKED SPUR

breeze. The bell of St Mary's Church chimed seven times.

A. put down his pencil and left his seat. He walked through a room with computer terminals. Less than half were occupied by typists. A radio was playing. A. passed empty, glass-sided cubicles, a dormant photocopier with boxes of paper, artificial pot plants. Turning left, there were more cubicles on his right and toilets on his left. There was a kitchen with a sink, water cooler and coffee dispenser. While the machine poured coffee into a plastic cup, A. went to the window. Beyond a narrow area of flat roof was a courtyard surrounded by offices. In the distance there were towers to the east.

Carrying the cup by its rim, A. took the coffee to a cubicle. He dialled a number on the telephone on the desk. He replaced the handset without speaking. He drank some coffee and looked out at the girders of a half-finished building adjacent. A crane swayed a little in the wind.

(39)

"What are you looking at?" the cook asked A.

She paused, tray in front of her full of plates, plastic cups and crumpled napkins. She followed A. gaze and looked to an office building, windows orange rectangles in the evening sky. Over it an aeroplane left a pink contrail.

"Very pretty."

She smiled.

A woman in a suit walked past, heels clicking on the parquet walkway. She used a paper napkin to hold a plastic cup. The cook resumed clearing the tables in the dining area.

"Where do you come from?"

"Sierra Leone."

"Oh."

A. looked out of the window.

"Do you like it here? In London," A. asked.

"Lots of work. It's okay for now."

"Do you have family here?"

"Yes. Most are here now, some in America."

"Do you think you will go back?"

"Some day. Not soon. Maybe to retire, when I am old. I will buy a house there. But things have to change there."

"It's bad?"

"So bad you wouldn't believe."

She was looking at the cloud shapes reflected in the building's glass.

"That will be years yet."

She turned away and carried the tray to the kitchen. Somewhere a door swung open and a peal of laughter issued. A. crumpled his cup and dropped it in a bin.

(40)

A. was seated, eating. Recessed halogen lamps lit empty tables, chairs and sofas. From the kitchen was the sound of the cook singing. A television was mute, pictures of an applauding crowd.

A. finished and walked past darkened meeting rooms, cubicles and typing area. In the reprographic room, the only light came from a scattering of standby LEDs, red, red, red, orange, red. In the manager's office a logo inched across a black computer screen. In the foyer, a fax machine gusted warm air, emitted a sliver of green light then fell dormant. Plastic palms moved in a breeze by an open window, silhouettes against lit windows across the street.

(41)

"It's half past eleven now," said a man wearing a T-shirt. His hair was grey and cut short. There was a motorcycle helmet on the floor at his feet. "We've had the last delivery of the evening. There'll be nothing else for us. You might as well shoot off."

A. put away his notebook and thanked him. Two others in the office left before A. A. pulled on his jacket, said goodbye to the man with grey hair and walked through the dark typing area.

A. stepped out of the lift into a tiled lobby. At the reception desk was an East African. He looked up from his religious tract and smiled at A.

"Goodnight, sir."

"Goodnight."

A. pressed a button next to the front door. The mechanism buzzed and A. walked out into the street. The air was cool. The sky was cloudless and starless, tinted streetlamp orange.

Turning right along Gresham Street, A. walked by a building site hoarding on his right, the Guildhall on his left. "The City Tup" was closed and dim, chairs on tables, legs pointing up. A couple of bar staff were at the bar, smoking.

ADAMS

A single taxi was the only traffic on Gresham Street. King Street, Ironmonger Lane, Old Jewry. Laughter. Three weaving shadows. At the bus stop in Prince's Street, a woman in a light dress and high heels pulled a shawl around herself, shivering. From a bank doorway, a rivulet of urine ran to the gutter. A street-cleaning vehicle was brushing the pavement outside the Bank of England.

There were splashes of vomit on the steps of Bank underground station. Three splashes were each separated by two steps. They became progressively smaller descending.

At the ticket barrier, A. stooped to retrieve several coins from the floor. By the escalators, a suited man was frowning at a mobile phone, swaying. The clock read "23:36". A. descended the escalator, walking down the moving steps. Corridors echoed with footsteps, clacking stilettos, squeaking trainers. A. did not encounter anyone.

On platform nine, passengers waited for a Docklands Light Railway train. A. did not look at the display board. He walked directly to one end of the platform and stood one metre from the platform edge at a point it was slightly more burnished than elsewhere. Within a minute, a train pulled in to platform nine. The front set of doors positioned exactly where A. was standing. Passengers disembarked and A. entered, taking the front-left seat closest the window.

Other passengers embarked: a youth with gelled hair and large headphones; a South African man in overalls; a man in shirtsleeves, eating a burger out of a box; a barefoot girl with bloodshot eyes, carrying high-heel shoes; a suited man with a flushed complexion, holding a bunch of flowers, one lily dangled from a broken stem. On two seats, twin Peruvian men sat, still and unspeaking.

Doors closed and the train pulled away. Shadwell, Limehouse, Westferry. The flower man was asleep. Bangladeshi youths who got on at Shadwell alighted at Westferry. West India Quay, Canary Wharf. At Heron Quays, lights on the frames of half-built towers reflected in the dock water. South Quay. The barefoot woman left the train at Crossharbour. Mudchute, Island Gardens.

A. was waiting by the doors when they opened. He ascended the steps to the street two at a time. No vehicles on Manchester Road. House windows were unlit.

A. had keys in his hand when he reached the front door and unlocked it without breaking stride. He climbed stairs in the dark. On the first floor the smell of cooking, on the second floor the smell of drying laundry. His room was warm from the day. He opened the sash window. Eastward, red tips of the Millennium Dome marked an ellipse.

(42)

Hartley and A. walked from Hartley's studio to the Docklands Light Railway station Deptford Bridge. Through the glass wall along the platform edge they watched traffic on the road flow beneath them. Hartley was carrying a battered case.

When they got on a Tower Gateway-bound train, A.

asked Hartley if he had spoken to Piers Floyd.

Hartley shook his head.

"No, he's still abroad, isn't he?"

"I didn't know he was abroad at all."

"At his house in South Africa."

"Oh. He hardly talked about it."

"He plays his cards close to his chest, doesn't he?"

At Canary Wharf, the train filled with business people. The train followed the tracks west after West India Quay. To the left were warehouses in the process of conversion. Inside hoardings were stacks of paving slabs, each numbered. Then came a cinema and a multi-storey car park with a spiral ramp.

"What are you working on at the moment?" A. asked Hartley when the train pulled up at Westferry station.

"Paintings for a show in Austria. I've got some older pieces but I wanted to put in a couple of new paintings."

When they reached A.'s studio, Hartley put down the case. They looked at the paintings.

"This is the series you mentioned?"

A. nodded.

"Curious, isn't it? Using a square format. It's difficult."

"It seems to work with these images."

"They link, don't they? They're consistent."

"Yeah."

Hartley ran his hand over the breezeblocks.

"It would be a shame to lose this place. Good size, good light. Not too expensive?" he looked to A. "Well, we'll all be in industrial estates in Kent soon." Hartley nodded to the case. "You'll take good care of it?"

"Yes. Don't worry."

THE NAKED SPUR

When Hartley left the studio, A. opened the case and took out an electric drill. He drilled four holes in his door and fixed a bolt, hasp and padlock on the outside of it. He replaced the drill in its case, locked up and left for the station.

(43)

A. climbed down the step ladder from the attic with a skeleton in his arms. The skull, legs and all of both arms except for the left humerus were missing. It was discoloured and held together by wire and bolts. Bands of browned resin connected the ribs to the breastbone. He dropped the torso on his bed. He went to the landing and closed the attic port and folded the step ladder. He put the skeleton inside a black rubbish sack and carried it out of the house.

He waited on the platform of Mudchute station and took a train to Limehouse station. When A. took a seat on the train, the contents of the sack rattled. The old man sitting opposite stared at the bag then at A.

When A. got to his studio, he put the skeleton down on a chair and ate a chocolate bar.

(44)

"How's business been?"

A. was in a chair looking a framed woodcut on the gallery wall. The print, executed in one-point perspective, was of a woman at the top of a leaning tower.

"There's hardly been any since I saw you."

"You went to Paris."

Dent's dog trotted from a ceramic sculpture near the window to the desk.

"Did I tell you?" Dent leant back in his chair. "Yes, I had a week in Paris staying with friends. And all that was very agreeable. Well, the gallery was closed that week. All the collectors are away so I didn't lose any business. Well, as soon as I got back I went to a club and within ten minutes I said to my friend, I'm sick. I don't know how I knew, but I just did. The next day I could hardly move. My temperature was something ridiculous. The upshot was I was bedridden for a week and then I was just so weak I couldn't come in for another two. I only opened up again yesterday."

Dent glanced at a stack of unopened mail on his desk.

"So, there hasn't been any business to speak of. And no, no one has bought anything of yours. I had that large canvas in the window and had a couple asking about it but they didn't come back. I've put it in the store. I can't let the display get stale."

A. was looking at the reverse of the canvas which stood on an easel at the window.

"Don't worry. The painting is still here if they come back. You'd be amazed how often it happens that when I change the display people come back and say, have you still got that picture you had in the window. Sometimes it works to your advantage taking things away for a bit."

The dog sat on the carpet next to Dent, head cocked.

"Business always picks up at this time of year. I know what I'm talking about. Anyway, you've got that office job, haven't you? You're probably earning more than I am."

THE NAKED SPUR

A. circled fingertips on the armrests.

"You keep painting and I'll keep pushing your work. Deal?"

"Deal."

"Now get yourself back to the studio and paint something I can sell. Or at the very least, something I can have in the gallery. No more fannies."

(45)

When A. knocked on the door to Hartley's studio voices talking inside stopped. Hartley's shape appeared in the glass then he opened the door.

"Thanks," said Hartley when A. handed him the case. "I've got someone here to look at the paintings. It's the writer for the catalogue. I can't really talk now."

"I have to get to the office. Are we okay to meet on Saturday?"

Hartley said they were and closed the door.

(46)

Eleanor followed A. into his studio. He watched her. She looked at the square paintings on the walls then studied the space.

"It's a nice space. The light's wonderful." She was looking up. "Changeable as well, I suppose. You work from photos so it doesn't matter to you. Not in that sense."

She moved about looking from floor to skylight.

"It will be difficult to get anything like this for this rent. When we paid rent, I mean."

She was under the skylight.

"And you don't have leaks?"

"No leaks," replied A.

She stood over his palette. Pause.

"Yeah. The space. Hmmmn. I'm going to miss this place. Getting broken up is sad. I made some good stuff in my studio and it's a shame to lose the connection. You never know how a change of environment will affect your work."

Pause.

"What about--?"

A. nodded to the pictures on the walls.

Eleanor was standing next to a painting of a woman splayed on a bed, thighs parted.

She said, "They're. Quite. Forceful."

She folded her arms and waggled a foot, heel to the floor.

"They're ahmmm. Well. Distinctive, aren't they? You've really captured the ahmmm form, the ahmmm figure there. In black and white. There's not much room for metaphor."

She looked at the skeleton torso and then at the door.

"Yeah. Listen, I'll catch up with you later. I have to pack. It's time."

(47)

Hartley and A. made their way around the exhibition. The walls were painted slate grey. The paintings were highly coloured and in thick impasto encrusted on boards. Some of the paintings were small and in glazed boxes, yellow and green, umber and sienna. The draw-

THE NAKED SPUR

ings were rubbed raw and patched, soot dark in places.

Outside, it was raining. Orange Street. On Panton Street they saw an epileptic lying outside the "Tom Cribb". His hands were slapping the pavement. The soles of his trainers drummed up and down, light against the dark macadam. Two bouncers stood over him, watching.

Hartley and A. went to a pub. The television over the bar showed pixellated starbursts in a night sky, tracer fire. The caption in the corner of the screen read "KABUL".

(48)

There were three people in the room. A man with blond hair, reading from a computer screen, a woman reading a library book and A., filling, emptying and refilling leads into a mechanical pencil.

A woman entered the room, slipped some clipped sheets into a tray and left. A. collected the sheets and put them on his reading stand. After making one mark in pencil, A. clipped the pages together, stamped the top sheet and initialled it.

In the typing area, a couple of typists sat at a row of computers. A. handed the pages to one and walked on to the galley kitchen. He got a cup of coffee from the machine and climbed out through the open window on to the flat roof. He walked past windows revealing offices empty of furniture. At the far end he sat on the tarpaper roof and took a drink.

There was a heat haze over the City. A band of brown-grey rested on the horizon, partly hiding tower blocks to the east. Cranes were rotating. The low sun bounced off the cabs. Office windows showed desks, computers, photocopiers, binding machines with manuals, folders, cups and pot plants on windowsills. At one was a figure, head lowered. In the office car park, a motorcyclist was on a bike with its kickstand down. He removed his helmet and swigged water from a bottle.

A. finished his coffee and crossed the roof. He climbed back through the window and returned to the office. Through a glass wall he, saw the two figures seated, positions unchanged. He went to the floor below and the cafeteria counter. The porthole of the kitchen door framed the cook facing to one side. She rubbed her eyes with the heel of a hand. When she came out her eyes were sparkling.

"Are you okay?"

"Fine." She picked up a pad. "We have pasta bake tonight."

"One portion."

"What time?"

"Eight o'clock."

"You have others upstairs?"

"I'll ask them to come down."

She smiled and returned to the kitchen before A. finished his next sentence.

(49)

Damien: "That sounds fine. We can meet at the restaurant on the corner and have a drink. It's something I'm pleased with. You'll get to see it first. Adam told you about the show we've got?"

THE NAKED SPUR

A.: "Yes."

Damien: "A little short notice but as soon as Adam said he was available then things came together fast. We spent all yesterday finishing the invitations. I think I saw your name on a label. If you don't get one then just saw and I'll get you a handful. This is my first show in a while. It's been a few years. It's great to be showing again. I wanted to show something new. This is a bit of a departure from the college stuff. People say they love the old stuff but you can't stay in a comfort zone, can you? It makes a change from wrestling with advertisers and Arts Council money men. You heard the magazine has folded?"

A.: "No. I'm sorry to hear that."

Damien: "Yeah. The Arts Council withdrew their funding. Just as we were starting to sell out, reaching foreign markets, getting in big names to write for us. Yeah. I don't know. I guess we had a great run but there was so much more I wanted to do."

A.: "What will you do?"

Damien: "Take a break, I guess. I don't know. We'll see how things pan out. There's the exhibition and then, well, who knows? Anyway, see you at the restaurant then we'll go and see my piece at the photography studio. We can talk then."

A.: "See you on Monday."

(50)

Damien led A. down into a basement workspace. The air smelled of glue, fixative and vinegar. On a bench were two square photographs. They were mainly black.

At the edges were irregular blooms of brown and sulphur yellow.

"It was an accident, but it seems to work. Well, cultivated accident. I'm pretty pleased with them. You never know quite what's going on until things develop."

A. bent to bench level.

"And these are going to be mounted?"

"On steel. The company has just changed from using an adhesive that'll last for five hundred years to one that'll last for three hundred years."

Damien put his hands in his pockets.

"If I'd brought these in last month they would have got the old type of adhesive."

Damien yawned.

A.: "These are going in the show?"

Damien: "Yes. They're being delivered on Monday."

Damien yawned again.

"We better get out before the fumes put us to sleep," he said.

Heading down Great Sutton Street, Damien said to A. that he had seen Piers Floyd.

"He was going to write about his life. He had it lined up. A publisher had met him and wanted to print something. Then, all of a sudden, he didn't want it."

"What happened?"

"We think the publisher got a phone call. Pressure was applied. Someone didn't want the book published."

"Was it his cousin Mack?"

"Yeah. Well, I think it was him. Piers thinks it was him. It stands to reason. It's a shame though. He's got a fascinating family. He's a curious guy, Piers. Did you

THE NAKED SPUR

hear he sold me his car? The silver Merc? Yeah. It had no brakes. I mean, when I bought it, he said, you might want to have the brakes looked at. He didn't say they didn't work at all."

They stepped on to the road.

"I sold it," said Damien. "After I had the brakes fixed," he added.

They visited a small gallery. There was a group of works by different artists on display.

"Hey. Look at that."

It was a rectangular canvas coloured olive green with a splash of silver at the centre.

A. asked what it was.

"It's a Warhol."

Damien talked with the gallerist while A. circled the gallery four times.

(51)

Two turns off Brick Lane was a street of bare-brick Georgian terraced houses. The windows were tall. Casements and doors were matt greens and blues. Steps led to each door, cast-iron boot scrapers next to some.

A wooden sign hung from an iron fixing over the gallery door. A. entered a front room with stripped floorboards and spotlights in the ceiling. On the walls were two abstract paintings and two square photographs. The photographs were on steel supports, the paintings were fixed to the walls by mirror plates. One of the paintings was predominantly purple.

A. looked at the art and returned to the hallway. In a back room a figure was at a desk. There was the sound of typing. A. went back to the front room. He paused over the visitor book, then turned and left the gallery.

Two Bengali boys on the pavement looked at A. as he opened the front door. One of them held a screwdriver. They made for the corner and disappeared. On the dull-green window ledge, a long scratch meandered.

(52)

"I saw Piers Floyd yesterday. He was at the gallery. Two, three, lift."

Hartley and A. lifted the panel from its tins and carried it flat to four tins close to the window, where they set it down.

"He's sold his house in South Africa. He didn't say anything about painting. You heard he's building his own studio in Bermondsey? I haven't met anyone who's been there. The way Piers was talking about it, it sounded great. The light, you know. Now this one."

They picked up an MDF panel painted matt red and laid it on the vacated tins. Hartley altered the placement of the tins.

A train crossed the viaduct.

"He asked after you."

Hartley stood up and regarded the red panel. He walked to the corner and picked a cigarette packet out of the debris on the floor by the chairs, then found a lighter among letters and photographs on the coffee table.

"I liked your pieces in the gallery."

"Thanks."

Hartley crouched to brush something off the panel.

THE NAKED SPUR

"The lighting was tricky. The halogens gave a bit of glare on the highlights, caused some shadows. And the light changes so much. It's difficult to light for both a mixture of artificial and natural light and for pure artificial light. People don't realise."

Hartley tapped ash into a paint tin.

"Did Damien tell you about his photographs?"

"Something about corrosion."

Hartley looked at his hands. A bar of red crossed his palm.

"The invitation cards were his idea."

A. was at the crates, reading the labels. Hartley joined him and began to pick off the labels. The text was in Italian.

"Have you talked to the gallery about exhibiting? It might be worth trying."

(53)

"No, sorry. I don't recognise the name. A., you said? No. What year did you leave college? Oh, well, so many people graduate each year that I lose track. Sorry. Do you still make art? Oh, hey, good for you. Well, there's nothing wrong with painting. I guess you have to subvert it a little, that's all. I guess that's what all the good painters now are doing. Have you thought about exhibiting? Do you? No, I never heard of that gallery. Ah ha. Oh, let me think. Well, we're pretty booked up but we might be able to find a space in the programme. And you're a painter, you say? The last two shows have had paintings. We gave Ben McEwan a solo exhibition at the beginning of the year. Um. So. We like to mix it up a bit. We're thinking of focussing on new media for a while. We have a Spanish photographer and an Iranian video artist coming up next. Um, I'd never say never though. Sure, if you want. Well, we're open this weekend. Slides are fine, to get a general idea. And you have a résumé? And press clippings too? Oh, the slides and résumé will be okay. No, we're all about emerging artists. We show a lot of artists who have been around for less time than you, some people straight out of college. Oh. Sure. If you want. Write it here. Here, borrow mine. No, I don't know the Isle of Dogs. Ah ha. Well, that's not ideal I guess. We all have to compromise. Oh? I know about that. Yeah. My sister worked in real estate some time. No, in the gallery pretty much full time now. Oh yeah? Do you? He was here only a couple of hours ago with his gallerist. He was pleased with the installation. We didn't really talk. Did you? So it must be nice to see it on a gallery wall. Ah ha. He's great painter. We're lucky to get him just for one show, and Damien, of course. No, I haven't heard about any reviews. Most come out after the show is down. Oh. Yes. After noon. If the door is shut ring the bell. Okay. Thank you. Yes. You too. Goodbye."

(54)

She held the sheet of slides to the window.

"How big did you say these were?"

"Sixteen inches square."

"I like the other ones better."

The woman pursed her lips and turned to face A., slides at her waist.

THE NAKED SPUR

"Probably best to come back next year when you have some new work. That's if we're still here. We're programmed up to the spring. Do you know Manolo Chavez? He's this wonderful photographer who went to the same college as us, a year below you. He's been commissioned to make these photographs of flowers for Estée Lauder for their Paris headquarters. These things are enormous. They showed a couple of them at the Economist Building. They're going to Rome before they're installed in Paris. Do you know Rome? Well, he was paid a fortune. I hardly recognised him at the Victoria Miro opening. He's dressed in Paris couture head to toe now. My God, the boys go crazy for him. Anyway, he's agreed to show the test pieces he did for the commission. They're large for Polaroids of flowers. I wanted to buy one but they're too expensive. Anyway, he's our next show."

She handed A. his slides and an invitation card.

"Before his show we're doing a fundraiser, an auction here. We've only managed to restore this floor. We haven't done anything to the cellar. You can put something in for it, if you want."

She showed him to the door.

"Do come. Auction night is good fun. We get a mixed crowd. You'll know some of the people there. Manolo has given us something. It's a contact sheet which he's written on. It's exquisite."

A. went through the market, stalls filled with cassette boxes in Arabic, photographs of Mecca in plastic frames, plates and plaques with inscriptions. Women in burqas, men in sandals. Men in overalls and rubber boots unloaded carcasses from a lorry. A. turned away, treading on crushed okra.

(55)

There were figures under a gas heater outside the gallery. Women were smoking, men pulled hipster jackets tight. Damien waved to one of the figures. He and A. climbed the steps into the house.

The house was thick with people. The walls were full of objects. A drawing of a chair, a vinyl disc, a case with travel cards, a signed poster, a framed signature, a child's drawing of a house next to a printed text, an oil painting of a hamster, a sheet of writing, a map in marker pen, a handprint, a plastic car hung on a thread, an apple modelled in paper, half a colouring-book page, the plaster cast of an ear, a photograph of a light switch. On a table was a book of lists. Some entries had marks next to them.

Damien moved through the crowd. A. was by a set of handcuffs wrapped in floral fabric. A man with a pierced lip and eyebrows was ticking a sheet.

"How are you? I haven't seen you in ages."

Barry Janus was next to A. He had a beard and was wearing a jacket. His stomach strained his T-shirt.

"Hello, Barry."

"You've got something in the auction."

"Have you?"

"No, I don't have anything at the moment. I'm back painting again. Feeling my way back. Sorry about not keeping in touch. You know how it is. When you've got a girlfriend it kind of eats up your life. There's nothing left over for yourself, not really much for the art either. Look at her."

A blonde girl in a red skirt was talking to Damien and Hartley

"Sorry, but you guys don't really compare. Seriously, if it's a choice between hanging out with you guys in your studios and her naked…"

Barry Janus smiled.

"I'm working for a Swiss investment firm as an art consultant. They're giving me money to go around galleries and studios and buy art, stuff I think worth getting. That got me back into painting, looking at all that art. I've been painting again for six months. Nothing really finished. You need perspective. It takes a while to get your hand back in. The eye is there already but the hand comes later. It's like a muscle that you have to exercise."

He finished his wine.

"I need another."

When he returned with a full glass, he said, "Now I'm doing this advising, I'm in a position to help out artists. You guys. I can buy work. I knew when I took this job that I could use it that way. That was half the attraction for me. To back painters who are really worth backing."

He drank.

"That's important. People aren't looking at painting. But I'm looking."

He pointed to his eye.

"It matters to make a commitment, to lay down cash. Why don't you send me some slides?"

He took out a business card. A. put it in a pocket.

"I know that's what matters to painters like you, like us," said Barry Janus over the noise. "Hard money. If I'd had that money from painting straight after college then maybe I'd have carried on painting. Five years I didn't paint. It's too long. This way I might be able to stop that happening to other artists. Make sure you send me something. We'll work something out."

The crowd closed around him.

"A., isn't it?"

It was Nelson Nicobar in a linen suit, his cheeks flushed.

"It's good you've contributed to the auction. It's valuable that places like this keep going. There's some cracking pieces here. I've put some money down on a piece but I was outbid. A critic's money doesn't go far."

Hartley joined them.

Nelson Nicobar: "I haven't seen your piece."

Hartley: "It's in the hall. It's a bit packed there."

Nelson Nicobar: "It's a good turnout. Better than the last one."

Hartley: "Someone put in a bid for your print."

There was a burst of laughter, a ripple of applause.

Nelson Nicobar said, "I know who that was. I'll tell you about it later if she gets it. I'm sure she won't mind you knowing."

Someone was shouting "Darling! Darling!". Shoulders pushed against them. Damien approached them with a sheet.

"There are some names here. Some of this stuff might be worth something one day. Worth putting in a bid if you've got some money," he said. "We're going to The Golden Hart later. Coming?"

Outside, A. was under the gas heater. Barry Janus and Damien were in conversation on the kerb. A girl next to A. was sniffing. On the opposite pavement a group of youths in hooded tops headed to Bethnal Green, one twisting round to observe the figures outside the gallery.

"May I?"

The sniffing girl was looking at A. There was a silver phial in her hand.

"The breeze is picking up. I don't want any blowing away."

She leant against A.'s back, cupping her hands around her face, and inhaled.

"Thanks," she said, smiling.

She brushed a hand over the back of A.'s jacket and went inside, tucking away the phial.

A. shook hands with Barry Janus and Damien and walked to Commercial Street. A tramp had passed out on the steps of Christ Church. Around him a dog paced, whining.

(56)

There were cigarette butts, bottle caps and dried splashes on the paving stones. Inside, a woman was sweeping the hall floor around the gas heater.

"Follow me."

Swathes of bubble wrap lay on the gallery floor. A man was folding tissue paper around a papier mâché set of teeth.

"I'm sorry it didn't sell. It probably proved a bit traditional for our buyers. But thank you, anyway."

She folded the frame in bubble wrap and handed it to A.

"We raised almost five thousand pounds. That should keep us open next year. People don't believe me when I tell them how much mailouts cost."

Empty bottles were being dropped in a crate.

"Manolo's private view is next Thursday evening at seven. Thank you again and good luck with your painting."

On Commercial Street, a shop was being gutted. Turks with padded work shirts carried plasterboard to a van which sat low on its suspension. The interior of the building was a cave, wires dangling, floorboards gone. A trail of dust between van and shop door crossed the pavement.

At the traffic lights, a car with tinted windows thumped with bass. Its trim buzzed like an insect.

(57)

"I've never heard of a career proofreader. I mean, nobody ever said to the school careers officer, I want a life among the hyphens and semi-colons of due-diligence schedules. It doesn't happen that way."

The large man took off his spectacles and dropped them on the pile of papers on his desk

"In this department, there are temps, people who are killing time between careers or supplementing a vocation that doesn't earn and ex-print workers. It's not a profession you get into because you yearn for the pastures of a bridging-loan agreement or a rights-issue share prospectus."

He rubbed the bridge of his nose.

"You've got your art, Norman's got his book writing, Jenny's got her acting. None of those pay much. That isn't the point. You do it because that's your life. None of you made an active decision to be here, you just ended up here."

"Not that that's a bad thing," he added, leaning back in his chair. "In some ways it's a necessary thing. After all, there's no career progression, no performance bonuses. The old printers are serving out their time waiting for their pensions. Temps are covering their rents for a few months. I'm here because the hours suit me. I've got my gardening, the charcoal burning and so on. If I could be motivated, I might find something else to earn money but this is one of those jobs where you put down your pencil at midnight and walk out the door and you don't give a second's thought to the job until you sit down at the desk the next day at four in the afternoon. That's one of the advantages. You don't put anything of yourself into the work. You do your hours and check out. What does get to me is the cheese-paring attitude of the company but the work itself is, well, reading documents.

"The job has attractions."

He looked out of the window. The tip of Monument burned yellow against the orange-black night.

"Pretty elusive ones though."

He tipped his head back, eyelids lowered.

"But now I think about it, there is a certain Zen-like state of grace you reach on occasion. Correcting the typos in a page of contract is almost like weeding a lawn. At the end you're left with this exquisite, cleansed expanse of turf where before it was riddled with thistles."

Then he laughed and picked up his mechanical pencil.

(58)

The door was opened and A. approached Eleanor's studio. On its door was a note. A. looked up. The sheet had gone from the studio windows. A. faced the door, hands in pockets.

He walked through the courtyard. A bed sheet had been hung from a window. There was writing on the sheet: "SAVE OUR STUDIOS". He passed through the second gate and the door to the passage. Taking the keys out by his studio door, A. paused.

At the last door on the right, a chink of light cut the corridor. A. approached and pushed the door open. The nails and shelf on the wall were bare. The floor was marked by fans of aerosol spray and drops of white paint. In a corner, was a bag with aerosol cans, cardboard stencils, drinks bottles, a latex glove with a split. There was nothing else.

A. stepped out, went to his studio and locked the door.

(59)

When the jar was one-third filled with green liquid, A. dipped brushes in it. Pressed on the bottom of the jar, the bristles remained stiff. As they were twisted and pressed, the bristles started to splay. As they did,

THE NAKED SPUR

fine particles of grey plumed in the liquid. After some minutes, the bottom of the jar was under a layer of sediment. Removed from the liquid the brushes, A. scraped the ferrules clean of paint with a pocket-knife. The steel ferrules glinted under the lights. The brushes went back in the jar.

A. carried the jar from his studio down the corridor. He ran a tap, emptied the jar and washed the brushes until the bristles no longer discoloured the water. The bristles were rubbed with coal-tar soap then rinsed a second tie. He turned off the tap and picked up brushes, jar and soap.

Facing him was an old man. He was at the corner of the corridor. He had a smock on, which was spotted with paint. The man's long grey hair was carefully brushed. The joints of his hands were swollen.

"There's not long now," said the old man. "Time's very short. You know the score. Don't you know the score? Yeah," he said softly. "You know the score."

The old man turned to leave, stopped, looked back at A.

"Don't forget. Time's short now. Don't forget."

The old man walked away, back bowed.

(60)

A. put the skeleton torso into a black plastic sack and took it with him to the station. It was dark. On the south-bound platform, a man was eating a burger. At the end of the platform, a youth was smoking. The smell of cannabis smoke drifted through the air. A. rested on a seat and hugged the skeleton to him. A train approached.

A man was sitting on his own in a splash of vomit. He was asleep. The other passengers had gathered at either end of the carriage. All the windows were open.

When he reached Cutty Sark station, A. alighted the train and took the escalator up to ground level. There was a fine mist of drizzle in the air. It made circles around the streetlights.

A. walked past the Cutty Sark and the quay. A. passed the obelisk on the promenade and stopped by the railings. Lamps lit the path. The river was dark. He looked either side of him then unwrapped the skeleton. He stuffed the bag into a pocket and dropped the skeleton over the railings. There was a clatter. A. looked over the railings. In the dimness was a skeleton. It made a faint shape in the darkness. The skeleton had caught on a corroded iron bracket halfway down the riverside parapet.

A. paused and looked about him. Then he walked to the steps down to the river. It was dark. A. walked slowly, one hand on the promenade wall. It was damp. The steps were slick with mud and algae. Near the bottom, A. slipped. The bank was a mixture of sand and gravel. Water was lapping at the foot of the parapet. A. made his way to where the skeleton hung. It was out of his reach when he stretched up. He stood with hands on hips, looking at the skeleton, water slapping his boots.

He walked along the bank and thrust his hands into the water. After twenty metres, he stopped. There was a beam lying on the river bed. It was slippery with weed and covered with barnacles. He could not move it. He carried on walking, feeling with his hands. He found a plastic curtain rod tapping against the parapet. He retrieved it and waded back to the skeleton.

When he got there, he heard footsteps above. One was a pair of stiletto heels. He stood still. The steps stopped.

"What is all this?" A man's voice.

"You know what I mean." A woman's voice.

A sigh. The man said something inaudible.

"No."

He spoke again.

"I said no."

He spoke again.

"I don't care what she did. I'm not her or haven't you noticed?"

The man said something.

"Oh, really? That's not what I heard," she said.

Silence. The water was over A.'s ankles. He gripped the curtain rod.

"Don't touch me."

Pause.

"I said, don't touch me."

The man replied.

"So, that's the important thing, is it?"

The woman was crying.

"It's not a competition, you know."

The man did not reply.

There was movement, then footsteps.

The man called, "Come back."

Then another set of footsteps diminished. Silence.

After a pause, A. held the end of the pole and poked

at the skeleton. The bones rattled. He tried again. After another try, the skeleton fell with a splash into the river, that was now at A.'s knees. He waded back to the steps. On the steps, he paused, listening. Then he ascended the steps to the path. His trousers were wet and his boots thick with mud and weed. He walked west. Where the path reached the ferry dock, there were figures in the shadows. A woman was leaning against the railings. A man was crouching on the paving stones. His head was under her skirt. Her pants were around her stiletto-heeled shoes. The pair froze, the woman holding the man's skirt-covered head. The woman watched A. pass. A. walked along the path, leaving a trail of muddy footprints behind.

(61)

The man in the swivel chair started when A. knocked on the doorjamb.

"I was expecting you," he said.

The office was dim with smoke, blinds closed. Through the closed window traffic was audible. A fire engine passed fast, lights on but with no siren.

The man extended a hand.

"Hamish McGregor. You spoke to me on the phone."

McGregor got to his feet and unlocked a cabinet with a key on his belt. Inside the cabinet were keys on eyehooks, each labelled with a number. Most hooks had one key, some had two keys, a few no keys. McGregor took a key and relocked the cabinet.

A. followed him out of the office and down a flight of concrete steps. The pipes over the stairs were lagged with foil-covered insulation. There were deep finger marks in the foam.

Down more steps and through a series of swing doors was a corridor of unpainted breezeblock. There was the noise of hammering. A radio was playing dance music. There was a smell of resin, fibreglass and Chinese food. They reached a corridor with flour dusting the floor, worn black with damp at the centre. In the flour were prints of pigeon claws.

McGregor stopped at a door. The breezeblocks here were greasy and fractured. The door was dented. McGregor unlocked the padlock and opened the thin hasp. A. followed him into a room about twenty foot by twenty-five foot, irregularly shaped with a high ceiling. Against two walls were narrow work surfaces supported on poles, next to them were two tall, wooden stools. In one corner was a desk with a black top. In another corner was a steel sink on wheels, plumbing fittings in one sink with a shadow of rust around them. By the sink was a stack of baker's pallets. Light came from a row of wired-glass windows in iron pivoting frames, some starred with cracks.

McGregor flicked on a fluorescent tube.

Directly facing the door was a thicket of iron pipes which ran up a pillar to the ceiling. Just below the ceiling a number branched out and travelled through side walls. Brown stains ran from the window frames down the white walls. The floor was mottled with puddle marks. The work surface had cup rings on it.

A. went to the brown speckles on one wall at chest height. He brought his face close then touched a mark.

He rubbed his fingers together.

"That's grease. It'll come out if you give it a wipe."

McGregor was watching A. A. wiped his fingers on his trousers.

"How much of this is staying?"

A. opened a desk drawer. It was filled with flyers on luminescent yellow paper. "Special Selection £1.50.", "£2.50 for two, drink's 50p." Another drawer had a roll of plastic bags.

"That sink will be going. Someone is collecting that next week."

"Those?"

McGregor looked at the stack of pallets.

"Don't you want them?"

A. looked at them and then at him.

"Well, we can get rid of those if you want."

"I'll have the desk and the stools."

"Fine."

A. crouched to look at the stains on the floor.

"So." McGregor was turning the key in one hand. "So."

A. was looking at the marks, then back to the pipes. He scuffed the edge of a puddle stain with his boot.

"So."

A. stood up, eyes on the pipes.

"Two weeks rent free for me to fix up the space."

"I can do that. Fine. No problem there."

A. looked down at the floor. Pause.

"I'll take it."

"I'll take you back to the office and we can sign the contract. I have the paperwork ready. It's a standard form for all the leases."

McGregor switched off the light and went to the corridor. A woman in a cardigan was smoking. She leant to one side to look into the room. McGregor said something to her and she extinguished the cigarette under her shoe and walked away. A. looked at the windows and followed McGregor out.

(62)

Hartley pulled a pole from under the work surface. It listed then fell, flicking up a spray of crumbs as it hit the floor. A. pulled it to the centre of the studio. He looked at it then at the wall.

"It wasn't screwed to the brackets on the wall, just resting on them. It wasn't fixed to the poles either."

They pulled other pieces away from the walls and carried them to a skip in the parking area outside. They dragged the pile of baker's pallets into the corridor.

Hartley looked at the walls.

"They're covered with grease."

A. pointed to a bag. "I'm going to scrub them."

Hartley was by a small puddle of water near the pipes. "What's this?"

"The manager says it's rainwater. It got in through the windows over the weekend. He closed the windows when he got in this morning."

They both studied the windows.

"Were they open when you saw the space last week?"

"No."

Pause. The only objects in the room were the black-topped table and a bag from a hardware store.

"It's a decent space. My first studio was about this size."

"It doesn't get much daylight."

Parts of the windows were obscured by large shapes.

"Lorries park there."

"Could someone climb on them?"

"Possibly, but the windows are narrow. I don't think anyone could get through. They don't open all the way. The lighting isn't good." A. turned on the light. "I'll buy some daylight bulbs and rig them."

They looked at the pipes which ran six inches below the ceiling.

"Do they leak?"

"I'm not sure."

Hartley tested the door handle. Dents in the door showed it hollow between thin boards. The hasp was aluminium and bent. The doorframe was loose. When Hartley hit it, a sift of powder fell from the outside of the frame. Blocks around it had holes. Between courses there were cracks in the mortar.

"You'll have to do something about it if you want to stay. A bolt won't fix it."

A. ran a hand through his hair.

"If anyone really wants to get in," Hartley continued. "They can just take a hammer to the wall. Perhaps putting a new bolt and padlock on is the worst option. It makes it look like there's something worth stealing."

Hartley shrugged.

"I'll buy you a coffee. The Pierrot Café?"

THE NAKED SPUR

(63)

When the man with the van arrived, he and A. loaded the contents of his studio into the vehicle. They started with the largest canvases and moved the rest in order of decreasing size. The biggest took two men to manoeuvre down the corridor to the fire exit. The exit was propped open with a fire extinguisher. After the first six canvases, the men carried separately. Each painting was wrapped in clear plastic or bubble wrap. Paintings were pushed close together, fronts facing each other, edges overlapping.

It began to snow. As the canvases were carried inside, snowflakes turned to droplets on the plastic.

The remaining canvases were smaller; the men carried one in each hand. Then the paintings were small enough to be taken in low piles held to the chest. The driver climbed into the back of the van and stacked items while A. fetched them from the studio. A. carried out the chairs. The easel was wheeled out on castors. Then boxes with bottles and tubes, papers and magazines. Lastly, a roll of used canvas. The driver stowed it and rolled down the shutter.

A. returned to the studio. It was empty except for a couple of plastic tubs and a paintbrush stiff with paint. Where the canvases had stood were dust-free patches. A. unscrewed the bolt and hasp from the door, putting it in his jacket pocket and locked the door's lock, walked down the corridor, through the door and gate. He pushed the keys through the administration letterbox.

They drove through the thickening snow. By the time they reached Greenwich, there was a thin white sheet on the asphalt. The van left dark tracks. They drove to a car park and a loading bay. After they had emptied the contents of the van, A. paid the driver in banknotes taken from his pocket. They shook hands and the driver left. A. sat on chair and looked at the windows and the dust on the sills and on the brickwork.

(64)

A. half filled the bucket with hot water then carried it out from the toilet and down three flights of stairs. When he got to the studio, he cut open a hole in the box of sugar soap and poured half the contents into the water. He stirred the solution with a scrubbing brush.

A thump, then noise of a diesel engine starting and a block of shadow retracted from the window.

A. scrubbed the walls with a brush, standing on the desk to reach. He carried the bucket upstairs and poured brown water into the toilet bowl. He sluiced out the bucket and half filled it with hot water.

He washed the walls again, then wiped them with a wet sponge.

He took from a bag a coil of cable, plugs and light fittings. He cut the cable with his pocket-knife and stripped the wire ends. He attached them to the plug terminals and light fittings using the tip of his knife as a screwdriver. Out of the bag he took some light bulbs. When tested they gave off bluish light.

After A. had put some screws high in the walls and suspended the lights from them, he opened a tub of paint and painted the walls white. He sat and waited for them to dry. Then he gave them a second coat.

With the desk, chairs, easel and paintings on one side of the room, A. scrubbed the floor with sugar-soap solution. The floor had been painted grey and was banded with watermarks. Paint had scuffed off the bolt heads in the concrete. He rinsed the floor and moved all the objects on to the cleaned area. Then he washed and rinsed the unwashed area.

When he went to the yard to empty the bucket for the last time, it was dark.

(65)

The noise came again. A. put down his brush and went to the door. Silence. A. opened the door and sat down. He looked at the painting on the easel for a long time before getting back to work.

(66)

"Ben McEwan is dead."

Pierrot Café was busy, all tables occupied. The cook was banging steaming plates on to the counter. Hartley was warming his hands around a cup of tea.

"How?"

"He had cancer. You didn't know?" Hartley looked at A.

"I knew he had been ill."

Hartley lit a cigarette.

"Yeah. Cancer. He was in remission. He got married. He was painting again, painting better." Hartley shrugged. "We saw him only a few months ago, at the private view he had. He seemed fine. He was talking about the work, shows he had lined up."

Hartley stared at the burning tip of his cigarette. Sound of frying oil, sound of coins on a counter.

"Nelson called me. The funeral's today."

They looked to the street.

"He was younger than me by a few months."

A. drank his tea. It had started snowing again. A girl in a woollen hat walked by the café, face muffled by a scarf, head lowered. There were snowflakes on her eyelashes.

(67)

Water had run from under the studio door and trickled across the corridor to form a puddle.

"Looks like trouble, sonny."

A woman in a cardigan was smoking under the no-smoking sign.

A. unlocked the door. The middle of the floor was underwater. Water was trickling from half a dozen pipes below the ceiling and running down the side of the downpipes. A. skirted the puddle and craned his head.

"Bought a pig in a poke there," said the smoking woman, at the threshold. "They've had trouble with those pipes before. They should never have let the space out. The last people skipped off owing rent. Hamish is trying to get this space earning again."

A. studied the pipes. Her eyes narrowed.

"Do you know what's up there?"

"Where?"

THE NAKED SPUR

The smoking woman jerked her head upwards.

"Up there. Above."

"No."

"Toilets."

She laughed and pocketed her cigarette packet.

"Fuck knows how those sandwich people there before you didn't get closed down. Turns me cold, it does. Making food there. Gave me the right horrors."

She threw her cigarette in the water.

"Don't take this personal, sonny, but Hamish has fucked you over good and proper."

With a laugh she pushed open a door and left A. alone.

When A. arrived at the manager's office, McGregor was on the telephone. He glanced at A. in the doorway.

"I've, um, seen the, um, leak," he said, replacing the receiver on the telephone. "I'm sorry about this."

"Turn off the water."

"I have. I cut the water this morning when I arrived at eight."

"It's still coming in."

"That's what's upstairs draining. There's no fresh water coming out. It'll take a few hours to run itself dry."

He lit a Silk Cut.

"It's happened before, I heard."

McGregor hesitated.

"Um, yes. Once. A few times. Before, yes. It's vandalism, pure vicious spite. They smashed all the toilets, must have been Saturday night or Sunday. I've told tenants about inviting people over, about giving out the gate security code. We don't have full-time security.

I've asked. I ask every month."

His hands were trembling. The end of his cigarette jittered. He looked A. in the eyes.

"Security," he added, with emphasis.

(68)

Through the open gate and down a short, steep slope, A. went left and rounded the back of the building. His scarf was pulled over his mouth and his hands deep in his jacket pockets. In the car park were vans and trailers. Workers were throwing broken pallets into a skip. A man was changing a tyre. His hands were wrapped in oily rags, a knitted hat was pulled low over his ears.

Through the loading bay was a wide passage with doors in the side. A double door was open, straw spilling out into the corridor. Inside were crates and carved African statues and masks on shelves and on crates, all the flat surfaces were covered with straw. Hanging bulbs illuminated the space. A woman with fingerless gloves held a mask to her chest.

Men in uniform overalls were negotiating a bathtub in protective packing round a corner. There was the sound of a forklift truck clanking. Smell of hot resin. Hollow objects were being moved about, reverberating as they struck solid obstructions. Machinery sounds came from different directions. A stack of tins sat in a corner labelled in Chinese. The English text ran "POWDERED CHICKEN, SUPERIOR GRADE". A door opened with a burst of steam and noise and a Chinese man, in white overalls rubbed dirty at the front, came out to carry the tins inside.

THE NAKED SPUR

Along the corridor floor were plastic rat traps, lengths of plastic binding and scraps of cellophane among the sawdust and flour.

A. unlocked his door and closed the padlock on the outside. Pushing the door shut, he put down his bag. He walked to the centre of the room and looked down then to the pipes. The floor was dry.

He took a fresh canvas from the wall, adjusted the easel and set to work.

(69)

Hamish McGregor capped and uncapped his pen as he listened. He nodded. He glanced sidelong through the blinds. He sat forward. He sat back. He rested on an elbow, twisting the cap on his pen. He rubbed his chin. He cleared his throat. He nodded, face lowered. He adjusted the ashtray, aligned his cigarette packet and lighter in proximity, opened his mouth, closed his mouth. He rubbed the bridge of his nose between forefinger and thumb. He scratched his jaw, sighed, opened and closed his mouth. He tilted his head to one side. He picked up the cigarette packet, set it down, lid open. He nodded. He tugged an earlobe. He cleared his throat. He unfurled his hands. He looked at the wet tread marks A.'s boots had made on the floor when A. left the office.

(70)

Two men carried out the last of the boxes to a van. They left footprints in the flour dusting the corridor.

"Wait for me," said A.

ADAMS

He walked through corridors, through swing doors and up some stairs. The door to the manager's office was open. He placed keys on the desk.

"Sorry about this." McGregor reached into a drawer and handed A. a slip of paper. It was a cheque.

"That covers last month's rent."

A. folded the cheque and pocketed it. He retraced his way to the van. He climbed in the cab and gave the driver directions. The van pulled away.

The vehicle reached an entrance between grey-painted walls. They drove past industrial buildings, loading bays, parked cars. Turning left, the van drew to a halt in a concreted yard. Ahead was a giant shredder filling a container with paper. A breeze picked up a drift of confetti and pushed it around the space. The driver killed the engine. A man loading pallets of boxes into a lorry gave the vehicle a glance.

A. led the driver up a ramp into a building. On their right was a wide lift with accordion doors. "That's what we'll use," said A. They took the stairs to the second floor. Large windows and skylights lit the corridor by the stair and lift exits. The floor was tiled in grey and red linoleum. By the lift doors, it was scratched. Smudges of bright colours were visible: yellow, green, orange. The dabs trailed round the corner.

A. brought them to a grey door glazed with a pane of frosted security glass. Unlocking the door, A. led the driver into a large room with a high ceiling and skylights. One wall was dominated by big windows of pebbled glass. The other walls had no windows and were of breezeblock painted white. The floor was smooth concrete painted grey vinyl. In the corner was a gas heater and beside it two meters. Tube lights hung from chains fixed to beams under the pressed steel roof. Sunlight was coming in through the west-facing windows.

"It'll get hot in the summer."

A. nodded. The driver looked to his right. In the same wall as the door by which they had entered was another door. It was identical to the first.

"Two doors. Gives you a quick getaway if you need it."

They walked the space.

"What do you think?"

The driver looked about him.

"How about stacking the large paintings close to the windows," he said. "Uh, no. That'll block the light. Put the large canvases closer to the door and smaller ones nearer the window."

"And the desk under the windows, in the centre."

"Okay."

They left and walked back to the van and unloaded the largest paintings. They carried them to the lift. When everything was up, A. paid the driver and closed the door.

(71)

"Look how clean it is."

Hartley was standing in A.'s studio studying the floor.

"What a beautiful space. I guess my space looked like this once. Plenty of light and ventilation with those windows. No views though," he said, running a fingernail over the pebbled glass.

"You're paying about two-thirds what I'm paying. A bit more. It's worked out in pounds per square metre but I've got a rent freeze from when I moved in. So, I've almost double the space that you've got. I don't know what I'll do when they raise the rent. I can't pay more. I suppose I'll leave."

Over by the stack of paintings, Hartley said, "Your work fits well here. This is a good space for you. Oh, I brought you this."

Hartley handed A. a catalogue with an abstract painting illustrated on the cover. A. opened it. On the title page was the inscription "To A., best wishes, Adam Hartley".

"Thanks. That's kind of you."

"No problem. Shall we get a cup of tea? I'll show you where the cafeteria is."

(72)

When A. opened the door to his room there was a note on the carpet. A. picked up the note, placed it on the bed then removed his coat, shoes and tie. He sat on the bed and read the note. Then he read it a second time and put it in the bureau. He went to the bathroom, urinated, washed his hands and face, brushed his teeth and returned to his room where he undressed. He put a CD on at low volume and turned off the light. He climbed into bed and was asleep before the CD finished.

(73)

"The room's... well, you decide."

THE NAKED SPUR

The girl pushed the door open until it connected with the edge of the bed, less than halfway through the full swing. A double bed filled most of the floor. There was no other furniture.

"I don't think so," said A.

"I felt the same, that's why I took the other room. Sorry. Maybe you could have my old room."

Down the stairs came a woman with black hair tied back. The woman's cheeks were pink.

"Hello. I'm Elsa. Laurie used to live at my house. Now the room's free, do you want to see it? It isn't far."

"Sure."

"It's a few streets across. Close to the station. Very close to the station."

They said goodbye to the girl and A. walked with Elsa past brick terraces down the hill. The streets had parked cars on both sides. Outside one house was an aspidistra in a smashed pot. At most front doors were multiple doorbells. Then came a row of concrete, prefabricated garages, graffiti sprayed on the doors. The sun was low and shining in their eyes. A car backfired and it echoed down the streets.

(74)

Elsa led him upstairs to a low-ceilinged, white-painted room. There was a mattress on a bed, two bookcases and an armchair. The room was warm.

"They start about six o'clock. It doesn't bother me but I've been here years. My room faces the other way. I don't know how you would feel about the noise."

She indicated the two windows. Outside was a yard

with parked cars and a chain-link fence next to a railway station platform. Pulling out of the station was a train.

"That's not a problem," replied A.

The bathroom was small. On a plywood shelf was an assortment of crystals, polished stones and Buddha statues. The shower curtain was speckled with mould. Walking the four paces from the bathroom to the top of the stairs, A. looked into a narrow, book-lined study with a computer on a table at the far window. The books closest to the landing were about teaching, psychology, sociology and poetry. A. followed the woman downstairs.

The kitchen was painted light brown and orange. The refrigerator was covered with photographs of the woman sitting in tropical surroundings. There were postcards with foreign stamps. By a table were a number of bowls with cat food. A plant with trailing fronds was on the microwave, foliage obscuring the control panel.

"And this is the living room."

The wooden floor was smooth. On it was a rug. Two settees faced each other. Near the television set was an aquarium with reddish fish swimming in it. On the walls were some carved masks. A ginger cat, which had been sleeping, started at the arrival of the pair. It dashed through a cat flap in a glazed door which opened on to a tiny patch of grass, a path and some bedding shrubs in a garden.

"I've had these walls white for so long I think I ought to change the colour. People say white is conservative but I don't know. I think the room might be too dark if I change the colour."

THE NAKED SPUR

She pointed to a hedge outside. It was as high as the window.

"What do you think?"

A. walked to the garden door. He studied the garden path for almost a minute while the woman watched him.

"One hundred pounds per week, you say?"

"I'm afraid so, yes."

"And it's available now."

"Whenever you want it. I was going to have it as a guest room but I've got so used to having the money." She trailed off. Her hands were on her hips.

He said, "I'll get my bags."

(75)

Elsa closed her bedroom door and handed some keys to A.

"These are Ibrahim's. He's asleep now," she whispered. "We can sort him out with keys tomorrow. You keep those. He works nights. He stays over sometimes, but he has a flat in Hackney. Anyway, you're paying rent and he isn't, so these belong to you."

They walked down the stairs. The ginger cat ran down the hall.

"That's Archie. He's a darling but very nervous. He was a rescue cat. Two of my cats are from rescue centres. Poor Archie. He's lovely but he won't go near men. Fine with women but won't let men near him. You wonder what he must have gone through before he went to the rescue centre. I don't like think to about it. But he's happy now."

"Have you got all your stuff here now?" she asked him when they were in the kitchen.

"Yes."

"Right then. You work evenings you said? My goodness, what ever happens to your social life? I need my friends. They're the only thing that keeps me sane. I have to pop out now and take your deposit to the bank."

"Make yourself at home," she said, shutting the front door.

In the living room, a grey cat and white cat were asleep on separate settees. In the fish tank, a stream of bubbles poured upward.

(76)

"Don't bother with Barry. He's like that. I only see him once every two years. The last time I spoke to him he was telling me how to paint. Never mind he hadn't picked up a paintbrush since leaving college. He doesn't paint abstracts. I couldn't understand what he was trying to tell me."

Hartley swilled the coffee in his cup.

"Maybe he didn't get the slides. Maybe they got lost in the post. I don't know."

Hartley frowned and dipped a finger into the coffee.

"He went to Will's studio and gave him all this shit about the Swiss investment firm. Well, maybe it was true. I don't know. But he spent an hour going around Will's studio saying, this is good, this is no good, this is strong, this is a failure. And then he started to tell Will which colours he should be using. Barry said that to me too. You should use more pink, he said. What does

THE NAKED SPUR

he know?"

Hartley looked at his fingertip then wiped it on his sweatshirt.

"So, he spent an hour with Will telling him his ideas on art. He picked out four or five paintings and said, they're the ones. I'll be round to collect them next week. The paintings were going in the collection. And he never turned up."

"What happened?" asked A., placing the catalogue back on the chair.

Hartley shrugged.

"Will phoned him up and asked him what happened. Barry just said things were on hold and he'd be back in a week to collect the paintings. Don't sell the paintings, he said. Will had a buyer after one of the pictures. After another week of nothing, he calls up Barry and says, what's going on. Barry replied that there had been a mix-up and that he had never promised to buy the paintings."

Hartley made a face.

"So, Will had put off this buyer because Barry had earmarked his paintings for the gnomes of Zurich. It turned out either the gnomes had holes in their pockets or Barry Janus was full of shit."

"Did Will sell the picture?"

"I think so. He got hold of the collector and sold it to him at half price to apologise for screwing him around. I can't speak to Barry. Don't worry about him, he's been giving the same line to all of us. Maybe it's all true. With Barry you can't tell. Don't let it get to you."

He put down his cup.

"I wanted to get your opinion on something," he said, getting to his feet.

(77)

"It's a weird sort of set-up, you know?"

Ibrahim was boiling pasta.

"It's an agency that makes press cuttings. In America, they call them clippings. Press clippings. I love that. I love those little differences between American and British English. Working with words all the time, I guess you pick up on these things. Not so different to what you do in your office. You don't go looking for these differences but sometimes they sort of fall in your lap. Which is nice."

He lifted the saucepan lid.

"I do a lot of reading outside of work. Fiction, non-fiction, journalism. Do you read American fiction? I've been reading Mailer, Updike, Bellow, Auster, that lot. It's not so good for my eyes. But to read you've gotta use your eyes. That's the way books come. Easy, Vish."

The grey-haired cat was winding between Ibrahim's ankles.

"We provide cuttings to companies. You know, City firms that want to keep track of this or that company. All that jazz. And for individuals too. There's this one guy, very well known, famous—you'd know him—and he's like this nice guy. Mr Nice Guy. Always smiling, that sort of thing. But he's such a bastard when he doesn't get his cuttings on time. He phones up from the Bahamas and is really angry with our boss, saying we don't know how to do our job. Even if it's just fifteen minutes late, he's on the phone. And he's an important man. You'd think he had better things to do with his time. Really, you wouldn't believe it. And from the TV he looks so nice, such a nice man. Really."

He adjusted the cooker control.

"They work in shifts. I work nights. That's okay for me because I'm a night bird. A bit of a night owl. I'm pretty much adjusted to it now. It's difficult if you lose your routine. But we get a lot of time off so that compensates. Weekends aren't so good because you start to change your routine then you start back and work and have to change it back. Your body doesn't know where it is. What time it is, I mean. The summer's the worst. Trying to sleep when it's raging hot outside and the buses are putting out all their smoke, my God. And you get kids screaming outside your window. Well, I know they're not doing it to annoy me but sometimes it feels that way. When your sleep goes and your routine slips, you get a bit cranky."

He took a fork out of the cutlery drawer.

"I start at ten or midnight and finish at around seven or eight in the morning. How do you like that? And we get cabs, you know? Every day we get cabs. And it's the same company so you get the same drivers. You get to know the drivers. How do you like that? Yeah, you get to know their names, stuff like that. There's this Turkish driver, he wants to talk politics but I'm not having that."

He got a plate out of the cupboard.

"Some drivers they don't want to talk but most do. You'd be surprised. No, you wouldn't be surprised, actually. There are a few who don't talk but most want to talk a bit. Some of them can't really talk. They don't have the English. You know, they have a map and they can count but that's it. But you know even the ones who can't speak so good want to talk. You know, even if it's just something about the weather or what country they come from. From the drivers who don't know me, they always ask—well, not outright but they kind of sneak up to it—if I'm a Muslim. They're so ignorant. They think I must be a Muslim and I say no, Ethiopia has been Christian longer than practically anywhere else on Earth but they don't know anything. Ah, they're so ignorant. My God."

He laughed.

"You're not going on about the Turks again, are you, Ib? He's not going on about the Turks, is he?"

Elsa entered and poured herself a glass of water.

"No. Was I? No. I wasn't. No. There you are. I don't have a problem with the Turks, Elsa."

Elsa returned to the living room, the grey cat followed.

"Okay. Bye, Vish," Ibrahim muttered.

He poured the contents of the saucepan into a sieve. Clouds of steam rose from the sink.

"The drivers are pretty friendly, you know. But it's their living, right? They're not going to come right out and say bad stuff. The agency is their best customer. They tell you their stories. Mostly I just listen. I'm going to write a novel about it some day, with all these characters. London's a great place for that. I just sit back and listen to them talk, collecting material. And sometimes you come across a guy who's interesting, a bit out of the ordinary. There's this one driver who's an Iraqi Kurd and he's so knowledgeable about Persian literature and here he is, in the East End of London, driving a mini-cab. My God, this guy should be, you know, writing essays for TLS or The New Yorker or whatever."

Ibrahim set the olive oil back on the work surface.

"Have you seen the latest TLS? I have it in the living room, I think. But I'm taking it to work with me tonight. Um, so anyway, let me know if you want to have a read of it. They have this great piece on Saul Bellow. I say great, I haven't read it yet. But it looks great. Elsa?"

Pause.

"What?"

"Have you got the pepper in there?"

"I don't know. Yes."

At the doorway, Ibrahim looked back, plate in hand.

"Okay, I'll let you eat in peace now."

The sound of Ibrahim's slippers merged with the blare of the television. Condensation clung to the windowpane.

(78)

A. went down the corridor then turned left. At the end of that corridor was a staircase. On the ground floor, sounds of forklift trucks, dance music played at distortion-level volume. Left through swing doors. At the cafeteria counter, A. ordered food and waited, leaning on a wall. Hanging in the cafeteria were a clock, a calendar and some framed posters of sports cars. A woman in an apron was dealing tin ashtrays on to Formica tables. A. paid for his order and carried the food upstairs. He ate it at his studio desk, looking at the pebbled security glass.

He was painting when a man walked in. The man was wearing spectacles. His head was shaved.

"May I?"

The man was gesturing to an empty chair. He sat, looked about him, then leaned forward to examine the painting on the easel.

"From photographs. I did that when I was at college, before I specialised in design. We had a project to copy a masterpiece. While everyone else was squaring up tracing paper over illustrations and copying them over on to paper, I just photocopied a Van Gogh sunflower picture and painted over the photocopy with acrylic paint. I'd got mine done before some of the others had even started painting. The teacher went on about how accurate my transcription was, all that. He wanted to frame it and hang in the staff room."

He studied the studio.

"Good space this. We looked at this before we settled on the unit opposite. Green Graphic Solutions. You've seen the sign."

He fingered his cufflinks.

"Good light in here. I don't know why more artists don't take these units.

"You know there's another painter on this floor? He does nice stuff, abstract. We were going to buy one of his paintings for the office but they're a bit pricey. We're trying to persuade him to loan us one. He told us to talk to his gallery. We could use the office as a showcase, put up different artists' pictures. Maybe our clients would buy a few. We could split the money. Maybe you could lend us something. Only it would have to be a little less—" he was looking at a magazine on the desk, "—hardcore."

He raised his eyebrows.

"Think about it."

Pause.

"Ever project a slide on to canvas?"

There was a box of slides on the desk.

"Draw around the outlines on to the canvas. Try it. It's quicker than that way. You'll crack on a bit faster."

The man's cufflinks caught the light.

"Combination, that's the secret."

He nodded.

"Combination."

There was a knock and a second man entered the studio.

"Jon? There's a call for you."

"Come and see us," said the first man, standing.

When the men had gone, A. wedged a chair under the door handle.

(79)

Dent emerged from the storage space with two canvases wrapped in black plastic sacks bound with tape.

"And that's it?"

A. unfolded the typed receipt and read.

"Yes."

Dent added the canvases to the others against the

window.

"I'm sorry things have turned out like this. My accountant said we should have pulled the plug on the gallery last year. The place hasn't been open regularly and the usual collectors get out of the habit of visiting. Then when I pay the girl to come in and mind the gallery, I'm paying her wages and there's practically nothing coming in. The bills don't stop arriving just because we're shut."

He ran his hands over his face.

"When the property lease came up for renewal and the figure was higher, my accountant had to intervene. I hardly took anything last year. I've been selling my own collection to keep the gallery going and much of the time the place has not even been open. I've got a mortgage on the flat. The accountant said enough is enough."

Dent sighed.

"And Bruno died. I don't want to talk about it."

He pressed his eyebrows with thumb and forefinger, head down.

"I know you'd like me to buy something from you for myself, but I can't. I like your stuff but I can't help you. Maybe this is for the best. You need a gallery which going to push your work more, get you some reviews. My place isn't that sort of gallery."

A. put away the receipt. They shook hands. Looking out to the square with figures in coats and jackets crossing it, Dent's expression softened.

"I was thinking about Paris. I could rent my flat here and that would cover my mortgage and give me something spare. I could live okay in Paris. I have friends there. I'm so bored with the scene here."

Dent held the door open and A. picked up his paintings.

"Things change," Dent said.

When A. arrived at his studio there was a brown envelope with a plastic window under the door. There was a local council logo printed in one corner.

He put the paintings with the stack of others.

On the palette were brushes tacky with paint. A. placed them in a cut-off water bottle. They disturbed the grey deposit at the bottom of the turpentine. Using a palette knife, he scraped the rubbery skin of black and smear of grey from the glass, then rubbed it with a damp rag. After he cleaned brushes, he put a magazine in a drawer and lay on the floor in a patch of sunlight. The light was irregular. It wavered, dimmed then flared brightly. Sound of distant traffic, sound of lorry loading. Men called to each other. There were gulls on the skylight. Their claws and webbing were clear on the wired security glass, bodies indistinct.

(80)

"He's called Vishnu, after the Hindu god. We call him Vish. Once, when I lived at my old flat, we had to evacuate because of a fire alarm. I told the fireman that my cat was still inside and told him the name. The fireman went back in shouting, fish, fish! I know Vishnu is an odd name but who would call a cat 'fish'?"

Elsa stroked the cat, which had its eyes closed.

"I really believe he can understand what we say. Part

of it, anyway," said Ibrahim. "He's got that look. He reacts to what you're telling him. He's a wise old cat, that one."

"He is old now. Aren't you, Vish?"

The cat opened its eyes, looked into her face then closed its eyes.

(81)

The cook put a plate on A.'s tray.

"Eighty and with the juice, two ten."

A. fed a card into a slot. The number on the display adjusted to "£0.90". The card slid out.

"I'm going soon," said the cook. "When I started here I needed the work. But now... I know this guy who works in a hotel in Mayfair. The money's about the same but better hours, less travelling time."

She picked up a cloth.

"The hotel's already accepted me."

"Congratulations."

"Thank you." She smiled.

"Places like this, they're no good for us."

She was looking at the office through the window.

"For the bosses they're good but not for us. I'm glad to go. It's sad to leave some people here. You make friends."

"Maybe some will come to join you at the hotel."

"I think they might."

A. ate watching the television which was showing golf on mute.

THE NAKED SPUR

(82)

When A. moved the bookcase, something slipped behind it. A. pulled the bookcase away from the wall and moved to one side. There was something paper resting on the floor. A. reached down and retrieved the item from the gap. It was a pornographic magazine featuring amateurs. A. wiped the dust off the cover with a sleeve. "Charlotte reveals her secret fantasies" ran the legend next to a photograph of a blonde woman in lingerie and knee-length boots. The boots were vinyl and had a snakeskin pattern.

A. leafed through the magazine. A few pages had been torn out. A. turned the pages around the torn strips. Three pages had been removed. A. studied the cover. The magazine had been published seventeen months ago.

One page was of amateur contacts. Above brief paragraphs with serial numbers were small photographs. One was of a woman in black lingerie and stockings lying on her back on a carpet. In the top right corner were the bottom of two chair legs.

The front door opened. Elsa was talking.

"-never until it actually happened. Which is no use to me. And typical."

"Oh, yes," said Paula.

There was a pattering of cat paws on the floor.

"Hello, darlings."

A. moved to the chest of drawers and put the magazine in a drawer. Then he closed the drawer and went downstairs.

(83)

The laminated photocopy on the wall said that the gallery had been designed by a prominent architect. The small room had four concrete paving slabs on the floor and white walls. In the centre was a fibreglass sculpture of a figure covered in spray paint. Steps led up to a small office.

Chris Kaminsky leaned over his office desk and handed an envelope to A.

"We're not really working with painters at the moment. The brief is more sculptural and film work. But thanks for showing me your slides. Anyway, it's great to hear from you and to know you're still painting. Do you still keep in touch with Adam Hartley? Yeah, he's a great painter. Isn't he still with Monks Gallery? I haven't seen him in a while."

A. was on the way to the door when Kaminsky said "Put me on your mailing list. I'll come to your next private view."

(84)

Ibrahim was crumbling the dry leaves and seeds over the line of tobacco.

"I read this wonderful piece. It was in a book I've been reading."

He rolled the cigarette and wet the paper edge. The settee was covered with newspapers. On the stereo, John Coltrane was playing.

"Did you know the Italians used chemical weapons in Abyssinia? No, it's true. Not many people know about it. There's this passage, this quote, in the book I've been reading. This writer, I forget his name, but he was actually there. He saw these weapons being used and he writes about how the smoke over the bodies of men and cattle dispersing was like mist on a summer morning. And it's such a beautiful, evocative passage about such a terrible thing. Maybe it seems more beautiful because it's describing something horrible. I can't decide."

Ibrahim lit and inhaled.

"It's reportage but it's almost literature. It has the quality of poetry but about death. Death in Abyssinia."

(85)

"Come in."

Hartley stepped aside and A. entered the studio. The air smelled of linseed oil and white spirit. The window at the far end was open. On a couple of large panels lying horizontally, fresh paint glistened. Hartley and A. sat on chairs with ripped upholstery and blotted with colour. The coffee table overflowed with papers. Hartley switched on the kettle and spooned coffee granules into two plastic cups.

"How's the work?"

"Good. I just got in. I was working late yesterday. I've got three new paintings."

A. went over to the panels in the middle of the studio. The floor was tiled with hardboard, joins sealed with gaffer tape. The boards were blotched with gloss paint, crimson, electric blue, moss green, with hanks of newspaper embedded. The panels were on tins. Two panels were red, a third was orange. They gave off the smell of wet paint. The surfaces were glossy smooth, unmodulated. A. bent over one. In the redness was his reflection as a silhouette against the skylight above.

The kettle clicked off and Hartley made coffee. A. walked back to the seats, avoiding dribbles of new paint on the newspaper.

"Thanks."

A. sat on the wall above the telephone was a calendar. It was marked with the dates of exhibitions, private views, collection dates and studio visits. A shelf was full of books, some spines smudged with fingerprints in blue and pink.

"How's the work going?"

A. shrugged. A trolley was being wheeled down the corridor. The wheels squeaked on the linoleum.

"I've done another square painting."

"How many have you got now?"

A. took a drink.

"About thirty. I haven't counted."

"Have you talked to anyone about showing them?"

"I offered them to Dent but he turned them down. I've been to all the galleries already. None of them wanted my earlier stuff."

"And Dent has closed his gallery."

"Is about to or already has."

"You got your paintings back?"

"Yes. I'd rather have had the money for them."

"He wouldn't buy any?"

"No."

They drank in silence. Someone walked by whistling.

"Those are new."

THE NAKED SPUR

A. nodded to a collection of packing cases. The wooden crates stood upright, metal handles screwed into their sides. Arrows in red marker pen pointed upwards. On each crate there were labels with serial numbers and barcodes. The crate sides were peppered by stickers with numbers.

"They're back from the Vienna show."

"How did it do?"

"Okay. A few reviews. I can get you copies but they're in German."

"Sales?"

"A couple."

They drank. Hartley lit a cigarette and tapped ash into a tin. Nearby was a tub of blue paint, in it was an electric hand whisk. The top of a tub of blue paint was covered with cellophane. There was a scattering of cigarette butts, a biro, a roll of tape with a trickle of yellow gloss dried over it. A puddle of paint had formed a wrinkled skin that had been partly kicked away, leaving a thin, greenish smear on the hardboard. Heel marks had left multicoloured crescents.

Hartley finished his coffee and walked over to the new paintings. A. was a few steps behind. They looked at the panels. Hartley leaned over a red one, holding his cigarette behind his back.

"They seem to be drying evenly."

Hartley nodded.

"It depends on the weather, the heat and humidity. It's really variable."

At Hartley's feet was a latex glove with red paint on it. Against the wall rested a stack of panels, paint partially cleaned from their fronts, lengths of guttering, sticks with their ends coated in paint. A. nudged one with his foot. The stick came away from the wall but stood upright, dried paint attaching it to the floor.

Hartley stepped away from the panel. They went to the window, which Hartley pushed open wider.

"The fumes can get strong."

He tossed his cigarette stub out on to a flat roof. Close by, a train passed, blinking sunlight at them. On the window sill and the top of a gas heater was a portable stereo with dented speaker grills, spotted with white emulsion, and a heap of cassettes and CDs.

Hartley picked up a tin of paint from a trolley. Paint had dried to form a convex skin dusted with grit. Hartley poked at one with a kitchen knife. Skin yielded then split, oozing lilac fluid. Hartley put the tin and knife back. There were paint tins, stacks of containers, a bag of plastic palette knives, lids, a box of latex gloves. Wire whisk attachments were bent and dusty, purple, yellow and vermilion. Two uneven paint skins had been laid out on a sheet of polythene.

"I'm saving those," said Hartley. "I've been thinking."

At the door Hartley gave A. a sheet of kitchen paper. A. wiped under his boots, dropped the paper in a bucket.

"See you later."

(86)

The suited man pushed open the door.

"Is this some kind of art studio?"

He had a briefcase in one hand and brochures under

an arm.

"The one over the corridor is a graphics company. You get a good mix in this place, don't you?"

He took several steps forward. A. wiped his brush.

"My name's Jerome Richardson. I represent XL Assurance. May I ask whether you have a pension? No? How about insurance? Have you thought about how you might keep up rent payments on this unit, for example, if you were unable to work for a period? We have schemes starting from as little as five pounds per month after initial arrangement fee. We offer a range of flexible schemes to suit individual client needs. We have adapted our services specifically to cater to small-business workers, the self-employed and those working on contracts. We find that since we have geared our operations to those groups, the general level of service satisfaction has increased dramatically. Insurance is not a luxury but a necessity in these times of uncertain job prospects and short-term contract working.

"May I ask you how much your monthly income is?"

"Not much."

"Well, as I say, schemes start as low as five pounds per month. I'm sure you could spare five pounds a month, sir."

"I have a serious illness."

The suited man hesitated for a moment.

"In which case, may I recommend our sister company JP Gilbert Assurance? It handles higher-risk policy holders in a variety of easy-to-understand arrangements tailored to fit your personal circumstances."

Pause. He reached into his jacket and produced a

business card.

"This is my card. I'll let you think about it. Give me a call if you're interested. My name's Jerome and my personal extension number is on the card, also my mobile number."

He approached A. and extended the card to him. He looked at the painting on the easel. The painting showed a woman lifting her dress to reveal her crotch.

After a pause, the suited man said, "That's very, ah-mmn, realistic, isn't it?"

A. took the card. The man backed towards the door.

"Thank you for your time, sir."

(87)

"This is Resistance."

The man rose from the settee to greet A. He was six foot four inches tall with another six inches of dreadlocks heaped on his head. His hand swallowed A.'s. He gave a broad grin. He sat down next to Elsa, A. sat on the settee opposite.

"He is my very dear friend from Trinidad. He's in London to do some gigs. He's a reggae musician. That's right, isn't it?" she asked Resistance. "You'd describe it as reggae?"

Resistance nodded, smiling.

"He'll be staying here for a week."

A. said that was fine.

"Aren't I lucky to have such cultured, creative people in my home? A musician and an artist."

"It's nice to be back," said Resistance.

On the rug, the ginger cat rolled on its back, eyes

THE NAKED SPUR

fixed on Resistance.

"Archie's flirting with you," she said to him.

Resistance's laughter filled the house.

(88)

Hartley was looking at a painting of a woman lying on her back, pulling up her top. He smiled.

"It's not going to win any prizes, is it?" said A.

Hartley shook his head.

"Did you get one of these?"

There was a printed invoice in Hartley's hand.

"For terrorism insurance? Yeah, I got one."

"You'll pay?"

"Do we have a choice?"

Hartley held the invoice in front of him.

"No."

A. was looking at the dots of crimson leading from his studio door to where Hartley was standing.

"They want to see the blood flow," said Hartley.

(89)

When A. had finished the painting of a woman in lacy lingerie, he placed his brushes into a cut-off drinks can half filled with turpentine and checked his watch. He shut the windows and locked the door behind him, bag over one shoulder. Through the corridor and down a set of concrete steps led him to the yard. A man was washing a van with a hose. A. picked his way around the running water on the ground and entered Creekside. He turned left. On one side were studios, on the other

` flats then a framer's. The road curved
gates was a view of waste ground under
₎e. Then came more high brick walls,
⌐ird's Nest" and a roundabout. Deptford Church Street joined Deptford Broadway at the college building. Teenagers with bicycles and folders were smoking on the pavement. A. followed Deptford Broadway over the Creek and climbed steps to Deptford Bridge station.

On the central-bound platform, a man was standing. A second man arrived at the platform and greeted him. The two looked over their shoulders and pushed together between the covered seating stand and an emergency intercom box. The second man was taking something from a pocket. They pushed closer together then the second man left without saying goodbye. The first man went to stand at the platform edge. He looked at A. A. turned his face away.

The Docklands Light Railway train to Bank arrived. A. found a seat and took a paperback out of his bag. View of Greenwich then the tunnel under the river. The train emerged at Mudchute. There was traffic on Marsh Wall, coaches lined the kerbs. Africans in white robes and women wearing headscarves clustered on the pavement under the linden trees. Crowd barriers were being set out around London Arena. There was a banner draped on the building side which showed a tanned man with a wig speaking into a microphone. The legend ran "Mission of Christ. You'll believe in miracles."

Heron Quays station was surrounded by hoardings and plastic sheeting.

THE NAKED SPUR

Canary Wharf was busy with business people. West India Quay was empty. Westferry, Limehouse. At Shadwell station, the smell of coriander, turmeric and onion fried in ghee came through the open windows.

When the train terminated at Bank station, the man from Deptford alighted on the platform. He did not notice A. and walked towards Circle and District-line platforms, one hand deep in a pocket. A. went in the opposite direction. The clock in the concourse read fifteen thirty-five.

(90)

"They've printed it out in six-point again," said the large man with a sigh. "Silly beggars. There was a very good reason why they got an enlarged draft and they knew perfectly well what that was. It was because trying to correct six-point was making my eyes bleed. Then they give me the fair in the six-point original."

"They probably just printed it without thinking," said the man with grey hair. "The Japanese contracts have come in so they're snowed under next door."

The large man rubbed his face.

"Yeah. I'll enlarge this on the copier."

He got to his feet and left the room. The grey-haired man swivelled in his chair. A. was making a list in a pocket notebook. The rest of the room was empty. Half of the room had no ceiling lights on; the lamps over the reading stands were switched off. A helicopter was flying over the City. Its lights disappeared behind NatWest Tower then reappeared.

"I like the City best like this," said the grey-haired

man.

The large man returned with a handful of pages.

"No traffic, streets empty, no construction noise, no roadwork queues," the grey-haired man continued. "At midnight, I can just drive straight out, no traffic. Coming in at three thirty, I'm hitting the traffic coming out but before the rush. I started days here but evenings are much better for me."

The large man had settled at his reading stand, pages laid out.

"Seeing the City like this," said the large man. "It's like seeing a woman who's got this harsh, unforgiving face during the day go to sleep. Once she's asleep, the lines smooth away and you're left with this tranquil, beautiful woman."

The large man rocked back in his chair, a half smile playing on his lips.

"Yeah," said the grey-haired man. "Then you stick your cock in her."

They laughed.

(91)

A dirt path beaten flat led to a corrugated-steel wall, rough with rust.

"You know where it is?"

Ibrahim was at the refrigerator.

A. looked from the calendar to him.

"That's down by the alms houses. The pub there, it's right next to it. It's by the river. I like being so close to the river. When I'm in Hackney, sometimes I wonder where I am. You know? Surrounded by these Nigerians

THE NAKED SPUR

and Ghanaians and Kurds and Russians and Poles and so on, I could be in Paris or New York or somewhere. But when I'm in Greenwich Park or down by the Trafalgar Tavern looking out over the Thames, I think, ah, this is London. And I know where I am. And I like the green of the park too. You don't get that in Hackney. Not at all. Don't get me wrong, Hackney's got its good points but greenery isn't one of them. I feel like I can breathe here. Hackney is so polluted. Trafalgar Road is too, but that's just a little part of Greenwich. I feel like, when I'm in Greenwich Park, that I'm in a giant lung. And there's that view of the London from One Tree Hill. Do you ever go up there? You look out over the city and see the history there before you. St Paul's Cathedral, the Observatory, Canary Wharf, the Naval College, the factories in the East End and with the river running through it. That's London. But the fried-chicken places and the mini-cab offices and the west African grocery shops in Wood Green, they're also London too. That's what makes London so interesting. London's not like Venice, not that I've ever been to Venice but you know what I'm saying. Really, you could write a book about it. I've thought about it, about writing a novel. I have ideas, too many ideas.

"Also, Hackney's so noisy. I get back from the office and they're digging up my road with pneumatic drills and there's sirens going off everywhere. Working nights means I'm trying to sleep through the busiest time of day. You can't, like, open your window and ask the buses and the workmen and the school children to be quiet because I'm trying to sleep."

He laughed.

"I want to. God knows I do. And there's people walking around on my ceiling. I mean, they're on the floor above, you know. So, this is quiet for me. I can get some kip and breathe the air."

Ibrahim poured out whiskey into his glass.

"The calendar's out of date. I told Elsa but she likes the image." He took a sip. "I do too."

A. cut a slice of pie and transferred it from foil tray to plate.

"I'm back now, by the way," Ibrahim added. "I kind of made myself scarce while Resistance was around. I don't know if you noticed. I had stuff to do in Hackney. Stuff at my flat. I had to see my dealer."

He laughed again.

"Anyway, Resistance is a big guy. This is a small house. He takes up a lot of space."

"He wanted to spend more time with you."

Elsa was bringing plates to the draining board.

"Maybe next time," said Ibrahim. "I know what it is, why he wants to talk to me. It's that Rastafarian thing about Ethiopia."

"Oh, Ib, he just wants to hear you talk. He'd love to hear about Haile Selassie. It's a big deal for them."

"Yeah, I know."

"He's not going to give you that Lion-of-Zion line. He just wants to hear your stories."

"Well, I did talk to him a bit."

"Yes. Thank you."

"Resistance is all right. Some of them come on a bit strong. I don't have time for all that. Distorting history and whatever."

He drank.

"Anyway, I'm going to get back to my book. I'll see you later, A."

"See you later, Ib."

(92)

Hartley placed the full glasses on the table and sat down.

"Cheers."

"Cheers."

"Not drinking alcohol?" Hartley asked, looking at A.'s glass.

"Not any more."

"Chris Kaminsky said no."

A. nodded.

"Maybe he wasn't right for your art."

Three men wearing dirty T-shirts and trousers spattered with plaster, entered the pub. With each step their steel toecaps gave dull rings. One of them ordered three beers and they turned to watch the screen in the corner. Projected on it was the image of football players warming up on a pitch.

"Nelson Nicobar has published a new article, in Art International."

"Oh?"

"You don't read his pieces?"

Hartley shook his head. A. took out of his jacket pocket a folded photocopy. Pushing beer mats aside, he spread it on the circular table.

"You haven't seen it?" A. asked.

"No. What's it about?"

"About what another critic wrote. Something about Marx, some French writers. I don't know."

"That's Nelson."

Hartley drank. In the projection, a face filled the screen. A graphic strip gave statistics

"You didn't send this to me?"

"No."

Hartley looked at A.

"Someone sent it to me in the post. I thought it might have been you."

"No. Did you recognise the handwriting on the envelope?"

"The label was printed."

Pause.

"Does the article mention you?" Hartley asked him.

"No."

"Does it mention me?"

"No."

"Does it mention any artists we know personally?"

"No."

They looked at the sheet on the table. A corner was wet with beer. Hartley shrugged.

A. asked, "Do you want to read it?"

"No."

A. refolded the paper and returned it to his pocket. The barman was wiping the bar. On the screen team sheets came up in giant pixels. The workmen had taken the table nearest the screen. A girl with hair dyed red and a leather armband round her wrist was talking to one of the men.

"You want to watch?"

THE NAKED SPUR

"No."

Hartley led them to the part of the pub furthest from the screen.

Hartley asked A. if he read Art International.

"Sometimes. I get old copies from Barbican Library. They sold last year's issues for three pounds."

"The old ones are the best. You can read them and see if the judgements turned out true or not. You remember Calvin Hipwell from the year above us at college? I found an old magazine saying that his work was exceptional and that he was a hot new name. No one's heard from him in five years or more. There's still time for you. All you have to do is stay the course. If the work's there, the audience will come to it eventually."

They drank and looked at the pool table. It was covered with a sheet. When they finished their drinks, A. bought a fresh round.

"I wrote to Art International," he said putting down the drinks. "I asked the editor if I could review books for them. Reviewers get free copies."

"What did he say?"

"He didn't reply."

A. took a drink.

"Are you artists?"

It was the girl with dyed hair. She was leaning on the bar beside them. She had on a black singlet. Her eyes were rimmed with kohl.

"We try to be," said Hartley.

"I like art," said the girl. "I was good at art in school. I got a 'B'. I would have got a 'B' in my final exam but I moved around between schools. So, I never took exams."

Silence. The men drank.

The girl sighed and looked at her empty glass.

"I've finished my drink," she said.

The men said nothing.

"I've got some drawings in my room. I copy pictures from magazines. Do you live near here?"

"Over the river," A. said.

Hartley said nothing and drank. Pause.

"Where do you live?" A. asked her.

"I live in a care home in New Cross." Pause. "I'm over sixteen."

She was looking at the men while playing with her armband. On the inside of her wrist there were little white scars almost covered by the armband.

She sighed again.

"I've finished my drink."

Hartley set his glass on the bar, got to his feet.

"I better get back."

"See you later this week."

They waved goodbye and Hartley left.

The girl looked at A., picking at the armband.

"Do you want to walk me home?"

(93)

In a narrow alley off Cheapside, A. came across a man. The man was wearing a suit and was lying on his back. He was a fat man, hair cut short. His tie had been loosened, its length flipped up, end lying at his ear. The streetlights picked out a spray of coins which had spilled from his pocket.

THE NAKED SPUR

A. looked down on him.

The man was snoring.

There was a clatter of footsteps. Two tottering women crossed the alley, supporting each other, silhouettes against the cobblestones. Somewhere, a street-cleaning vehicle was operating.

The man's breathing became thick. He coughed a line of spit over his chin. He grunted. His fingers curled to form fists. His breathing gradually became less laboured, returning to its former rhythm.

A. knelt beside him. He watched him, not moving.

Then he stood and walked to Bank station where Africans in green overalls picked litter with grabbers from the concourses. He caught the last Docklands Light Railway train south. When he went to bed, it took him a long time to sleep.

(94)

The girl on the escalator smiled at A.

"Yeah, I had a good time."

A. waited at the top of the escalator for her. He was passed by a youth in a baseball cap and a man eating french fries from a carton.

The girl dismounted the escalator and leaned towards A.

"Hi. I'm Elizabeth."

"Hello, Elizabeth."

As they exited the ticket hall of Cutty Sark station, a member of staff clipped a chain over the escalator and switched it off with a key. Outside, the streets were deserted.

"Do you know anywhere we could get a drink? I fancy a drink."

She swayed against A.

A. mentioned a bar on College Approach. The girl said it was closed Tuesdays.

"Maybe you could find something at home," she said.

"Maybe."

A. touched her back and she pushed into him, putting her arms over his shoulders. They kissed.

"I'll call a cab."

Elizabeth brought out a mobile phone. She looked him in the eyes and said, "I don't usually do this. It doesn't mean anything."

Walking from the cab down unlit steps, she stumbled. A. caught her. The house was dark. A. switched on the hall light. In the living room, the cats' eyes reflected green discs at them.

On his bed, they sat. A. gave Elizabeth a glass to use as an ashtray. She talked and A. rested a hand on her leg. After the third cigarette, Elizabeth put the glass on the floor and lay flat on the bed. She took off her skirt and pants.

"Don't you want to take off that?" A. asked, looking at her top.

"No."

Afterwards, she said she could not stay.

"I have a presentation tomorrow. It's really important. I have to get up early. You can stay with me tonight."

She asked A. to find her mobile phone and a card with a mini-cab number on it while she went to the toilet. A. looked through her handbag. Amongst the tissues and cosmetics was a security pass. It read "Alpine Office Engineering. ELIZABETH BERGUERREN. PROJECTS CO-ORDINATOR." A. looked at the photograph of her face printed on the plastic. He ran his thumb over the barcode.

They waited in the fog for the cab. Elizabeth knew the driver. On the journey, she talked to the driver while A. looked out of the window. The Naval College, shops and restaurants of West Greenwich, closed and dark, Creek Bridge. They arrived at a new block of flats overlooking the river.

In the lift, Elizabeth looked at A. and said, "You have amazing eyes."

"My friend's in tonight," she said, as they entered the flat.

"In there." She pointed A. to a door facing the front door. In the room there was a double bed. The floor was covered with suitcases. The windows gave a view of Docklands and had no curtains.

They woke early. Morning light came through the windows. She was naked. Her breasts were small, triangles of pale skin surrounded by tan. She covered her stomach with a towel but as they had sex it slipped off to reveal a paunch. When A. ejaculated in her mouth, she gagged, twisted her head aside and coughed semen and saliva on to the pillow. She removed the pillowcase, spat into it and wiped her mouth. She bundled it and dropped it to the carpet.

They showered separately. A. ate unripe bananas while Elizabeth stood on the balcony. All the furniture was new, some with protective wrapping on. The cooker hobs were clean. The spice jars in the rack had plastic seals over the caps. A. finished eating and went to the balcony. On the quayside, workers were moving scaffolding. A. stood behind Elizabeth and cupped her breasts. She said nothing and continued smoking.

(95)

"Can you get me some cigarettes on your way here?"

"I'll try. I get out of work at midnight. All the stops and pubs are closed then. What do you want?"

"Twenty Marlboro Light. I'll give you money when you get here."

"I'll try. How was the presentation?"

"Okay. Yeah, okay. I'm so tired after last night. I need to sleep."

A. was in a cubicle. Through the glass he watched an unlit corridor, figures in a patch of light at one end.

"Flat seven-three, floor seven, Three Creek Wharf Tower."

"I've written it down."

"When will you get here?"

"Quarter to one."

Pause.

"Okay. I'll be in bed."

"See you later."

"Yes."

(96)

A. walked from Cutty Sark station along Creek Road and took a street next to a pub called "The Hoy". The

THE NAKED SPUR

road had been recently laid. Asphalt was sticky under his shoes. The pavements were unfinished, walking to the flat entrance, he kicked stones. He pressed the "7" button. The door clicked open.

Upstairs, Elizabeth was in a nightshirt, standing at the door to the flat. They kissed.

"Did you get the cigarettes?"

"Nowhere was open."

She climbed into bed and pulled the cover over herself. A. undressed and got in next to her. He put his hand over her pubic hair. She rolled away, turning her back to him.

"Turn out the light," she said.

He did. He stroked her back and she curled away from his hand.

In the darkness, she said "I said you could sleep here. I didn't say anything about sex."

Silence. Towers of Docklands formed grids of light in the sky.

"I'm tired."

Pause.

"I think you should go."

He got out of bed, flicked on the light and dressed.

"Bye."

"Bye. Turn the light off."

She didn't turn to look at him.

He switched off the light and left the flat.

(97)

At the end of the gravel drive was a large house. A. walked to the front door and entered a hallway. There was a desk with a visitor's book. The rest of the desk space was covered with cards, brochures and invitations. Through a doorway to the left was a woman taking cards out of a box. She raised a hand to A. A. nodded back then walked through the right-hand doorway into a gallery with a tiled floor. Beyond that were three rooms, one large, two medium-size, at the back of the house. A. went to the French windows. The lawn was tousled and the bushes unkempt. From the trees flew two magpies. They hopped over the grass, tails wagging. An initial had been scratched on the window glass.

Back in the entrance hall, A. looked into the left-hand room. The woman was peeling labels from a sheet and applying them to cards. A. knocked on the open door. The woman looked up.

"Don't tell me," she said. "You're an artist and you want to exhibit here."

"Maybe."

"In which case, maybe you want to put your name on our mailing list. You could put in for our open shows. We have two every year, one in the summer, one over Christmas. We show quite a range of stuff, conceptual art through to watercolours. If you've been to art college then you're almost certain to get a piece selected. We get a lot of amateur artists submitting. Between you and me, most of them aren't very good. Usually we show some to encourage the others. Some know people on the selection committee. Others are friends of the gallery. You know the way things work."

She crumpled her empty sheet.

"If you want a solo show then you could send a selection of slides to the exhibitions committee. I have to warn you the waiting list is two years. That's if you get accepted. Then we'll pair you with another artist or two and you share the space. We get all sorts who submit. We can't take anything blasphemous, sexually explicit, offensive or racist. We'd lose what little funding we get from the council. The council will probably cut us from the budget next year anyway, but we don't want to give them a reason to do it."

She took a fresh sheet and returned to the cards.

"Also any artwork that is dangerous to the viewing public is excluded as it would contravene our public-liability insurance. So, that's a no-no. You wouldn't believe the sort of things people consider suitable for the gallery. I'm no prude, truly I'm not, but you think some people are just out to shock. I'm not shocked by it but I know the majority of our viewers would be. They're a fairly conservative bunch in this area. We don't get the metropolitan crowd coming down here, more's the pity, so we have to cater for the visitors we do have. Without them buying the occasional picture and submission fees to take part in our open shows, the gallery would have to close."

She rapped the cards on the table and took more from a box.

"What sort of art do you make? Paintings?"

"Figures."

"Okay, well, as I say, put your name on the mailing list and send some slides to the selection committee. We'll see how it goes."

A. said goodbye and departed, leaving the visitor's

book untouched.

(98)

A. exited the lift and walked to the reception desk. One of the guards brought out a clipboard. A. took a security pass out of his suit-jacket pocket and put it on the clipboard. A. signed the sheet, opened the glass door and stepped onto the street where he turned right.

(99)

A. opened the front door, bag of shopping in hand. Ibrahim was in the hall, gripping a bottle of Jack Daniels by the neck. He was shouting up the stairs.

"Well, do what you want, Elsa. I don't care. I don't care anymore. You start with all this stuff—your female stuff—and you try and make me crazy. Well, I've had enough. You can't do this to me anymore. It's just not acceptable. It's not acceptable. It's not acceptable behaviour. You're not rational when you're like this. My God, you're the crazy one here. So, don't you start at me. You peck, peck, peck like a little bird at me—drilling into my head. Why do you do this to me? My God, what is it? What is it with you? All the time. You peck, you know that? That's what you do. You peck at me. Why do you do it? Do you want to get a response from me? Is that it? Well, it's not working. You're not going to get under my skin. I refuse to be drawn into these little games you play. Or you try to play. But I'm not playing."

He gesticulated with the bottle towards the empty

THE NAKED SPUR

landing above.

"And another thing. Why did you mention that thing to Joseph that I specifically told you not to? You know how touchy he is about other Ethiopians here in London. That's why I said, don't mention that thing. And then you come out, in the middle of this discussion about something else in front of a whole room of people and say the thing I told you not to. Then you act like it's no big deal. Well, it is a big deal, Elsa. You don't understand. It's people's lives. My God. Then when I say what was that all about afterwards, you act like I never told you. And you call me the crazy one. You know how difficult it is with his father and everything. My God. He practically jumped out of his skin when you said that thing. Did you see? Did you see his reaction? He couldn't leave fast enough. You act like you know something about Ethiopia that I don't, like I don't know my own country."

A. closed the front door behind him. Ibrahim looked round and raised his hand to him.

"Anyway," Ibrahim shouted up the stairs. "A.'s back now, so that's enough. I don't want any more said on the subject. We'll talk about it later."

He walked off to the living room.

A. ascended the stairs. In the study, Elsa was at the computer. She looked over her shoulder then turned back to the screen.

(100)

There was a letter taped to the glass of the studio door. A. peeled it off and opened it. The envelope was manila and had a heraldic device on the back. The text of the letter had paragraphs of bold type.

A. knocked on Hartley's door. There was no answer. A scrap of card had been fixed to the door with masking tape. A. read the card then detached it, slipping it into a pocket.

There was a queue at the cafeteria counter. A teenage boy was collecting an order. He put paper bags and polystyrene cups into a cardboard box with a torn-off top. A. ordered and took his tea to where Hartley was sitting. He gave Hartley the letter. Hartley read it.

"What will you do?" said Hartley, putting down the letter.

A. shrugged.

"Can you afford it?"

A. shook his head, pressed his hands flat on the Formica.

"The gallery pays mine. Well, they buy a painting and I use the money to pay it."

Hartley pushed away his plate and lit a cigarette. A man at a neighbouring table addressed Hartley by name and got a light from him.

"No sign of any sales."

"Where?"

"Anywhere. You've asked around? Well, I guess that's it."

A. drained his cup.

II

(1)

A. was shaving. He tilted the mirror and air from the open window cleared steam from it.

Coughing from the next room.

A. hesitated, washed the double-sided razor in the water and raised it to his jaw.

Coughing again, dry and barking.

A. stopped, dropped the razor in the basin and waited. Soapy water occluded the razor. When the pale oval was still, A. reached in to retrieve it. The coughing subsided.

(2)

A. had fallen asleep on a park bench. His head had drooped. Blurred discs of sunlight rocked over him. A woman with a pushchair walked by.

A. jerked his head up. A squirrel stood upright then skittered up a horse-chestnut trunk.

Slouched on the next bench was a man keying a text on his mobile phone. The man was dressed in a tracksuit and white trainers. By him sat a little girl with a pigtail wearing a corduroy dress and brown, buckled shoes. She was swinging her legs to and fro. She caught sight of A. and after a few seconds smiled at him. A. smiled back.

The man glanced up from his mobile phone, looked at the girl then at A. He frowned and made a comment to the girl and they both stood up, the girl brushing the seat of her dress. They started away down the hill. The man had his hand resting on her shoulder blade. She looked over her shoulder to A. A. waved his hand. The girl turned her face away. They became smaller. A. lowered his head into his hands.

(3)

A. took an orange-coloured scotch bonnet pepper out of the paper bag and washed it under a running tap. He dried it and cut off the stalk. He finely chopped the pepper with its seeds inside. He put a saucepan on the hob at medium heat and poured a thin layer of olive oil into it. He peeled two cloves of garlic and finely chopped them. He put the chopping board over the saucepan and with the knife scraped the chopped pepper and garlic into the hot oil. He stirred the pieces in the oil with a wooden spoon. He took a medium-size onion and topped and tailed it with the knife. He slit the outside of the onion along its length and peeled off the outer skins. He stirred the oil again. He halved the onion along its length. One half he placed flat on the board, cut it twice one way then twice crossways. He stirred the oil again. He repeated the procedure with the second half of the onion then added it to the oil, which was now orange-yellow in colour. He stirred the contents, breaking up the onion layers. He opened

THE NAKED SPUR

a can of peeled tomatoes and another of red kidney beans. The can of beans he drained then rinsed twice, draining them twice. He stirred the saucepan contents. The tomatoes A. cut with a knife, pressing the soft bodies against the inside of the can. He stirred the onion until it was broken up and the pieces all translucent. He emptied the can of tomatoes into the saucepan. Then the beans were added. From the refrigerator, A. took a half-empty tube of tomato puree. He squeezed the contents into the mixture and threw away the empty container. To the mixture, he added a sprinkling of salt. A. took a coffee spoon from a drawer and added a quarter of a spoonful of sugar. He stirred the mixture, covered it and turned down the heat. After it had simmered for half an hour, A. measured half a cup of brown rice and added it to a pan of boiling, salted water. He boiled the rice for ten minutes, drained it and rinsed it in boiling water from the kettle. Then he put it on a plate. To the rice, A. added half the contents of the first saucepan. He poured a glass of water and sat to eat. Later, when the uneaten half of the chilli was cool, he transferred it to a bowl and put a saucer over it, then he placed it on the top shelf of the refrigerator.

(4)

"It must be very satisfying to work with your hands, not to have to deal with words."

Ibrahim was standing at the back door smoking.

"To do something physical, that's like, you know, an artisan making a shoe or, I don't know, a table. I get the urge sometimes to make things, with my hands. I don't know what." He inhaled. "Then the urge goes away."

A. tapped the linen tight over the stretcher with his hammer. He was squatting on the garden path, surrounded by square canvases.

"It's a whole different way of putting ideas across. Art. You must show me more of your stuff."

A. dipped a brush in the watery solution of primer and began to coat the canvas fronts. The white cat walked through the grass and stopped by a canvas to sniff it. A train arrived at the station. Sound of a warning signal, hiss and thump of doors, footsteps.

"I'm just getting ready for work. What about you? Haven't you usually gone by now?"

Ibrahim studied his watch.

"I quit my job."

"Oh? Really? Hey, that's great. I wish I could. You're lucky. But you've got some savings, right?"

A. propped the canvas upright against a shrub and reached for another. The white cat was looking behind the canvas.

"Some."

"That's great. I'm pleased for you. But be careful," Ibrahim waved with his cigarette. "I find that money never goes as far as you expect it to. In my experience anyway."

The grey cat approached the open tub of primer. Ibrahim watched him.

"Be careful, Vish. I don't want to have to wash you, man."

He issued a laugh.

"How great it must be to be a cat. Imagine that. No

work, no money, just food and sleeping. And killing the occasional mouse. You got it good, Vish," he called to the cat.

The cat glanced at him and stalked away.

(5)

A.: "Thanks for your letter."

Mack: "No problem. I heard you left your work and I thought up this idea about how you might be able to make some money. So, I thought, I'll put it in a letter and see what you think about it. I don't think anything I wrote is impractical. I was looking at those photographs of your square paintings and thought they were exactly what people I know would want to own. I'm in that world. There are people I work with who bid money on e-Bay for vintage clothing, records, magazines, all sorts of stuff, just to kill time. I've bought stuff and got really into it and then a few days later something gets delivered that I'd forgotten about. Just small stuff. But I know guys who do that every day. That's normal for them. They've got money to burn and nothing to spend it on. They don't go to art shows much, they work long hours and they're not into all the pretentious art-gallery stuff. Conceptual art puts a lot of people off art galleries. So, I thought, I'm sure some of these guys would commission paintings of their girlfriends, in the style of your square paintings. Money is no object for these people, trust me. I know it's not really your scene and you're not so keen on the promotional side. That's why I thought that maybe there could be some sort of agent acting as an intermediary. And then I thought we could make a feature of this buffer between the buyer and the artist. It would heighten the mystery, that way you would be hidden behind this front man. Actually, front woman might be better, someone glamorous. That way we are already intriguing the male client and the female clients aren't intimidated. We need to gain their trust if they'll give us photographs. But I think it's something people do anyway. I was thinking about the way you present your pictures on those thirty-five-millimetre transparencies. I love those. There's something really tactile and intimate about them. They're a bit retro but at the same time you've got those contemporary, in-your-face nudes. It's a great combination. So, I was thinking how about Dahlia going round the bars in Soho with this box of slides and a little viewer, like the one you've got, showing people these images. And she'll arrange for these people to get their own photographs painted in the same way. She would make all the deals, take the photographs from the clients, get the money and deliver the art. For that, she would get a percentage. She works in an office during the day. It leaves her evenings and weekends free. She would have leaflets with details and prices and so on. Something for people to take away with them. Or maybe people could get some slides. We could get a painting to someone's flat, a really cool place, then people could come round and see an example face to face. We could make out that this was a collector who had already bought work. We can use my house for that. Dahlia could act like I was this collector who had commissioned some paintings and wanted people to see them. Dahlia could

THE NAKED SPUR

have a Polaroid camera with her in case clients want to commission work on the spot. We could have a delivery service where a camera is delivered with two packs of film and we collect it the next day with a few of the photographs they've selected and you paint from those. That becomes part of the service. Maybe a client wants Dahlia to photograph them, I don't know how Dahlia would feel about that. I don't know how we would work that. I'll talk to her. Anyway, she has time in the evenings and I mentioned her going to bars and talking to clients and she was really into it and she's seen the art you've done. I didn't go into the details because I wanted to talk to you first, find out how you felt. The beauty of this is that you never need to meet the clients. Also, the paintings are small enough for you to do at home now you haven't got the studio. What do you think? Are you into it?"

A.: "Yes."

Mack: "It's got a lot of potential and it could mean quick cash for you, which is your priority. The great thing is that it is actually work you already do. You'll be doing what you usually do only this time getting paid for it. This is what you already do, paint on to canvas nudes from Polaroids. You're confident you can do these paintings if we get some orders?"

A.: "Yes."

Mack: "We need to sit down together, the three of us, and talk about the plan. We have to get it just right. I spoke to Dahlia and we're going out to see a film on Wednesday. We're meeting in Soho first. You're free Monday evening?"

A.: "Yes."

Mack: "We're meeting at my office at seven."

A.: "Seven."

Mack: "My office is number eighteen Brand Street."

A.: "Eighteen Brand Street."

Mack: "In Soho. I'm on the second floor. Press the button for MG Associates and the receptionist will open the door."

A.: "Fine. I'll be there."

Mack: "See you then."

(6)

A trumpet chord woke A., then it was cut off. There were footsteps in the study then Elsa was shouting, "Turn it down, Ib. What are you playing at?"

From downstairs: "I was warming up the valves."

"Ib, it's a stereo not a Theremin. You switch it on and set the volume to the appropriate level and it plays music. An appropriate level, mind you."

"Yah, but first you gotta warm the valves. It never plays as well if you haven't turned it up loud first. That warms up the valves."

"Ib, I bought it new only three years ago--"

"Four."

"--Four years ago. It doesn't have any valves. It's all circuit board."

"The speakers--"

"The speakers are even newer."

"They're not so good."

"Not any more. Not since you started abusing them."

"I don't abuse them. I warm them up. The music al-

THE NAKED SPUR

ways sounds better when you've warmed up the tubes."

"No, Ib. No. Don't do it. We've got neighbours. I've got neighbours. They aren't your neighbours."

"Like anyone's going to complain about a bit of Charlie Parker. Some people have no taste."

"That's not the point. You need sleep not jazz."

"Jazz is better than sleep."

"You can get all the jazz you want at an appropriate level."

The music started again at low volume. Footsteps in the study. At the start of the next track the volume rose. Footsteps again. Then the volume decreased. After a while the footsteps came again. A. rose and went to make breakfast.

(7)

On the wall was a large figurative painting. The coffee table was covered with books and magazines. In the corner was a close-up photograph of red paint mixed impasto, brush marks prominent in raking light.

"One of the old ones," said Damien, following A.'s gaze. "It's a bit scratched. Take a seat."

A. sat in an armchair.

"You were telling me about this project of yours. It sounds wild."

He laughed, filling a kettle in the adjoining kitchen.

A. picked up a Nabokov novel off the table.

"I don't know how far it will get," said A.

"I have slides with me, if you'd like to see."

"Sure."

A. replaced the book on the table.

"This is a nice place," said A., unzipping his bag.
"It's a shame it's going. It's been sold."
"Where will you live?"
"I'll be looking after a flat in Notting Hill. Jammy, aren't I?"

Damien brought in the coffee and A. cleared a space on the table. Damien looked at the slides and A. depressed the cafetiere plunger.

"And you want to show these?"
"Yes. No. We're not sure."
"And you talked on the phone about some sort of commissioning service from Polaroids?"
"Yes."
"They've got that feel," said Damien, changing slides. "Have you had any commissions yet?"
"No. We haven't started yet."

Damien squinted at a slide.

"They're pretty explicit, aren't they?"
"Some are."

Damien poured out the coffee.

"They'd be difficult to place, you know, with a gallery."
"So it seems."
"Maybe going straight to private collectors is best. I'll have a think, see if I can come up with any contacts for you. I don't think they'd be impossible to sell but you'd have to approach it the right way. You'd have to make clear that it wasn't just porn. That's the tricky bit. Pitching the tone. So often that's all that separates what's on the walls in Hoxton from on the shelves in Bethnal Green newsagents. There's not much to choose

THE NAKED SPUR

between them. But I'll ask around for you."

"Thank you."

"Did I tell you about this place in Notting Hill? It's an exclusive boutique selling erotica. Strange stuff. Miniature vibrators you can put on key rings, stuff like that. It doesn't advertise. Well, not that I've seen."

He took a sip of coffee.

"I haven't been there myself," he added.

"Do you have the address?"

"No."

"The name?"

"No."

"The street name?"

"Ah, no. No. I can't remember. I could get it for you. I have a friend who lives round the corner. It won't be far from where I'll be living."

The telephone rang. A. sat in the living room while Damien answered it in another room. Once the coffee was finished, A. folded his hands and looked at the painting. Then he leafed through a magazine.

Damien came back.

"Did I tell you Gavin Turk gave me a piece for the magazine? I'll find it for you."

They went to Damien's bedroom. Damien searched the books and papers under his bed but could not find the sheet.

Leaving the building, A. crossed the street and entered the art store. He bought a tube of white oil paint and a brush. Eleanor was not there. When A. asked the girl at the upstairs cash till when Eleanor had left the store, the girl said that she had never heard of Eleanor.

He did not look at the magazines and walked straight to the underground station.

(8)

"I couldn't believe it. I couldn't believe she said it to my face. All she eats is potatoes. Can you imagine? She's such a slob. It's the end. It really is the limit."

Laurie and Elsa were making tea in the kitchen. A. was eating a slice of cherry pie and reading The New Yorker.

"And then to cap it all, I came down yesterday morning and she's—" Laurie glanced to A. "She was having sex, loud sex, with the door to her room open. At eight in the morning. And apparently she'd only met this guy while she was waiting at a bus stop for a night bus the night before. My God. Can you imagine?"

Elsa sighed, shaking her head.

A. asked Laurie which bus stop the girl had been waiting at.

(9)

When the first train to Charing Cross arrived at the southern platform, A. boarded it. He sat on a seat at the left side of the train. He watched the brick buildings of Greenwich pass with increasing speed. Mumford Flour Mill on Deptford Creek, industrial buildings, forecourts with lorries and hand trolleys. The light in Hartley's studio was off. Then came a view of Deptford Church Street with its trees, "The Bird's Nest" at the roundabout and distant Deptford Broadway. The narrow platforms of Deptford station. Later, came an expanse of silver rails under an indigo sky. The hospital tower with its jutting top loomed over the thronging platforms of London Bridge station. Beyond Waterloo East, arches of brown iron rose over the train. Rust speckled the edges of graffiti tags. "IRON LIKE A LION IN THE DEN." Hungerford Bridge was a mass of naked girders and scaffolding. Charing Cross station.

Past the ticket barriers was the concourse. People gazed up to the departures board, cardboard cups of coffee in hand, bags between their feet. A beggar walked among them, rattling coins in a cup. Outside, the light was going. The air was cooler. A. edged between taxis and crossed the cobbled forecourt of the station. Over at the lights, then up to Trafalgar Square, right at St Martin-in-the-Fields. He walked up St Martin's Lane on the left side by the National Portrait Gallery. On a triangle of the pavement near the exit of Orange Street, artists drew pastel pictures on the pavement and portraitists and caricaturists drew tourists. Tourists milled in streets near Leicester Square. At Cambridge Circus A. went left up Shaftesbury Avenue, right up Greek Street and then left into the centre of Soho.

(10)

Eighteen Brand Street was a door between a coffee-machine shop and a hair salon. A. stepped into the entrance hall and pressed a button on the intercom. He spoke into the grill and the door buzzed open. In the lift to the second floor, A. straightened his clothes, looking in the mirror.

A blonde girl in reception showed him to a sofa in the lobby. She got him a coffee. He had almost finished it when Mack came to meet him.

"Come through."

He led A. to a small office. On the shelves were DVDs, CDs, ring binders, manuals and video cassettes. On the top shelf was a row of vintage trainer boxes.

"And those are the slides?" Mack asked when A. brought out a small plastic box.

"Some. The recent paintings haven't been photographed yet."

Mack put a slide against the illuminated computer screen.

"That's what we want."

In a tiny plastic rectangle was the torso of a woman. She was lying in a bath, her back arched, light catching on her wet belly, shoulder and nipple.

Mack brought his eye close.

"Yes. That's it. It's that."

(11)

"What sort of time period are we looking at between commissioning and receipt of picture?"

"The painting could be done in one day, let's say three days to be safe. That gives me a margin to paint a new version if the first doesn't work."

"Okay. Three days for the painting. How long do paintings take to dry?"

"A week to be safely handled."

"A week?"

"Minimum."

THE NAKED SPUR

Mack sighed.

"No way of speeding that drying time?"

"Not really."

"And you only paint in oil colour, right? Not anything faster?"

"I could try acrylic, that dries in a day. But I couldn't guarantee the quality. I don't usually use acrylic paint."

Mack scratched his head.

"So, seven days for drying."

"Minimum of seven days."

"At least seven days for drying. Three days for painting. There'll be a delay between receiving Polaroids at the outlet or with the agent and you getting them. If you're not going to the outlet, and Dahlia can't come down to Greenwich every time she gets a commission, then the photographs will go in the post. Two days for that, three if it's a weekend. So, we're looking at thirteen days so far."

Mack rocked back in his chair. Outside, taxis were driving along the darkening street.

"How does twenty days guaranteed turnaround between commissioning and delivery sound?"

"How about three weeks, twenty-one days, between outlet or agent receiving deposit and delivery of work?"

"Okay. We'll do that. Twenty-one days."

(12)

When a petite girl with dark hair arrived, Mack was writing a list.

"Hey there."

"Hi, Dahlia," said A.

ADAMS

The girl walked in and kissed Mack on the lips. A. looked down and brushed his trousers. Dahlia picked up a few slides and studied them in a small box with a translucent side, a slot and an eyepiece.

"These are just great. Mack showed me some photos but this is better. These are so much more vivid. They're almost alive."

She smiled at A. then took a seat.

"How many of these have you got?"

"About three dozen. I'm not sure."

Mack broke in. "The main thing is the commissioning service. I can't see how we can sell those paintings that already exist. How can we convince people that these paintings have been commissioned by private collectors and then in the next breath offer to sell them?"

"Maybe there is a way," responded Dahlia. "You told me about that shop."

"I forgot to tell you, A., I've found this great shop down Marshall Street called Zoltar the Magnificent. It sells weird things, vintage clothes, retro furnishings, little model guns plated with gold, animal skin rugs, seven-track cartridges, Betamax videos. They have film posters there. I think they sell paintings too. Maybe I could pose as a collector, a very private collector, selling off his collection of paintings of ex-girlfriends. I could say I'm getting married and my future wife is forcing me to sell my pictures."

Dahlia smiled and tossed back her hair.

"They sell bizarre things, funky. It's got the right feel. I'm sure they'd take these. Maybe. There was an article on the place. I cut it out when I thought of

THE NAKED SPUR

the commissioning service. I thought we could make a connection."

Mack sorted through some magazines on his desk.

"I'll get you a photocopy when I find it."

Holding up a slide, he said, "It might be better to separate these old paintings from commissions. We could use examples but we can't offer them for sale to commissioning clients. What we need to do is sell some pictures through other outlets not connected with the commissioning. We shouldn't mix them up."

Dahlia nodded.

"We'll find a way," Mack said, tapping the pencil on his list.

Dahlia asked, "How do you feel about having your name on these paintings?" She held up the slide viewer.

A. shrugged.

"No one knows who I am. I don't have a gallery. Using my name is the same as being anonymous."

"We could do it anonymously to add some mystery or we could invent a name," said Mack, holding the pencil between his hands.

"Either is fine," said A.

"We could just call you 'A'. You know, just the first letter of the alphabet. Just a single letter. 'A' for artist. So small it's almost nothing. 'A' for anonymous. That way, you almost don't exist."

Dahlia said, "What about banking? If people are writing cheques as payment, what name is going to go on them?"

"We can put my name on them. Or the agent's. We'll sort that out later," said Mack.

Dahlia planted an elbow on the desk and put her chin on her hand.

"Maybe they could write my account number and sort code on the cheques," suggested A.

"I'm not sure that would be accepted," Mack said.

"Oh."

"Well, I'm not keen on wandering around at night between bars carrying a lot of cash," said Dahlia. "So, you'll have to think up a solution."

"We'll find a way," said Mack. "Maybe there is some method by which we could set up an account and all the funds get transferred to your account automatically. I don't know if that's possible. We'll look into it. Our finance guy is pretty sharp, I'll e-mail him about it."

Dahlia was running a thumbnail along a slide-mount groove.

"We have to think about some sort of leaflet setting out terms and conditions of the service. That way clients will know where they stand. It will reassure them. We don't want to make it too dense or legal or people will get nervous. It should be factual but not too heavy. Approachable. Dahlia can help with the layout and the wording. She's good at that. You're okay with that?"

Dahlia, chin in hand, nodded.

"Write a few ideas for the terms and conditions," said Mack to A. "Try out different wording. We'll decide on the best. The terms could be combined with blurb so they become brochures. Put something on paper and we'll go through it together next week. We can meet for a meal."

Mack brought up the diary on his computer.

THE NAKED SPUR

"Thursday at seven okay for you both?"

"Yes."

"Yes."

"We'll meet at the Pop bar. Get me some more slides and have a go at that text."

Mack got to his feet.

"And keep painting. Can I keep hold of these slides and the viewer?"

"Yes."

"There's a few people I want to show them to."

(13)

"So I think that what now needs to happen is that we keep the agenda moving forward and push these decisions through and make sure that the principles if you like, the things that we determine in principle at the summit, are actually translated into genuine change on the ground."

Sunlight was shining on the painting on the wall. The reverse of the top stretcher bar rested on a screw twenty inches above a radiator draped with a sheet. A. mixed white and black paint on the saucer at his feet.

"Now I also know, I think I would be right in saying that many of your questions will be on Iraq, so I will just say a few brief words of introduction there. I sense that some of you believe we have taken all the key decisions but just haven't got round to telling you. That isn't the case. The position is this. There is constant dialogue and discussion. We, at every level of government, have been and remain in close dialogue with the United States of America about this issue, and where we are in absolute agreement is that Iraq poses a real and unique threat to the security of the region and the rest of the world."

A. dipped the brush in a jar of clear liquid and pressed out the liquid on the saucer rim. He added some to the half-mixed paint in the central depression in the saucer. Then he poured four drops of oil from a bottle. He stirred the paint until it became an even light grey.

"We have to face up to it, we have to deal with it and we will. The issue is then what is the best way of proceeding. Now, I can't promise to answer all your questions in detail at this stage because, as I say, key decisions are yet to be taken. But I can and do promise that as the situation develops, the fullest possible debate—"

A. charged his brush and applied highlights to the left half of the woman's vulva. The left side was fully exposed, the right partially obscured by the G-string that the woman in the magazine photograph was pulling aside. The centre of the painting was almost complete. The parted thighs, foreshortened stomach and the lower part of her face were rough outlines, without volume or detail.

"Look, the most important thing is that what ever we do, we do with the broadest possible basis of support. That is clear. That is what we did in Kosovo. That is what we did in Afghanistan. We had the international community with us and obviously it is better to have the international community with us again. The important thing, however, because this is a problem for the world, is that the United Nations has to be the route to deal with this problem, not a way of people avoiding dealing with this problem. After all, it is the

THE NAKED SPUR

United Nations resolutions that Saddam is in breach of. So it makes perfect sense to say that this is an issue for the international community and should be dealt with in that way. All I am saying is it has to be dealt with because we cannot have a situation where people simply turn a blind eye to a situation in which Iraq continues to develop these weapons. I will say a bit more about that later, but you know it is worth at some point going through for people the history of the last ten years and then I think we answer the other point that I think people make perfectly reasonably, which is why now this is a really important question."

A. cleaned excess paint from the brush, wiping it on a sheet draped over the radiator below the painting.

"Well, let's wait and see, Jamie. Let's wait and see what happens on that front. I think we are entitled to perhaps some trust as a result of what has happened before. There have been two major pieces of military action that I have been involved in. One has been Kosovo, the other has been Afghanistan and on both occasions not merely did we have the fullest possible debate in all forums that you would expect that debate to take place, we acted with broad international support."

Resting his left forearm on his knees, A. bent forward. Little and ring fingers of his right hand touching the unpainted linen, holding the brush with three other fingers, A. painted the labia in shallow arcs, top to bottom.

"I don't know how much of the difficulties are attributable to worries about international stability. There are obvious economic factors at play as well. But I think there is a good point behind your question which is the terrorism of the eleventh of September had a big economic impact, that is why, as I say, these questions may seem far away from our domestic national interest, but actually they are intimately connected with it."

(14)

"Weird, isn't it?"

A. nodded, chewing.

"Injera."

"Injera."

Elsa nodded. She was taking plates from a cupboard.

"The first time I tried it, I thought, my God, it's so sour. But after ten minutes you adjust. I tell you, I get cravings and I've only ever eaten it a couple of dozen times. I don't know how Ib gets by without it."

"Oh yeah, I get cravings too."

Ibrahim walked into the kitchen and started to help himself from foil containers on the work surface.

"There's no food anywhere else in the world that tastes like this. Everyone who tries it says so. It's African and a little bit Indian because Ethiopia's on the coast and there's a bit of Arabic influence too but it's unique. The styles and the ingredients mix."

Ibrahim tore half of a large pancake and put it on his plate. The pancake was light yellow and speckled with holes.

"The injera, for example. That is made from wheat that grows in Ethiopia. Teff. I think that wheat grows hardly anywhere else in the world. It's got a unique taste. It's hard to get the flour here in London. And we use it fermented. So, you see some of the ingredients are unique to Ethiopia. And people in Europe don't know anything about it, but really, Ethiopian food is one of the great cuisines of the world."

He picked food up with a patch of injera, folded it and used his fingers to raise it to his mouth.

"Well, in my view it is," he said, eating. "I guess I'm biased."

"Well, Ib, I'll go along with you on that. On how good the food is. And on you being biased," said Elsa.

Ibrahim tilted his head and closed his eyes, mouth full.

"It's my country. I guess you can't help it. You're the same about the UK, right?"

After swallowing he added, "But it is great food."

(15)

A. asked Mack, "Will clients trust us with their photographs?"

"They'll have to. We'll return their photographs but there's no way they'll know whether or not the image was scanned or photocopied. That's just the way it is. We won't copy their photographs but they won't know that. We might have to work some system where the clients can operate anonymously through a receipt system. Each photograph submitted is given a number and the client gets a receipt. That way the client is anonymous. The client can either pick up the finished painting from the outlet or agent on production of the receipt. The client could give an address for delivery."

"What about payment? Isn't the buyer's name going

to be on the cheque?"

"Yes, but if the payments were going through an outlet then there's this barrier between client and artist. The outlet wouldn't see the image. The artist wouldn't see the cheque. A Chinese wall. That would be sealed in an envelope and sent to you. That means the outlet isn't just a place that stocks brochures, the outlet would also do the banking and take a commission. That's a bit tricky but maybe there's a way around it. I'll have to give that a bit of thought. Perhaps we can say only cash payments and collection of work from outlets. It preserves anonymity and it means clients will feel more confident about handing over images. It might prove a deal-breaker, having names and addresses and nude photographs going to one source. It looks like a scheme to entrap people in blackmail. People are a lot more relaxed about nudity these days but even so, it's a sensitive area. Leave it with me. I'll talk it over with Dahlia. She might have some solutions."

(16)

Down Crooms Hill there were houses to A.'s left, park railings to his right. The fallen leaves had compacted into russet mats. An elderly couple walked in the park. He stopped, leant against the park railings, breathing deeply. He looked at the house before him. There was no one at the windows.

At the bottom of the hill he turned right into Nevada Street. He went into an antiques shop. Upstairs rooms were lined with books. He picked one and began to read.

THE NAKED SPUR

Later, A. heard a noise. He put away the book and returned to the stairs. The door at the bottom was locked. A. checked his watch. It was one o'clock. A. pushed the handle, then knocked. After five minutes, he climbed the stairs. He found a book and curled up on the carpet in a patch of sunlight.

Later, the door downstairs was unlocked. A Chinese man in a blazer stopped in the corridor outside the room to examine a nautical print. A. stood up and descended the staircase.

(17)

At the end of Park Row was "The Trafalgar Tavern", bow windows overlooking the Thames. Young people were sitting on the promenade drinking, eyes squinted against the sun. Men in sunglasses were laughing. A woman in sandals was adjusting a sun hat on a toddler in a pushchair. A pigeon was pecking at an ice-cream cone. A. stopped at the railings by the river and looked east. There was a pontoon landing stage, parapets green with weed, brown with mud, gas tanks further on. The river curved away to Silvertown. A. looked south-west and the sun was in his eyes. Canary Wharf Tower and the half-built towers beside it were hazy. On the narrow path, people were moving in files in both directions, pausing to negotiate the drinkers sitting on flagstones near "The Trafalgar Tavern". A. walked west. The promenade widened where steps from the Naval College went down to the river. A. paused there and looked to the opposite bank. A pleasure cruiser passed, sending waves of wake which slapped against the steps. There was a growl and a snarl then the sound of a child squealing. People turned to look. A Staffordshire bull terrier was confronting a young child. The dog was on a leash held by a big man in shorts, T-shirt and a cap. His face was glistening with sweat. A woman in a flower-print dress was clasping the child to her. She said something to the man. "What the fuck are you talking about, you bitch?" he replied. The child was crying. The dog was straining at the leash. The man's arm tensed, forearm bulging under red skin. The woman answered. "Oh, yeah?" he said. "What would you know about it?" The child wailed. "Shuddup!" the man yelled. "'Ee din' do anyfink!" The child closed its mouth, eyes wide. The woman said something else. The man shook his head and spat on a paving stone. Then he strode away, pulling the dog after him. After a few yards, he halted and shouted back. "I love my dog more than you love your kid, you cunt!"

(18)

"You know," said Ibrahim. "People think that Ethiopia is this barren desert. Not at all. They remember the pictures of the famine and think that is how the whole country is all the time. Uh ah. Overall, Ethiopia is a green country."

He looked at A.'s face.

"Oh, yeah, very green. Mountains, lots of rain, forests even. It's quite temperate. The Addis Ababa is at a pretty high altitude so it's quite cool."

Ibrahim cleared his throat.

"You get a touch of colonial architecture in a couple

THE NAKED SPUR

of places on the coast, not much. You know, Ethiopia wasn't ever really colonised but you can find these buildings if you know where to look. The Italian occupation was hardly anything. They planted their flags and built a few villas and courthouses and skedaddled after a few years."

Ibrahim was lying lengthways on a settee with a glass of whiskey balanced on his chest. Occasionally he looked away from the copy of The New Yorker in his hands to the television. On the television, a forecaster delivered the weather mute.

"People know the famine and Haile Selassie and that's it. Some of them don't even know that. It's where King Solomon's mines were. Yeah, a real place. You can go out there and see these giant clay pits, all red, and actually see where the slaves worked. I haven't seen it myself. I saw photographs and people have told me about the mines. It's a bit of a ways to get out there. Through jungle, stuff like that. A bit of a hassle, really. It's not really me. Oh yeah. It's out there. If you want it."

Ibrahim took a sip and looked at the television over his half-moon reading glasses.

"I met Selassie. Yeah. As a boy. A number of us were presented to him and we all lined up and bowed. He gave us each a gold bar. I got a gold bar from Emperor Haile Selassie. How do you like that? Well, actually, more a stick of gold. Like that."

Ibrahim held out two fingers separated. He shifted his position.

"I don't have it any more. I wish I did. Not for the money though. If I still had it I wouldn't sell it. It's quite something to have met the Emperor. But I didn't say anything to him. It wasn't like, you know, I had a conversation with him." He chuckled. "Even so."

He laid the magazine on his lap.

"We moved around a bit after the Revolution. With the Emperor gone and Mengistu in government it wasn't such a hot idea to go back to Ethiopia. So, you know, we travelled."

The grey cat entered through the cat flap.

Ibrahim said, "Hello, Vish. Where have you been?"

The cat blinked at him.

"I think it's about time for another glass of sour mash. What do you say, Vish?"

The cat blinked and padded out of the room.

(19)

The woman in the antiques shop filled a bag with books and added up the cost on a calculator. A.'s gaze was directed at an enamelled sign for beer above her. She gave him the figure and A. pulled out some banknotes.

Before she took the notes, she said, "You know we don't give refunds?"

A. said he did. She took his money and rang up the sale on the till.

"You won't be able to sell these on. With those library stamps, no other dealers will take them. They're cancelled and withdrawn from stock but since the whole library went, they didn't stamp each book. Besides, stamped books aren't worth anything. You know that's why these are so cheap?"

She gave him change and he carried the bag across the

THE NAKED SPUR

park to his room where he put it in a corner and draped a coat over them.

(20)

There was movement in the corner of the room. A. twisted on his chair. The grey cat padded up to him. It looked from him to the saucer of paint. Then it looked to the painting. It walked to the bed and craned its head to see what was on top of the mattress. It jumped on to the bed and sniffed its way across the bed, then crossed to the table where it climbed on and walked to the window.

A. returned to painting a female torso. It was in bright sunlight. Behind the figure was a view of a sloping field of grass, with copses at shoulder height. The figure was bare chested with white pants on, left hand on hip, right arm raised out of the image. Sunlight was shining down over one shoulder picking out the collarbone and ribs of her left side. Upward reflected light under the breasts and on the lower part of the underwear came from below the edge of the image.

Sitting on the table, the grey cat was watching birds on the fence.

"Hey, Vish."

The cat glanced at A. then returned its attention to the birds.

A. extracted a bristle from a brushstroke on the canvas and wiped it from his finger to radiator sheet. He washed the brush and examined it. Its bristles had been worn short. Close to the ferrule were the remains of broken bristles. He tested the tip. The bristles hardly flexed. The bristle ends at the ferrule were clogged with old paint.

The birds flew away. The cat stood up and walked on to the bed where it curled up.

A. pushed the brush into the sack of rubbish by him and picked up a new brush. He split the cellophane packet with his teeth and slid the brush out. The bristles were firm between his fingers when he pinched it. With gradual manipulation, they loosened. He brushed it on his leg, riffled the bristles with a finger then rinsed the bristles with turpentine.

The cat was asleep.

A. resumed painting.

(21)

The bookseller shook his head and handed the book to A.

"I bought them legally."

"I know where you got them. I'm not accusing you of having stolen them. That's not the point. It's just no one wants books that have been blind-stamped throughout. Look at this, every illustration has been stamped."

The bookseller opened one of the books on the table. A violet oval overlapped the edge of a landscape printed in black and white.

"The flyleaf is torn. There's marginalia. The dust-jacket has been laminated. They don't sell. We don't want what we can't sell."

"You've got books in the art section that came from the same library. I've seen them."

The bookseller's expression changed.

"I said no."

The bookseller massaged his neck.

"Really, it's a question of rarity. Those ones in our art section we cherry-picked because they're rare. They're not worth much in that condition, perhaps a third of the price of a regular copy in good condition. They're catalogues raisonné, reference material, stuff that's out of print. It's nice to have them because it surprises the educated browser. Now, get me the Bacon catalogue raisonné, even blind-stamped, and I'd give you two hundred quid without even looking at it. This--" he indicated the pile on his desk, "—is tat."

"You can have them cheap."

"You could give them to me and I'd tell you take the fucking lot and throw them in the bin on your way out. I can't sell them. Don't waste my time and don't bring them back."

(22)

"Where did you get those?" asked Ibrahim, pointing to the avocados on the table.

"The grocer with the barrow on Trafalgar Road."

"Oh. Not the shop on the north side of the road?"

"No. Why?"

"I just wondered. Do you ever go there?"

"The African place?" asked A.

"Yes."

"Sometimes. They sell scotch bonnet peppers."

"Yes. I just wondered."

"What?"

"Well, how you found them."

"Fine. I hadn't noticed anything about them."

"The only reason I ask is that they've been a bit funny with me in the past. I think it's because I'm Ethiopian. I just wondered if you, as a white guy, found them odd."

"No."

"Oh, well. Maybe I caught them on an off day but every day I go in seems to be an off day." Ibrahim paused. "They're Nigerian, I think. I didn't ask. West African anyway."

He rubbed one temple.

"I'm quite partial to some West African things. I have a craving for the piri-piri chilli sauce, you know? I read somewhere that you build up a tolerance for certain chemicals. You get a buzz from them. I'm like that with piri-piri. Ethiopian cuisine is quite spicy but piri-piri is from the west side of Africa, I think. Anyway, I didn't mean to interrogate you on the subject."

As he was leaving the kitchen, he stopped and patted the door jamb.

"But if you notice anything about them, you know, if they say anything to you about me, you'll tell me, won't you?"

(23)

Mack and Dahlia were seated at a window table. Dahlia was leaning back in her seat. Mack was bent over the slide viewer.

"What are you drinking?" Mack asked A.

"Tomato juice."

Mack disappeared into the crowd. A. sat down, folded his jacket over his lap. He adjusted his watch strap.

THE NAKED SPUR

"Thanks for your help," he said to Dahlia.

Dahlia smiled.

"It's a pleasure. We're both really into the idea. It could be interesting for all of us."

She took a drink. The music became louder.

"It's good that you're doing this, you know, painting bodies the way they really are."

She indicated the slides.

"I've been to museums and I look at the nudes in gilt frames and I think, I've never seen a body as perfect as that. And the figures are standing next to classical ruins and I'm thinking, aren't they cold? Why have they dropped all that drapery over the pillars? It's just false. But in these paintings, the ones you do, the figures are real. They've got wrinkles and moles and stretch marks. They've got fat and operation scars. These figures are wearing their own clothes, sitting on their own furniture, not surrounded by props. You can look at these bodies and not feel intimidated or jealous. I think it's important to be honest. These are real people not models. It's how people look in everyday life."

She looked around her.

"The figures in your paintings could be anyone in this room."

She said, "Mack explained to me about the lighting, about how the camera flash flattens things but in pornography everything is lit brightly to show, you know, details. Then I realised why these paintings don't look like paintings, like classical paintings, or like porn. And he said something about the cropping, about how in amateur photographs the cropping is bad and the compositions are unbalanced and that's why they look so different from porn, which is all set up and lit and so on. He's got the film director's perspective. I noticed stuff about the paintings but he can explain it."

Dahlia gestured.

"I'll do my best to keep Mack from going off on a tangent. He's been so busy. I know you're relying on this money."

A. was looking at her hands. Her nails were shiny with lacquer.

"We'll find a way of making this work. You can't live on nothing."

A. turned his face to the window.

Mack returned with drinks. A. unfolded a sheet of paper on the table. Mack and Dahlia passed it to each other, reading.

Mack said, "It's a bit dry. It could be more—" his gaze wandered over to a girl in a light dress, "—adventurous. Play up the saucy aspect. Be a bit kinkier."

"It needs to be fun and inviting." Dahlia folded the paper and tucked it into her handbag. "I can work on it at the office."

She looked at A.

"It's okay. Honestly. The factual stuff is clear. It just needs a lighter touch. Relax a little."

"It needs a feminine touch," said Mack. "Ready to eat?"

THE NAKED SPUR

(24)

"The trick of selling is not to look like you are selling. Hold back a bit. That's where the rumours come in. I've got Lucy asking around about these great paintings she's heard about. So, that sets us up a little. It does some work for us. When I go to this potential outlet—or when Dahlia goes—then the people there have already heard about these paintings. The rumours are out there now doing some of our work."

Mack sprinkled soy sauce over his noodles.

"The one thing we don't want to appear is desperate." He paused, chewing. "Or amateur."

A. put down his chopsticks in his empty bowl.

Dahlia raised an eyebrow and said, "Hungry, were you?"

A. dabbed his mouth with a napkin.

"If we think this through," Mack continued. "The paintings, the commissioning, will sell itself. It's a great product. I know the money's out there waiting to be spent. This is a great angle. Art, money and sex. It's the ultimate erotic gift, individually tailored, perfect."

He belched into his napkin. Dahlia frowned. Mack continued.

"I get this social-chronicling aspect, the using-found-material part and so on. And as an art project that's great. But from the buyer's point of view, these are just exclusive, individualised gifts. The wonderful thing is you don't have to compromise the artwork at all to do this project. You already make this sort of painting. What you make can be both things. It's this conceptual art project and it's these erotic gifts. We're slipping them this subversive art and they're just buying a picture to hang in the bedroom. It's a scam but it's not a scam because it's genuine on both sides. The selling, the commissioning, the whole scheme is a giant conceptual art work."

Mack emptied his tumbler and filled it from a water jug. Dahlia tapped her chopsticks on the bowl rim.

"But no one's being taken for a ride," she said.

"Of course not," replied Mack, adding more soy sauce. "I'm just saying. We can appreciate the irony, the different levels this operates on. We can see it from the inside. But it's all for real. The scheme operates as a straight business but it's also an art work in itself. And A. can earn some money from his art. We're thinking eight hundred or six hundred and fifty pounds per painting, yes? And it's art he'd be making anyway, so he doesn't have to sell himself out."

He sniffed.

"Galleries take fifty percent, right? So, he's getting a better deal this way. The agent can get twenty percent so it's worth her while. The more she sells, the more she earns."

Dahlia pushed away her bowl.

"I thought we said twenty-five percent," she said.

Mack gestured with his chopsticks.

"We'll talk through the figures once we settle the price and what the agent actually does. Twenty percent, twenty-five percent, whatever."

He carried on eating.

"I thought we said twenty-five," said Dahlia, looking

at her bowl.

Dahlia and A. sat in silence while Mack ate.

Leaving the restaurant, Mack said, "We've got a Polaroid camera at work I could borrow. If this takes off we could buy one. Don't worry about the money. You've got materials, right? But we'll get deposits with each commission so you'll have your material costs covered even if the client rejects the painting."

They moved out of the doorway. Figures entered the restaurant.

"What happens to the work buyers commission but turn down?" A. asked.

"We'll cross that bridge when we come to it," answered Mack.

Dahlia pulled up her collar.

"You'd have to destroy them," she said.

"If a buyer has rejected the work and not paid for it, who owns it?"

Dahlia gave A. a hard look.

"You'd have to destroy them," she repeated.

"She's right," said Mack, "No one's going to volunteer to appear in a nude painting with the possibility that if they reject it there's a chance it might turn up in the future. You'd have to destroy the painting. It doesn't matter who owns it. You can't show it and you can't sell it to anyone apart from the client who commissioned it. So, you can't do anything with it. It has to go."

"And that's going in the terms and conditions," added Dahlia.

(25)

A. used the ruler to measure a square on the photograph and then to guide his pen across the surface. The image was of a woman standing on a table raising her dress. Camera flash had flattened her to a cut-out and put a stripe of shadow on the wall behind.

A. squared a second photograph, of a woman in a short dress standing against a built-in wardrobe, one leg outstretched, hand on hip.

He put the second on a stack of magazines and began to brush in the outlines of the first on a blank canvas.

Noise of wheeled bins being emptied into a truck.

He went to kitchen and prepared a meal.

A. finely chopped up half a jalapeño chilli, scored then crushed a clove of garlic and put these in a jug. He added salt and pepper then squeezed half a lime into the jug. He poured some olive oil and a few drops of balsamic vinegar then stirred the mixture with the knife. Without cleaning the knife, he halved an avocado and stabbed the stone with the knife tip. He drew out the stone and dropped it in a rubbish bin. He put the avocado halves on a plate and poured the vinaigrette into the semi-ovoid hollow in one of the avocado halves and began to eat it with a teaspoon.

From the living room came the sound of "In a Silent Way" by Miles Davis, footsteps, quiet laughter, a lighter being struck.

A. ate, taking drinks of water from a glass on the table.

Footsteps approaching.

"Ah, you're here. It's you, I mean. I heard these sounds

THE NAKED SPUR

and I'm thinking who is this. Of course it's you. Who else would it be?"

Ibrahim smiled, in one hand a glass of whiskey, in the other a cannabis cigarette.

"You know I think I am losing my marbles. Don't you think? Eh? What do you think, Vish?"

The grey cat at his ankles looked up to Ibrahim.

Ibrahim laughed.

"Vish doesn't care, do you?"

The cat sauntered to the food dishes.

"Has he got food?"

Ibrahim craned to see. The dishes were overflowing on to the floor.

"Oh, that was me. I refilled their dishes when I got in. I was thinking all the way back from the office, the cats must have food, the cats must have food. I was sitting in the cab, thinking that."

Ibrahim inhaled from his cigarette, closing his eyes against the smoke.

"Vish is fine. He's got food. He doesn't care."

The cat walked out of the kitchen.

"That's right, Vish. You go have a sleep, man. I might be joining you."

A. scraped clean the inside of the avocado skin and began to eat the second.

"Wow. That looks nice but I'm not hungry. I had a sandwich at about four. That does for me."

Ibrahim glanced up the stairs.

"That's right, Vish. You settle down for a kip."

He took a sip of whiskey. He waved the glass in A.'s direction.

"You know, this is like two in the morning for me."

The clock in the kitchen showed twenty minutes past noon.

"There are some guys in the office who get off work and take a taxi up to Smithfields at nine in the morning. There is a pub there that's open in the morning for meat porters at the market. What a great job title. Meat porter. How old fashioned is that? It's like a job from the Middle Ages. That's right, you can go in at six in the morning and get yourself a beer and a steak. And guys do that. Not me. I'm never one for pubs. I like the idea, you know. With all those Irish writers it's a big thing. I like the idea but I don't like it so much in practice. Don't get me wrong, I like alcohol but I'm never a social drinker. I like to listen to my own music. Jazz is the thing. That's what you need to listen to."

Drops fell from his glass to the table cloth.

"And you can't smoke this in a pub."

Ibrahim held up the joint.

"That's right, isn't it, Vish?" he said, addressing the absent cat. "He knows me."

He put down his glass and tapped his ashes into the bin.

"Oh, I meant to show you a picture. You know this photographer Elliott Erwitt? The American, I don't know, realist, whatever. I got this book of his. I must show it to you some time. It's at the flat. Anyway, it's great. He takes these snapshots and it's art. Really, really. Maybe there is some hidden principle at work that I can't detect. To me, they look like things you'd just dash off with an instamatic. I guess there's more to it

THE NAKED SPUR

than that but they feel very real and ordinary and yet amazing too. The pictures are of planes and chairs and so on. That jug—no. That jug with the tablecloth is too much. Too rich. He couldn't photograph that. It's not prosaic enough. Anyway, he's dead. Or is he? But you get the idea."

A. drank water and looked at him.

"Anyway, that's not what I wanted to show you. Wait here. Don't go anywhere."

Ibrahim put his cigarette in an ashtray and left the room. He came back with a stack of photographs.

"These are mine, my photographs of everyday life, things I see. It's amazing what you see just walking the streets. You get the most amazing juxtapositions. Going through Hackney, you get the West African shops, fruit on the pavement, those textile shops where they sell these really intensely coloured fabrics. I try to carry a camera with me all the time because you never know when the most wonderful image will come up. There are times when you see something great and you don't have a camera with you. I don't want to be caught out, so I keep my camera around. Have you seen them already? I have to show you this one photograph."

Ibrahim shuffled the stack.

"Ha. That's Elsa. But of course you can see that."

He laughed softly.

"Oh, that's us at Bob's. Such a beautiful house. I'll take you there. He's a writer. That's Elsa with her make-up on. It makes her face look like a Kabuki mask. That's Greenwich Park. Those are of Vish. Greenwich, again."

There were about three hundred photographs in the

stack.

"There's this one I have to show you. I thought I had them in order. I did have. No. Ah. No, not this. It's a photograph of a door I saw one day. A green door in Dalston. But it's like, oh, I can't describe it. There's something magical about it. Something intangible. This photograph is like my own Elliott Erwitt—a Dalston Erwitt."

He continued dealing out the photographs on the table.

"We have a system, don't we, Vish?"

Ibrahim laughed then started to cough.

A child walked down the alley. All that was visible between the slats of the venetian blind was the crown of his head. He was bouncing a ball.

"Ah. Here. I have it."

Ibrahim placed a photograph in front of A. It was of a green door in a brick wall.

"There's something magical about it. I was thinking about it all yesterday. What do you think? No, don't tell me now. Take a look." Ibrahim picked up his glass. "I need a top up."

A. looked at the photograph and listened to Ibrahim bumping against the wall as he walked to the living room.

(26)

"I'm not so sure about this idea for photographing people. It seems a bit complicated. Also, Dahlia isn't keen. I mean, it would probably be all right. It isn't the sex angle that bothers her. Dahlia is worried about going

THE NAKED SPUR

into people's houses alone. I could act as a chaperon, stay outside or something but I can't guarantee to be available. I get work abroad. It's too difficult. I don't know how we'd work it. So, I think we'll just say they submit their own photographs. We don't want to make the scheme too elaborate. It would be bad if we offered the service then for some reason we couldn't do one part of it. It's letting the client down right at the start of their contact. We can't have it getting inconsistent, one person gets the photography done by Dahlia and the next person doesn't get it because I can't chaperon. Best to scrap that aspect."

A. was in the telephone box on Trafalgar Road watching paramedics push a man in a wheelchair to a waiting ambulance. Queuing traffic discoloured the air.

Mack continued.

"I went into that shop I told you about. I gave them this line about some paintings I'd heard about. So, we'll see. If someone goes in talk to them about the commissioning service, they'll already know something about it."

A lorry was edging out to the centre of the road, attempting to overtake the stationary vehicle. The oncoming traffic did not yield. A man had stepped out of the fireplace showroom to watch the disruption.

"A few people at the office have seen your images and they're really into them. I don't think you ought to let the galleries put you off. Galleries are looking for, well, I'm not sure, but they want something else. People are really into the work, all you need to do is connect with those people directly. You don't need the galleries if you can get work directly to buyers. When viewers see these paintings they feel a connection. Fuck the galleries."

The lorry moved out and the approaching traffic braked. A volley of horns sounded. A couple of cars followed the lorry then east-bound traffic started to move. The west-bound traffic was solid and unmoving, queuing out of sight.

"Are you speaking to me from a motorway? Are you actually standing on the hard shoulder of the M25 using a roadside emergency phone? Get yourself a fucking mobile phone before you die of carbon monoxide poisoning."

(27)

In the room was a single bed, a kitchen table, a kitchen chair, an armchair heaped with papers and magazines, two bookcases, a chest of drawers with a pivoting mirror, a wicker dressing screen, a typewriter in a carrying case, a suitcase, a bag of books, two sacks of clothes, a line of garments hanging from a rail set into an alcove, a laundry bag on a stand, a bundle of linen, a stack of stretcher bars, eighteen boxes and thirty-seven square canvases. Balanced on one bookcase was a large painting wrapped in plastic. On the table was a desk lamp. On the dressing table was a television. Under the table was a portable CD player/radio.

A. moved the paintings to the bed, then stacked the boxes until the sides of the lowest began to bulge. He put the bags of clothing on top and pushed the dressing screen close to them. The suitcase went between screen and chest of drawers. Paintings were restacked by the

THE NAKED SPUR

door. Papers on the armchair were put under the table with the typewriter, linen, stretcher bars and radio.

When A. went to the door, paintings prevented it from opening fully. The armchair A. moved to the centre of the floor. He stacked six canvases on a window sill, turning the outermost ones back outwards, showing unpainted linen to room and window. Then A. put four further paintings on top. The lowered roller blind covered them from sight inside the room. Remaining canvases he leaned on the wall below that window. The table he pushed against the second window.

He wiped clean the painting saucer and rubbed brush bristles clean on the sheet over the radiator. Out of the chest of drawers, A. took a manila envelope. He counted out of it a number of banknotes and replaced it in the drawer. From the bookcase, he collected a handful of forms.

On the doormat was a letter. He picked up the letter and read the envelope. He raised it to his face and smelled it. Slipping the letter into his jacket, he left the house.

He entered Greenwich Park at Maze Hill gate and walked westward. There was a kidney-shape boating pool drained of water. Its basin was painted blue. Sun was drying the paths. A crocodile trail of French schoolchildren in pastel-colour anoraks walked up to the Observatory. A group of skateboarders dressed in black practised jumps.

A. left the park at King William Walk. In the telephone box by the gates, he dialled a number. After waiting, he hung up and left the telephone box. Nevada Street. Burney Street. The clock tower of Meridian House jutted into a sky racing with cumulus clouds. He climbed the steps into Meridian House and went to the second floor.

In the open-plan office, he sat on a chair and waited. The man on the chair next to him was very thin. The bones of his wrists and his cheekbones stood out. There were tattoos on his neck. He was staring vacantly, gnawing his hands. When the man stood to go to the claims desk, A. saw his fingernails were abraded stubs.

The officer at the inquiries desk studied A.'s forms then told him to sit in another part of the office. A. sat under a wall-mounted fan. A note had been taped to it. After twenty minutes, A.'s name was called out. The woman asked him questions then he signed some documents.

Outside, A. bent over behind a bench on the corner of Burney Street and Royal Hill and retched. Nothing came up.

The house was empty when he arrived. A. climbed on to his bed fully clothed and curled up. He was shivering. After a while the shivering stopped and he was asleep.

(28)

A. put the top three coins of the stack on the payphone into the machine and dialled.

"Mack, please. Yes."

He shuffled the coins across the top of the payphone over its scratched paintwork.

A. read the number written on an information panel

THE NAKED SPUR

in the telephone box. He hung up and one coin was returned which he added to the others and put in a pocket. A minute later, the telephone rang.

"I've been thinking about another way of getting people's attention," said Mack. "We circulate these rumours about this collector who has amassed a large group of these square paintings. He's commissioned the artist to paint all the collector's ex-girlfriends from photographs. He's got a whole wall in his bedroom covered by twenty paintings. Just imagine."

Mack paused.

"So, he's your biggest collector. He's buying stuff off you every month. If you ever go off on holiday or are sick and can't paint then we'll just tell clients that you're tied up with this collector's commissions and you can't do any extra work at the moment. Think about it. It's beautiful. I mean, the angle is beautiful."

(29)

Inside the plastic case was a roll of film, which A. extracted. He put the camera in his lap and opened the back. It sprang open and A. inserted the film cartridge and fitted the end of the film into the spool. He closed the back and depressed the shutter release button three times, winding the film on between shots.

Putting the camera on the bed, A. hung a painting on the wall screw. He turned on the spotlights and stood on a chair to adjust them. Then he retracted both roller blinds fully and cleared the sill of canvases. Then A. opened the windows. He took a large sketchpad and folded under the cover sheet to show a white page. He moved the chair to the wall and balanced the sketchpad on the chair back and the radiator. He looked at the reflected light from the paper and altered the position of the pad.

A. sat on the bed and screwed a shutter-release cable to the camera. He set the aperture, the exposure time, timer and sat against the wall, camera on his raised knees. After focusing the lens, he slightly tilted the camera. Keeping every part of his body still, he depressed the cable button. An LED flashed increasingly rapidly and the shutter clicked once then clicked again. A. breathed out. He photographed the painting twice more then he took thirty more exposures of thirteen square paintings in the room.

He stacked the canvases then rewound the film manually, sprang the back open and extracted the cartridge which he put back in its case. Putting the lid on the case, A. zipped it into a jacket pocket.

(30)

Waiting ahead of A. in the queue were a man in a striped shirt, wearing oblong-lensed spectacles and a girl with facial piercings. When A. got to the counter he handed over a pink carbon receipt and watched the soap opera playing on the wide-screen television near the ceiling after the assistant had taken his receipt to a back room. The assistant came back with a bag containing a small red box with a white lid. A. handed over some money, pocketed the change and crossed to a table adjacent to the front window. He pressed a button and the tabletop illuminated. Out of the box, A. took thirty-seven slides.

THE NAKED SPUR

Two had ends of film strip. He tossed these into a nearby bin and spread the remaining ones over the table. He placed over one slide a viewing lens, which was chained to the table, putting his eye to it. By A.'s side was a cycle courier in Lycra shorts putting a packet into a satchel. He was looking at the table. He smiled then took three steps to the door, his hard soles tapping on the pressed-metal floor. A. swept the slides into a pile and put them back into their box. He switched off the light and stepped out on to Wardour Street.

(31)

"Don't ask. He'll get us Stella Artois or some shit like that. I have contacts who can get us crates of Kronenberg, free. The last thing we want is him volunteering his services. Keep him out of it. The people I know handle top events, launches, film premieres, not fucking office parties full of sales managers trying to finger the typists."

A. slid the photographs and the box of slides across Mack's desk.

"He's not even invited to the opening."

Mack pressed the "Enter" key.

"These guys can get us blow-up details of the paintings and print them on fabric. We can have banners hanging up around the room. There could be tables with brochures. The blow-ups will be great. They can bring out the grain of the canvas like ben-day dots. We'll have to get high-quality photographs. We've got a photographer we use. He could do it."

He shuffled discs and put one into the computer. The

image of a room came up on the screen.

"This is the launch of a film Simon worked on. You see those screens. We can get ones like those. Those tables, the chairs, the lights, they're all hired. We could get those. We wouldn't need much. They're all geared up to deal with these events. It would be straightforward. They do some of this at short notice. Different sizes of venue, numbers of guests and so on."

Mack cleared the screen and took the top photograph from the pile on his desk.

"I'm thinking he's a businessman. I don't know why. That's how I'm seeing him in my mind's eye."

The painting was of the flank of a black male, limp penis in profile.

"It's got that feeling about it."

He fanned out the photographs on his desk.

"You get wondering about these people, what their lives are like. They're so intimate, these images, but impersonal too. With these strips over the eyes, you wouldn't recognise these people if they walked by you in the street. I think up stories about them. And I wonder about the person on the other side of the camera, the person who took the original photo. Strange. You get this one image and no information. Maybe that's what makes them interesting, don't you think? It gives you room to speculate. I imagine that their lives are as routine as ours are. More so, probably. If you had a page of biography for each image, I don't think I'd be half so curious about them. I look at the furniture and the clothes and the stuff on their shelves and I try and piece together what sort of person they are. I guess what their

THE NAKED SPUR

jobs might be. The women with stretch marks have had kids. You wonder what their circumstances are. These paintings are like the opening frames in a movie where you don't know who the characters are or what is going on."

He gathered them together.

"If you leave these with me, I can get these scanned. We'll try and work them into the brochure. Perhaps we could have two pictures, one outside, one in. When a person opens the flaps, the two halves open to reveal the image on the inside in exactly the same place. The one on the outside could be alluring but demure and the inside one could be full-frontal nudity. You could do two paintings of the same woman, on the outside in lingerie, on the inside nude. I could get you the photos to work from."

He smiled.

"I'll get the scanned images to Dahlia and she'll look at layout. We'll have to adapt the wording."

"We don't need to work from photographs," Mack added. "We can use video. Clients could submit a video and you could select a frame to paint."

"I can't work from a screen. It needs to be printed out."

"We've got machines here that can do it. You just need to run VT and pause where you want and press a button and out comes a printout. It's straight forward. I'll show you."

"Okay, if you think any client would do that, we might put some in the brochure about it."

"We need a name for the service." He tapped a printed

sheet. "This is no good. Something creative, something that isn't being used by anyone else. We don't want the same name as some escort agency or tacky strip club in Romford."

Mack rocked in his chair.

"There's a girl I know."

He tilted back his head.

"She might have a name we can use?" A. asked.

"Yes. She's got her fingers in a lot of pies. She's a smart cookie. I've been meaning to tell her about this to see if she'll give us a steer. It's her sort of thing."

Mack scratched his beard.

"Things are coming along. We're almost there."

A. rested his head in his hands and watched Mack start typing.

(32)

"There they are. Two powerful beams of light blazing straight up into the night sky. They are dazzlingly bright and stretch up into the heavens as far as the eye can see, visible from space apparently. It makes a haunting, eerie contrast with the site of ground zero. Two great towers of steel, glass and concrete obliterated and now, one year on, replaced by these twin beams of light blazing into the sky over Manhattan."

A. got up from his bed and sat facing the painting above the radiator. In the painting a woman in underwear lay on a velveteen sofa. On the carpet was a circular rug, tassels on its fringe tangled.

"Robert, looking at these pillars of light, can you tell me how you feel now?"

THE NAKED SPUR

A. painted the figure's hair lying over the cushion.

"I don't know how to explain what I'm seeing to your listeners. It's a beautiful sight and it's a terrible sight."

Parallel, descending strokes. Medium grey. White. Light grey. Turpentine. White. Turpentine. Light grey. Medium grey. Turpentine.

"Perhaps no one has ever seen anything like this. It's beautiful but it comes out of loss and waste."

A. switched off the radio and dropped his brushes in the jar. He went down to the kitchen and cut himself a slice of pie.

(33)

The telephone box was on the corner of Park Row and Romney Road.

"Wait."

A. inserted a couple of coins from those on top of the telephone.

"The address."

"Of the boutique?" Damien paused. "No, sorry. I did say I would, didn't I? I'll ask if you want. I can call back. But you don't have a telephone. I could send you a postcard. I'll do that. You want it quite soon, don't you?"

"Yes."

"I'll do my best. I'll find out today and put it on a postcard. Give me your address."

A. spoke his address into the telephone handset. A bus drove west on Romney Road, lifting leaves from the tarmac in its wake. A metal shelf by the telephone was smudged with ash.

"I'll be quick about it because I'm off to Monaco for a week. Just a little thing. I've never been there before. Okay, I have to go. Give me a call in a couple of weeks' time and tell me how it went with these boutique guys."

When the dial tone sounded, A. pressed redial and entered a number. The answering service replied and A. snapped down the telephone cradle but the coins had already rolled into the coin safe. He tried the returned coins slot. When he withdrew his fingers, they held a cigarette butt.

(34)

"You need some money," said Mack, shutting his office door.

He sat at his desk and began to work on the computer.

"Have you ever heard of e-Bay?"

"Yes," said A. "I don't know anything about it."

"I use it all the time. You understand the principle, right?"

"I think so."

"Okay. So, I go on and bid for, I don't know, a pair of trainers and I can watch the bidding and put in a higher offer if someone else outbids my first offer. Clear?"

A. nodded and settled in the chair next to Mack.

"So, it's an open market. Anyone can offer and bid on any item. I think only certain categories are prohibited. I had a look. Drugs, porn, war relics, body parts. Art gets sold all the time."

Mack clicked on to an Internet page of thumbnail images and bid details.

"So, here we have some art. It's just old tat. Amateur

stuff. This is just an example for you."

Mack pointed to an item on the screen.

"That's up for a hundred and twenty-three dollars. Everything's in dollars here. Here you can see the bids and this is the deadline. If it doesn't make its reserve then it remains unsold. Like a regular auction, right? So, search category 'nudes'. We'll have to wait for a while. Here we are, fifteen items located. Right. They're not so good, even I can tell that. But that's not the point. You see how things work?"

A. nodded again.

"As this commissioning system is going to take a while to get running properly, I thought we could sell some of your art through e-Bay while we're waiting. At the moment we've got this problem because you have ready-made paintings but no way of selling them because they are supposed to be already sold. We're putting over this idea that those paintings were commissioned and belong to private collectors. So, how can we sell stuff we just described as already sold? What we do is, we put together this cock-and-bull story about how this guy commissioned these paintings of his girlfriend and now they've split up and the guy's new girlfriend has told him the paintings have to go. So, he's selling them on e-Bay. All the time it's us doing the selling. I sell the paintings and you get the money. What do you think?"

"It sounds fine. I don't have a computer though."

"No problem. It's easy to set up an account. We could do it now. Or we could use my account. It's no problem. We set up this back story. The guy, his ex-girlfriend, the commission, the new girlfriend and so on. That's part of the deal. So, the background is also acting as promotion. We can't do it obviously. It's indirect. So, the back story is entirely false but we are genuinely selling the paintings and the buyer gets what he pays for. It's not a hoax. It's a marketing angle. We're selling the painting, getting some money, but better still, we're selling the rumour."

A. shrugged.

"We put a reserve on, maybe one hundred and fifty dollars. It's got to be pretty low. We're not selling a big-name artist. In fact, we're not giving the artist's name at all. Bidding might take off but to be realistic, we've got to expect to sell for a low price. If they don't sell then you keep the paintings. No one's lost out."

Mack lifted a pen.

"What are we talking? One hundred and fifty dollars? One hundred and seventy-five?"

"Whatever you think we can get."

"I think we should go for the lower figure this time. If the auction works then we can try other paintings at higher prices."

Mack wrote on the notepad.

"I was thinking of those two paintings of the stripping woman in white underwear. They're of the same woman, right?"

"Yes."

"So that backs up our story about this guy commissioning paintings of his girlfriend. It all ties in. You're okay to sell them?"

"Sure."

"Let's call it one hundred and fifty dollars for each. And the guy will split them, yes?"

"Fine."

"We have the images scanned on disk. I remember seeing them. I'll dig them out. So, is this a plan?"

"Let's go for it."

(35)

There were no letters on the doormat. A. could hear a sighing gasp, cut off. He closed the front door and went to the living room. The room smelled of cannabis smoke and whiskey. The curtains were half drawn. A cat lifted its head when A. approached the room, then curled itself on the settee. On the television screen a man in a suit was giving a press conference in mute.

There was a rattling sigh.

Ibrahim was asleep on the sofa. In the ashtray, a cigarette had burnt itself to a neat column of ash. Aslant on the settee arm was a glass of whiskey. Ibrahim was wearing slippers and mismatching socks. His V-neck pullover was spotted with cigarette burns.

A. lifted the glass off the settee, placing it on the rattan occasional table.

Ibrahim stirred.

"Is that you, Vish?" he muttered.

A. stepped away and went up to his room. He put a bottle of turpentine by the radiator. He opened the window. Paint on the brushes was viscid. Turpentine poured into a jar, A. put the brushes to soak. He put a fresh dab of black paint on the saucer and started to paint. The image was of a woman's torso from above the hips to her shoulders. Between her small breasts was a circular pendant on a leather cord. One forearm was slightly raised in mid gesture. Some of her long brown hair lay in front of her shoulder. To one side was a dark curtain, to the other a wall. A. worked on the highlights of the hair, referring to the magazine page.

There were halting footsteps. A sleepy voice.

"Time for bed, Vish. Yes, time for bed."

The toilet flushed. A door closed.

A. switched on the radio.

At five o'clock, the front door slammed. A. went to greet Elsa.

"I have a terrible headache and if I don't go to bed as soon as I finish my tea I will feel so awful tonight. And I've promised to meet Paula. I suppose Ib is in my bed."

"Yes."

She opened a box of herbal tea bags.

"How long has he been there?"

"About an hour."

"An hour! Oh, why does he do this? That means he's been awake for about twenty hours. No wonder he's always ill. What a pair we make. What's he been doing since he got in from the office? Oh, don't tell me, drinking Jack Daniels and smoking jah. What will we do with him?"

She carried her cup into the living room. The cats woke.

"Hello, darlings. Has Ib been fumigating you?"

She opened the garden door.

"I have to get back to painting," said A.

"Paint anything good?"

"Nothing finished yet."

(36)

"I thought you were doing it."

"No, we said you'd do it and we'd look at it together when we meet."

Pause.

"Oh. Did we?"

"Yes."

"What did I say?"

"You said that was fine and that you'd work on it before we met."

"Oh."

Sigh.

"So, you haven't written anything?"

"No."

"Well, okay. Do you want to work on it this evening before we meet?"

"I can do."

"Will you? Because if you don't do it then we'll have nothing much to work on tomorrow."

"I thought we were working on the brochure."

"Well, yes that too. But I thought we wanted to get those paintings up on e-Bay as soon as possible."

"Yes. Okay. I'll work on the back story for the seller."

"You're sure?"

"Yes."

"Okay. Then have it with you tomorrow. We don't want to waste time by writing the whole thing up fresh."

"Agreed."

"So, see you tomorrow with the story."

"See you at the office."
"See you then."

(37)

"You should cut out all this untitled shit. I don't know what's what."

Mack was looking at a handwritten list of serial numbers.

"I'm confused. The painting of the girl in the lace basque is OW15 in the first list, O/23 in the second and the slide is called B. Can't we just give it a name? 'Sarah' or something? Or just 'basque'. Something, anything. I'm going to call it 'basque' so we know where we are. None of this matters but we'll go crazy if we carry on with these numbers. So, 'basque'. Pendant. Ahmmm, 'Brazilian stripping'."

"But she's British Asian."

"Brazilian sounds better. This can be 'chick in lacy bra', yeah? Babe on carpet. Stripping milf."

"What's a milf?"

"I don't know. They use it on the Internet. I don't know what it means. The Internet has these different classifications. Lady is demure, girl is pretty sexual, woman means she's engaging in sexual activity. Ahmmm, there are milf and some others. This is 'Latina seated'. I know she's Asian but here she's Latina. This is 'male torso'. Woman in slip. Black male. I'm going to make a shortlist of the ones I think best for publicity. I'll ask around, see which paintings people find most intriguing. I've had a positive response from people in the office who've seen the photos. Those gallerists have got their heads stuck so far up their arses they can't see anything. Screw them. You don't need them."

(38)

"The idea is that you're anonymous. That way, people are responding to the art and saying to each other, who is doing this. It's going to add to the mystery and add an element of intrigue. So not only have you got the commissioning aspect, you've got the sex aspect, which is going to draw a lot of people in. On top of that you've got rumours about who's making this art. Believe me, it will work a lot better than having your name signed on the bottom of each picture and someone searching on the Internet and finding your CV. We want there to be the hint that maybe a well-known artist is doing this in his spare time. No offense to you but it'll get a bit more attention than just than, oh, it's this guy who went to this college and has had these shows and so on. You're not a big draw. Better to push the rumours. So, all the time, the question is being asked, who is doing all this."

(39)

When he was alone in the house, A. took three square paintings down to the garden. He laid them face down on the path and used a tack-lever to pry out tacks attaching linen to stretcher. The detached canvases he rolled together. A. cut the last of a roll of new linen into squares and attached them to the stretchers with the extracted tacks. Then he prepared them with two coats of primer.

ADAMS

It was dusk. Dew was forming on the grass.

He brought in the stretched canvases. In the yard, A. pulled a rubbish sack out of a wheeled bin, folded up the loose canvas squares and put them in the bin. He placed the rubbish sack over them.

He washed his hands twice. He made a salad. He talked to Elsa when she arrived. He drew five pages of sketches from contact magazines. He shaved and showered. Elsa had retired for the night and A. was lying in bed with the lights out when the radio news broadcast that in America a man in a grocery-store car park had been killed with a single shot fired by an unseen assailant.

(40)

A. shut the door and dried his hair with a bath towel. He flicked a switch on the radio.

"--surgeons who operated on the boy said that the three-hour operation to save his life involved the removal of the boy's spleen, pancreas and parts of the stomach. The boy remains in a critical condition in intensive care."

A. sat naked on the bed, towel tented over his head. Downstairs, the washing machine was on spin cycle.

"--occurred outside Benjamin Tasker Middle School in Bowie, Maryland. Initial police reports suggest the sniper used a high-power point-two-two-three calibre rifle as in previous shootings."

The washing machine was hammering at the wall, whining, rattling. A. wound the towel around his head.

"--within the next hour a statement is expected.

Chief of police, Charles--"

A. groped for the controls and silenced the radio. He stretched out on the bed, legs together, cupped his genitals in his hands, towel enfolding his head. He lay like this for a long time.

(41)

"So, what I'm thinking now is that we get an outlet to stock brochures, handle inquiries, receive payments and they hold finished paintings ready for clients to collect. Maybe one of your paintings could be on display at an outlet. That would attract clients. When they ask at the counter about it, the person at the till gives them a brochure. It will save Dahlia a lot of work. She can operate as a freelance agent. She'll have the brochures but she won't be the sole point of contact. It's best to spread this scheme between one or two outlets and an agent. That way you're not relying on one person to do all the selling for you."

(42)

When A. went to the telephone box on Trafalgar Road and telephoned Damien, Damien told A. that he had been in a car crash in Monaco. "Passenger in a car that hit a stationary vehicle at 40 miles per hour. Hurt so much. Unbelievable." "I've only just returned to London. I've been sick as a dog for a few days with food poisoning." He said that very day he had put the name and address of the boutique on a postcard addressed to A. A. thanked Damien and asked him about the accident. They said goodbye.

A. went back to his room. As he cleaned his brushes, the radio reported a Vietnam veteran had been shot dead filling his car tank with petrol in a town called Manassas in Virginia.

That evening A. asked Ibrahim if he could use some of Ibrahim's olive oil on his pasta. Ibrahim said that was fine, so A. used the oil.

(43)

A. sat in the dole office, feeding the strap of his bag back and forth between his hands. He watched a narrow-faced youth in a baseball cap pickpocket a woman.

The woman was in her fifties and wiping away tears as she talked to a girl at the inquiries desk. Behind her chair, the narrow-faced youth went on one knee as if to tie the lace of a trainer and slipped a scab-knuckled hand into the woman's handbag. He brought out a purse and hid it under his tracksuit top. At the door his path was blocked by a burly security guard. The guard said something. The youth raised his shoulders and splayed his arms, mouth open. The purse thumped on the carpet. The guard put a foot on the purse and spoke into his radio, eyes on the youth.

A black teenager with a bandanna approached the guard and started abusing him. Heads turned to watch, people fell silent.

A second guard arrived. The youth in the bandanna made a dash for it, shouldering past the first guard. He hit the door and bounced off, ending sitting on the floor, eyes round. As the second guard reached for him,

THE NAKED SPUR

he got to his feet, yanked the door handle and ran out. His trainers thumped and squeaked on the stairs, the sound growing fainter.

A.'s name was called and he signed on. The man signing him printed out some sheets and gave them to A.

When A. was leaving, he passed the woman holding her purse, talking to the first guard. The second guard and a policeman were restraining the narrow-faced youth against a pin board. On the pin board were posters of smiling faces.

(44)

When A. left Meridian House he went south-west along Greenwich High Road. He went into a bookshop with the sign "Halcyon Books". He found a paperback, checked the price written in pencil on the flyleaf and paid for it at the cash till.

Leaving the bookshop, A. retraced his steps back to Meridian House then followed Royal Hill towards Blackheath. On the corner of Circus Street, a couple of tourists were consulting a guidebook.

Gloucester Circus was divided in half. On the south side was a crescent of old brick terraces with front doors above steps, high windows and railings. The north side was modern blocks of flats. In the centre was a semi-circle of lawn and trees behind railings. A. walked the north side. A group of West Africans climbed out of a white Mercedes. They were wearing gold jewellery and black leather.

A. entered Greenwich Park through Circus Gate on Crooms Hill and crossed the lawn. The grass wetted his boots. Ragged nimbostratus cloud blew from the south. On a bench, a woman sat motionless. She had a wide-brim hat, a tan raincoat with the collar up, Jackie O. sunglasses and tan gloves. A scarf covered her lower face.

It was raining when A. arrived home. Cats were play-fighting on the living-room rug. On the television a western was showing. The air smelled of cannabis smoke and drying laundry. A. went upstairs. He half-opened a window. On the radio a presenter announced that all traffic on Interstate 95 and Route 1 in Virginia had been halted by police as the search continued for an unidentified sniper. Vehicles were bumper to bumper for fifty miles. Leave for all police officers in the region was cancelled. At five o'clock confirmation had come that the day's victim, the eighth, had died of his injuries.

A. painted the clavicles and cleavage of a woman lying on a carpet in her underwear.

Later, "Quatre Ogives" played in the dark. Wind was blowing through the leylandii and rain beating on the windowpanes.

(45)

"You'll like this," said Mack.

"What?"

"I said, you'll like this."

A. covered one ear and hunched over the telephone receiver. An eight-wheel lorry filled with rubble idled next to the telephone box.

"Where are you? I can hardly hear you."

"Trafalgar Road."

THE NAKED SPUR

"I was talking to this girl. Did I mention Georgette? She's in PR and she works on shoots. That's how we know each other. I told her about our project and she was really into it. I was picking her brains, bouncing a few ideas off her but it sounds like she wants to get involved, if that's okay."

A boy on a bicycle cycled along the pavement.

"We were talking about names. She thinks they're really important to get right. She's doing some research and she'll get back to me with examples."

Traffic was moving again.

"She mentioned a place that might take brochures and act as a contact point for the commissioning service. It's a place called Heliotrope X. I don't know if you've heard of it? It's in Notting Hill. A new branch is opening in Islington. They sell all sorts of beauty products but they specialise in erotica, lingerie, creams, body rubs, oils, sex toys. This is exclusive stuff, expensive, not high-street tat. They have the sort of customers we want to reach. I haven't been there but Georgette has. She wrote an article about the shop for a style magazine. She's going to show it to me when we meet next week."

An old woman with a shopping trolley was resting on a low brick wall.

"That's another thing. Georgette's a journalist too. She works with style magazines. She thinks she might be able to publish a piece on the service. She thinks she could pitch it to either the hip style magazines or the women's weeklies. She could take either the outsider-art or the product-review aspect. It could go either way. She knows both markets."

Traffic pulled to the kerbs to allow an ambulance passage.

"It sounds positive. When are you meeting?"

"Next week, she has to look at her diary. We'll meet and have a look at the Heliotrope X article. We can think about how we could pitch the service to them. By then we should have a name."

"Next week."

"It'll happen. Trust me. She's worth waiting for."

(46)

A. woke up. It was dark. He sat up. He was fully dressed. He sat on the edge of the bed. The radiator clicked.

He went downstairs. Ibrahim was watching television. On the screen, children and policemen were running doubled over to a yellow school bus. The picture cut to a motorway solid with stationary vehicles. A. went to the kitchen and drank a glass and a half of water.

On the television, a police officer was speaking into a battery of microphones.

A. went to the upstairs bathroom and vomited up the water he had drunk.

A. did not sleep that night. He lay on his side and stared at the bars of orange light cast on the wall and sheet over the radiator. The radio whispered into the dark.

(47)

"The what?"

A. was standing in the telephone box, looking through

THE NAKED SPUR

scratched glass at the clouds. He was turning over a coin in his hand.

"The Naked Spur."

"Tell me more."

"You like it?"

"Yes."

"It sounds classy and absurd. A bit knowing. A bit camp. It comes from a western."

"A film?"

"Yeah, some fifties' western."

A thin man walked up to the gates of the park. There were two large bunches of balloons on strings above his fists. His raincoat hung on him loosely. The balloons hid his face. A. watched him as he passed.

"I can go with that."

"You're happy with 'The Naked Spur'? We could ask Georgette to do more research and get back to us."

There was a tattoo of a bird on the back of the balloon man's right hand.

"No need to look any more. 'The Naked Spur' is fine."

"That was my favourite out of the options. It has a real ring to it but it shows we don't take ourselves too seriously. It works both ways. No one's using it either, which is important. We can use 'Naked Spur' as the project name and you can be anonymous. I've e-mailed a few of your photographs to Georgette. She'll know what is best to use on publicity material. She's a good judge. That painting of a woman in a lace basque, I'm getting her opinion on it. She knows clothes. We don't want to use that image if she says the lingerie is cheap.

She knows her stuff. We don't want to give the wrong impression with our publicity images. That's where Georgette's PR experience is valuable. It's her world."

A. pushed himself into the corner of the telephone box, craning his head. The balloon man was standing inside the park gates. All that was visible of him was one hand, the tip of a boot and some balloons. A girl was handing him a coin, looking upwards. She was smiling.

There was a sharp rapping on the glass. A tall youth was standing close to the telephone box.

"I'm running out of money. I have something to show you next week, when I come to the office. I'll bring it with me."

"I'll see you then."

By the time A. had retrieved some coins from the top of the payphone, the youth was already opening the door.

(48)

"At nine thirty in the morning local time a man at a petrol station in Fredericksburg, Virginia, was shot and killed. Exactly a week ago, a woman was shot in Fredericksburg by the gunman who is being called in the American media the Beltway Killer. She survived but is being kept under observation in hospital and is described as in a serious though not life-threatening condition. A police press conference is due to begin in an hour's time."

THE NAKED SPUR

(49)

"He looked at me funny. I'm not making it up. He gave me, you know, this look, like, I know what you're about."

"Oh, Ib, what are you talking about?"

"I'm not making it up. Why would I make it up?"

"He handed you the pizza. You gave him the money. He gave you the change. You shut the door. That's it."

"Elsa, do you think I would make this up?"

"Frankly, Ib, yes."

Elsa spread her caftan about her and brushed away the approaching cat. She took a slice of pizza from the box.

"You're paranoid because they're Turkish at that place."

"No, no. That isn't it at all. You've got it completely wrong, Elsa."

Ibrahim sat back, plate on lap.

"I don't see why we go there anyway. They're not that good." He laughed. "Who ever heard of Turkish pizzas. I mean, come on."

"It's close and it's cheap. Besides, if we start ordering from somewhere else they'll notice we've stopped going there."

"So? What's that got to do with it?"

"Because," she said, taking a bite.

"It's just a good thing they aren't Somali," said Elsa.

Ibrahim shook his head.

"Nah ah. I'm not rising to that bait, Elsa."

He ate, then said, "You think you know what the situation is but you don't. really, you don't. It's not that

I have anything against Somalis. Ethiopia and Somalia, they're just such different countries. They are so different you wouldn't believe it. The people, the food, the religion, everything, the climate even. If you'd ever been there you'd know, but you haven't."

"You haven't been to Somalia either."

"That's not the point. I don't need to go. I know already. You think I don't know about the countries there? You're impossible to talk to."

He drank some water.

"It's not prejudice. It's just being different and being glad of it."

A. was standing in the doorway.

"Can I look something up?" he said, pointing at a book.

Elsa looked at him with a frown.

"Of course, why are you asking?"

"I brought you that Norman Mailer interview I told you about. I found it at last," said Ibrahim, waving to a magazine on the arm of the settee opposite.

"Thank you, Ib. Your fish are sick," A. said to Elsa.

"I know," she said. "They're changing colour, poor darlings."

Ibrahim's gaze was fixed on the television pictures of soldiers standing in a desert.

"And what can you do about it? It's not as if you can take them to a vet. I mean, what's he going to do? Scrub them or something? And how do you get them there? Do you, you know, carry them there in a water jug?"

"Don't be horrible, Ib."

THE NAKED SPUR

Elsa looked at the fish.

"I should clean the tank. Yes, that's what I'll do. I'll clean it on Saturday. You'll help, won't you, Ib?"

"Oh, sure." His attention did not move from the screen.

"Look up what you want," said Elsa to A.

A. took the book off the video player. He turned pages then paused, reading. The text in the book read: "The Naked Spur, US 1952, 91m. A bounty hunter pursues his across Colorado in conventional Western, with greed the main motivation."

Afterwards, Elsa asked, "Find what you wanted?"

"Yes, thank you."

"Would you like some pizza? We've got plenty. Ib, ordered too much again."

"Thank you. If there's any left over I'll have that if I may."

"Of course. Don't wait till it's cold though. Get yourself a plate."

"You heard the boss," Ibrahim said. "Go get a plate."

While A. was in the kitchen, Ibrahim got some water.

He said to A., "Boy, this sniper is really going for it, you know. You heard about the latest?"

"No."

"This woman, shot in a car park outside a shop. In front of her husband. Can you imagine?"

Ibrahim raised the glass to his lips.

"Yeah. Dead. Like that. Boom!"

He shook his head.

"My God, this guy's not taking any p' really going for it."

When they got back to the living room, Elsa had changed the channel. They watched a film while cats slept on the rug.

(50)

"A PO Box."

There was music playing in the background. Mack was speaking loudly.

"A PO Box. That way people can send you stuff directly. You won't even have to speak on the phone. Just register it as 'The Naked Spur'. There will be an address on the brochure, so clients can take it away and talk it over with their partner and then they can post material to the PO Box and you collect it. It costs about fifty pounds for six months or a year, I think. I'll cover the cost. That way there isn't a direct link to you."

"Okay."

"You could set it up in Greenwich then you wouldn't have to go far to collect your post. We'll have to check up on the details. This way no one needs to know your address. It allows you to operate without an agent. You could work through brochures. It makes you almost independent, untraceable and anonymous."

(51)

Chestnut boughs lay on the ground. Splintered breaks, pale against the grass, oozed sap. Wind was pulling at the leaves and blades of grass. Walkers stumbled. Air roared in the trees, thrashing foliage. Leaves and twigs cartwheeled over the ground. On One Tree Hill, a number of trees had been toppled, roots were wind-whipped and scattered soil. There were pebbles lodged between roots.

The drained boating pool had tapering crescents of debris against its walls.

(52)

A. stepped off Greenwich High Road into the Post Office. The swing door cut the noise of buses and lorries idling on the street outside. A. joined a queue and watched a number come up in red on the electronic display.

"Cashier number six," announced the automated PA system.

The queue shuffled forward by half a step. By a scattering of orange recorded-deliver labels, a woman with hair in a ponytail was forcing a packet of crisps into the hands of a toddler. The woman had a sleeveless vest. On her shoulder the words "Karren-Jo" were tattooed within a heart. Below it was an oval bruise. The child was in a pushchair. A zircon earring in one ear caught the light.

"Cashier number two."

A girl was sending parcels to South Korea. She added items to the stacks on the narrow counter and put them on the scales. An Indian woman read out the prices to her through a grill in the glass. The girl gave a nod and added the parcel to the collection.

A man in a combat jacket was arguing with a cashier.

"They said this office. I went to New Cross and they said they couldn't cash it because of the number. The number's wrong. They said go to the Job Centre and they'll check it. Greenwich they said."

The large cashier wiped his forehead with a bare arm. "Show me."

"I won't give it to you. I know how it goes. You take it and you lose it and I have to go back to the Job Centre and they'll tell me-"

"Cashier number one."

The woman ahead of A. in the queue tugged her dress away from a symmetrical sweat patch on her back. She sighed loudly.

The man in the combat jacket was tapping his fingers on the counter as the cashier consulted a colleague at the other end of the desks.

There was a slapping sound, then a child was crying. The woman was standing over her child, flat hand raised. Scattered over the labels on the floor was a spray of crisps.

"Pick 'em up, you li'ul shit," said the woman.

The child was belted into the pushchair. He made no move. He closed its eyes, drew a breath and wailed again.

"I ain't buyin' you anuvver." The woman put her hands on her hips. "That's all you're getting till teatime."

The woman paused then looked at the queue, which was watching her. The woman with the sweat patches lowered her gaze to a form in her hand. An old man in a tweed jacket frowned and looked at his watch. A. looked back at the woman.

"Cashier number six."

One step forward. The fat cashier was back with a

THE NAKED SPUR

supervisor. They were leaning towards the glass where the man in the combat jacket was holding up a giro.

The child was leaning over to grasp the fallen packet of crisps. He stretched out his hand. His fingertips brushed the plastic. His face was a mask of concentration. His mother lit a cigarette, eyes narrowed against the smoke. The boy shifted his weight and leant out further, fingers splayed. He reached for the packet, straining against his restraint. The woman pushed the chair to the doors. The boy twisted his head to watch the packet, his mouth open. The chair juddered as the woman used it to ram the swing door. The boy shook in his seat. The door did not open fully at the first push. A tall youth outside held the door open for her. She exited without acknowledging him.

"You're having a laugh. Tell me you're having a laugh." The man with the giro was jutting his face to glass.

"Cashier number two."

At the counter, A. asked about PO Boxes.

"Didn't you see the forms? Do you want a form?"

The cashier swivelled on his stool and took a brochure from a set of pigeonholes behind him. He slid it under the glass screen. A. picked it up.

"Do I need to give a home address?"

"Business or personal?"

"Business."

"No. Just a signed authorisation by the company and a document of incorporation giving the company's registered address."

"Registered address."

"Yes."

"Do I have to give a name?"

The cashier looked at A.

"A company name would do."

"No personal name."

"For company business, no."

"Would…"

The cashier blinked.

"It's all in the form."

He reached over and pressed a button.

"Cashier number two."

"I just wanted–"

There was a woman with a parcel wrapped in the brown paper standing close behind A.

"All in the form, sir."

A. walked away. The Indian cashier was collecting the girl's parcels through a window in the screen. A. checked his watch and then the change in his pockets on his way out.

(53)

"I've set some rumours circulating. The first is that one we talked about. There's a big private collector who has commissioned two dozen paintings from you. It's this amazing collection that people talk about but only a few people have seen. The next rumour is that these paintings are being done by a well-known artist on the side."

"Who?"

"It doesn't matter who. You can attach the rumour to four or five different painters. It could be any one of them. The last rumour is that you have a number of famous collectors."

"Who?"

Mack sighed.

"It doesn't matter who. I just picked out some names from a magazine on my desk as I was talking on the phone. To be credible they had to be big names with money who spend time in London or live here. So, now we've got these rumours doing work for us, we need to get the service operating soon so we can capitalise on them. Get e-mails to the right people and they multiply. Just think how many of those stupid pyramid e-mails get sent every day. Same principle. Viral advertising."

"I suppose," said A.

"You heard about the Arab-favour story? You know the one. Everyone's heard this. A guy is walking behind an Arab in London and the Arab drops his wallet. The man behind picks it up and tells the Arab he's dropped his wallet and hands it back to him. The guy is taken aback because the Arab is thanking him so profusely. Thank you, thank you, he says. How can I ever repay your kindness? The Arab opens up his wallet and in the plastic pocket is a photograph of an old Egyptian man in traditional clothes. The Arab says, this is the only photograph of my grandfather. He was a very special man to me. Very kind. I don't know what I would have done if I had lost this photograph. For this great favour I will do you a favour. Do not come to London on Tuesday. Something terrible will happen in London on that day. I cannot tell you more but please do not come to London on that day or you will be killed. Something terrible will happen on that day. The Arab is clutching the other man's hand and looking him in the eye. The Arab says goodbye and disappears. So, the man goes to his office and writes this e-mail to all his contacts and says, pass on this story. Warn everyone you know. A terrorist attack will take place in London on Tuesday. And of course, everyone forwarded this e-mail or a version of it to half the people on their e-mail address list. Every office in London had someone who got a version. I heard that the number of people who called in sick that day in London was something like thirty percent more than the average for a Tuesday. And I guarantee you that there were twice that number who wanted to take a day off but couldn't quite bring themselves to do it. All because of this bullshit e-mail. It was a hoax of course, or some bloke had a trick played on him.

"Truth doesn't come into it. It's whether people want to believe something might be true. Just enough to plant a seed of suspicion in their mind. That's how all those conspiracy theories get started. People want to believe that something is going on that no one will admit to but is happening anyway. They love knowing a secret even if that secret is utter bullshit. It's got the whiff of the forbidden fruit, right? The government is hiding something but we've found out the truth. They haven't found out anything like the truth. We're just going to tweak reality. It's going to be so close to the truth. It'll be beautiful. E-mail rumours are a virus. Let's get our infection in the bloodstream."

THE NAKED SPUR

(54)

"Did you see the great storm last night? It was terrific. It rocked the cab all the way back here."

Ibrahim and A. were standing on the landing.

"I was going to take my camera and photograph it. Some trees in Greenwich were blown right over. Bob told me. He called me just now and said get out there with your camera."

Ibrahim rubbed the bridge of his nose.

"I'm not going to. I'm going to get some kip now. But, you know, the funny thing is that the news predicts there's going to be another storm just like it tomorrow. So, I'll photograph that one. I've got a day off tomorrow, well, a night off. Tonight, actually. The weather's been pretty wild recently. I guess that's the way things are going. It's not so good but it makes life a bit more exciting.

"All right. I don't suppose you saw my reading glasses anywhere, did you? I have a feeling that I might have left them at work. That would be a crazy thing to do. I don't know."

He looked about him.

"Storms. Storms."

He shuffled into Elsa's room and closed the door after him.

(55)

"When will I meet Georgette?" A. asked Mack as they walked down Dean Street.

"We can arrange something if you like. I like keeping

things separated though. It helps to keep up the act of the anonymous artist if the agents and arrangers genuinely don't know who you are. If they've never met you then they can't let anything slip. That's why when we meet with Heliotrope X, we'll work out our strategy then tell you about it afterwards to check. We won't suggest anything you don't agree to. That way, we're working semi-independently."

Three taxis drove by. They went to an ATM where Mack took out two hundred pounds in twenty-pound notes.

"You don't even have to meet Georgette. I'm kind of thinking it might be better if you didn't. If we keep the promotional side separate from the production then there's no risk of leaks. The public side and the artistic side can be kept apart. That way we can push your service without being too much influenced by you and you can make art without having to deal with any public contact. We can have a buffer between you and the outlet so you never need visit the place or contact them. It can all be done through me or Georgette."

They headed south.

"Really, I've thought about it."

"If you think it's best."

"I thought you'd agree. Georgette is curious about you and keen on the work but if I'm at the hub then you can concentrate on painting and leave the arrangements to me. I'm not getting anything out of this. I'd just get a kick out of getting this thing going and getting it talked about and seeing things from the inside. You'd get your work out there and get some money. So, everyone's happy, right?"

Turning into Brand Street, Mack asked A. how many paintings he would need to sell to live on.

"If we were selling at eight hundred pounds per item and the agent was getting a quarter, say, that would give you six hundred pounds per painting as your share. Your rent is what, one hundred pounds a week? So how many paintings would you need to sell to keep yourself solvent?"

"Three paintings every two months, maybe two per month."

"That's nothing. We could easily do that. It'll be a bad month if we get less than three commissions. And you could paint, what, one canvas, two canvases each week?"

"Five, maybe more."

"If we could get you the business that would be great money. I don't think we'll do that much business but I think we can get you three paintings per month."

He adjusted his glasses.

"Sometimes I think this scheme is just absurd. Then I think, why shouldn't it work? It's just selling paintings. People have been doing it for hundreds of years, right? This is just a new spin on it. And everything has to start somewhere."

They went into a newsagents. Mack leafed through a music magazine while A. studied the magazines on the top shelf.

"How is that e-Bay page going?"

"Fine. I've been so busy I haven't been on e-Bay for a week or more. No more surprise packages arriving for me from America and Sweden. When you get a bad habit you've got to get yourself a distraction when you quit, otherwise you're always thinking back to how things were. It's like that when you split up with a girl. It's best to change a couple of things in your life so you're not always in familiar situations and usual routines. I've been so tied up with this new pitch I haven't been on the site for weeks."

The newsagent handed Mack his change and Mack put a packet of chewing gum in his pocket.

"I was talking about that with Simon. About distraction strategies."

"Actually, I was talking about my paintings."

Mack frowned.

"Your paintings?"

"On e-Bay."

Mack's expression changed.

"Oh, fuck! I completely forgot about it. Sorry, man. I'll get right on to it. Seriously. Sorry about that."

(56)

"We need something special in the way the work is delivered. You have that slide-transparency aspect of presenting the work. I'll work on the brochures with Georgette. We need a finishing touch for the work itself, something old-fashioned and classy, something unexpected. What do you think? The Naked Spur needs something distinctive to set it apart. Can you think of anything? Maybe a special way of delivering the work or framing it or… I don't know, there's a part that's missing and I can't put my finger on it but I know we need it. There's something there but I can't see it. I can't quite see it."

(57)

"Your children are not safe anywhere or at any time."

(58)

While A. was making breakfast, Ibrahim came into the kitchen.

"Not working today? Oh, no. You quit your job, didn't you? Wow. Yes, of course you did. How could I forget? Man, my memory is going."

Ibrahim started to leave the kitchen.

"Oh, by the way, I'm sick. I'm off work. My doctor said I have this infection. I don't know. Anyway. I'm not going in to work tonight but I'm trying to keep my routine going. So, I'm sleeping during the day still. I'd be grateful if you're around that you don't make much noise. I know you don't usually but if you were planning on making noise, you know, please don't."

He laughed which turned into a cough.

"Oh, boy! There it is. Can you hear it? Did you hear it? I really don't feel good. I'm going to get some sleep before Elsa gets back and starts with her damn television. I don't know what it is with women and television. I tell Elsa she should read a book. She's got lots of books, a whole roomful but she has to watch her soaps and her reality television.

"Right, I'm going up now."

"Sleep well, Ib."

"You too. I mean, thank you."

Again, his laugh became a cough. He stopped on the stairs.

"I'm going to shut the door to Elsa's room to keep it quiet but if Vish wants to come in, could you let him in?"

"Sure."

"Yeah. Vish can join me but the others are no good. They play. They get restless. They want to be let out. I can't be dealing with that. Vish is a good cat. He's a restful cat. He calms me down. He's the only one that can."

"Okay."

"Yah."

Footsteps then a door snicking shut.

While A. was cleaning the kitchen, the letterbox clattered. There was a bill for Elsa and a bank statement for A. A. read the statement, folded it small and pushed it into the rubbish in the bin.

He walked to Greenwich Park. Two men were gathering broken branches and placing them in a trailer. A man and a child were ascending Observatory Hill. The child had a kite in green and white.

The wind tugged at A.'s clothes and ruffled the grass. Cloud was moving overhead rapidly. A. turned up his jacket collar and buttoned his cuffs as he crested One Tree Hill and turned to view London. Stratocumulus cloud filed in ranks over St Paul's Cathedral and the City. The sky over Silvertown was lighter. He tightened his collar and headed south.

At the end of the tree-lined avenue, A. reached a triple

gate. Beyond that was Blackheath. A. ignored the footpath and crossed the turf making for the church spire. Half a dozen people were flying kites which swooped and dipped. Among a handful of spectators, a woman was crouched beside a child, pointing to the sky. The boy extended an arm and traced an arc with his finger.

The soil was wet. A.'s boots made deep heel prints. A flock of crows watched him pass, nictitating membranes blinking white over black eyes. On every concrete rail post and streetlamp, a bird perched. Near A., one bounded across the turf, wings spread. Air ruffled the flight feathers. It rotated its head and cawed, showing a black tongue.

When A. got to Blackheath Village, he stopped outside a jewellers. He stamped mud out of his boot treads on the pavement. When he entered, the jeweller raised his head and removed his eyepiece.

"How much would it cost to buy an engraved seal?"

"A seal? What for?"

"A silver seal for sealing wax. Maybe another metal."

A. made a pressing gesture.

"It would depend on how big it was, how elaborate the design."

The jeweller circled the hand holding the eyepiece, magnified skin in its lens. He followed A.'s gaze and put the eyepiece behind the counter.

"Could you do it?"

"I could get it done. I don't engrave myself."

The jeweller held out his hands palm down.

"When would you be wanting it?"

"As soon as possible."

A. took a handful of coins out and placed one on the glass counter.

"About this size."

The jeweller's eyes flicked down, head immobile. A clock chimed.

"What would you want to go on it?"

"Two initials."

"Any device? Flourishes?"

"Nothing else."

"Do you have a design in mind? A script?"

"No."

Both men looked at the coin on the counter. Under the glass was a tray of watches. Each was set at a different time.

"You'll want a handle for the seal. You don't want to burn your fingers. Ever used sealing wax?"

"No."

The jeweller smiled.

"A hundred pounds for silver. Less for brass, maybe eighty pounds. That's without the handle."

"That much?"

The jeweller spread his hands wide.

"What can I say?"

"Do you know anywhere in London that sells seals?"

"Don't you want a custom one?"

"I can't say. I can get back to you."

"There are places."

The jeweller stopped and gazed at a case of silverware.

"I could tell you."

He stopped.

"Places."

THE NAKED SPUR

A. returned the coin to his pocket.

"Well," said the jeweler, with a smile. "I shall be here if you change your mind. I don't go anywhere. Blackheath, man and boy."

The jeweller did not stop smiling until A. had left the shop and walked into the wind.

(59)

A. was sitting in the kitchen. On the table was a segment of pie in a foil tray. Next to it was a knife, fork, plate and a cup of tea. The sky was thick with grey cloud. Snaps of static cut the radio news.

"Yesterday's victim was a thirty-seven-year-old man. He is in a serious condition in hospital. He was shot while crossing a road outside a restaurant in the town of Ashland, Virginia."

The ginger cat went to the bowls of food and began to eat, eyes watching A.

A. stared at the knife lines in the foil.

"Police have said that a letter has been found taped to a tree near where the sniper is thought to have fired the shot, though they have not revealed anything about the contents of the letter."

Static crackled and there was a flash of light at the window. When the thunder sounded, A. picked up the knife and lifted it over the pie.

"Searches continue for a white van which police believe may be the sniper's vehicle."

A. cut a slice of pie. The cat left the kitchen and A. finished his tea and piece of pie, before replacing the remainder of the pie in the refrigerator.

(60)

"It makes an artistic impression, those canvases at your window. I always feel that when I walk up that direction. You see the canvases at the window and you think, ah, there's the house of an artist. Well, room, anyway. I like it. It's nice to be in a house where you know someone under the same roof as you is creating. So many people live their lives and create nothing over sixty or seventy years. It's a shame. They don't even do, I don't know, flower arranging. Not that I'm putting down flower arranging and so forth but, you know, not even that. I walk down the street and I look at people and I think, how many of you write or paint or make craft things, you get my point? But you never know. The strangest things happen. You read about all these unlikely people who spend days working as rubbish collectors and making art in private at home in their spare time. Like that guy Henry Darger, who was a janitor in America and when he died they found his apartment filled, crammed full of books and paintings and collages. There was an article on him in The Guardian. They say he wrote a two-million word novel. No, longer, I think. He was writing just in the evenings and nights and working in a hospital during the days. How do you like that? Millions of words. Most of it was completely mad, of course, but he created. Perhaps that's what kept him together. It stopped him ending up in an asylum or going out with a gun and shooting people. Americans are like that. They don't do things by halves, in my experience. So, on balance, I feel a person is better creating than not creating. That's my take on things, for what it's worth."

(61)

The man sitting beside him smelled of piss. Around one wrist was a bracelet of tinfoil. He rocked back and forth. He was called over to sign. As soon as he went to the desk, a security guard carried away the chair which had a patch of wetness on it, bringing back a replacement.

A woman came to sit by A. Her long hair was pulled back tight in a ponytail. There were dark smudges under her eyes.

"Have you been waiting long?" she asked him.

A. shrugged.

"They don't care," she said.

"How are you getting by for money? Have you checked your giros? You have to make sure they're giving you the right rate. Get a printout from them. Don't believe anything until you've seen it in black and white."

There was a tattoo of a heart below her collarbone.

"You got to be careful with giros. The place I live the post gets thieved. They know when the giros come. Those fucking junkies can smell a giro. They stay up all night waiting for the post. Soon as the post hits the mat they're there. I caught them at it. I caught them going through the post. I said I'd take a knife to them if I caught them again. I told the landlord but he weren't no fucking use. He don't care. He hardly speaks English even though he's been living here long enough."

Her eyes narrowed.

"He's hardly better than those junkies. I'm not a

racist. My boyfriend's black. It don't bother me. But he's a foreigner. All the houses he's got are in his wife's name. She's British. Well, I say British, born here but not British."

She sniffed then rubbed her eyes, mouth down curving.

"They're skavving the social. They got Poles in the basement but they're getting rent from the DSS for some Simon Jackson who ain't never lived there long as I've been there. And the Poles are paying rent. They sleep on mattresses, even in the kitchen. Honest. They showed me around. Hardly room to walk. They're construction workers working up at Heathrow on the underground extension. They work shifts. One sleeps at night, then the one who's been working nights comes back and takes the bed from the other one who goes off to work the day shift. One of them said to me it keeps the beds nice and warm and laughed."

She sniffed again.

"They speak better English than the landlord."

She looked at A.

"Do you have problems with your giros?"

"The money goes into an account."

"They want me to get an account. I told them the bank said no. They say that if I don't open an account with the Post Office they'll stop my payments. I won't do it though. They can't force me. If your claim is stopped they can take the money out of your account. I told them if they did that they'd be taking food away from my kiddies."

She moved closer to A.

THE NAKED SPUR

"Listen, you got kind eyes. Couldn't lend me twenty quid for a couple of days, could you? I got money coming. It'll be here Friday."

A. opened his mouth and his number was called.

As he got to his feet, the woman said, "Wait for me outside after you sign. I'll get you fixed."

A. went to the desk. Afterwards, as he left he saw her at a desk arguing with a member of staff. Walking home, he took a detour by Norman Road and the promenade by the Thames.

(62)

"—called by some in the media the Beltway Killer, who has struck in three states. Chief of Police Charles Moose made the following request." There was a clip of a man speaking with an American accent. In the background was the sound of camera shutters. "The person you called could not hear everything you said. The audio was unclear and we want to get it right. Call us back so that we can clearly understand."

(63)

"I really admire you giving up the office job. That was brave. That's one of the reasons I came up with the commission idea, to help you out. I don't know, have you thought about maybe getting a temporary job? Just to keep you going. You could ditch it when the commissioning takes off. Some office work, just temping. I'm thinking it might be December by the time money starts coming in from commissions. Maybe later. It's a long time and all the while you're burning money on rent. What's that place costing you – four hundred a month? No, more."

The connection momentarily broke.

"The traffic's started to move. I've got to change lanes. Hang on."

The signal cut again.

A. shifted stance.

Mack came back on the line. There was a radio on in the background. A presenter was reading a news bulletin.

"How much are you getting on the dole?"

"Fifty-six pounds a week."

"With rent at one hundred pounds a week, that means you're running forty-four pounds a week behind your outgoings even before you pay for food. How much have you got saved?"

"Four hundred pounds."

Silence.

"That's nothing. Can you get money from anywhere?"

"I don't know."

"You better think of something."

When the connection broke again it did not restore itself.

A. walked west down Trafalgar Road. A man was sitting on a crate in a derelict doorway. He was eating from a tin of fish using his hands. Oil had run down his beard and spotted the crotch of his trousers.

"Spare some change?"

A. dug into his pocket and brought out a handful of coins. The tramp wiped one hand before cupping it for

THE NAKED SPUR

the money.

"Much obliged," the tramp said.

He returned to his food. He lifted up an oily spine and threw back his head. In his open mouth, A. could see the shattered stumps of his teeth.

A. walked to the promenade outside the Naval College and looked at the corroded pilings in the pebble bank.

(64)

"The latest victim is a school-bus driver, who was killed by a single shot to the chest. Part of Silver Spring, Maryland has been sealed off while police-forensics officers conduct a fingertip search of the area."

(65)

The man sighed and put the books on his desk.

"Hardbacks. I have the soft-cover versions of most of these. These take up more space. People want something smaller, lighter, you know?"

He grimaced and picked up a biography of Stravinsky.

"Yeah, you see, I've already got this in paperback brand new. I'd be duplicating stock if I bought these. The difference in price between a second-hand hardback and a discounted paperback bought at trade price is almost nothing and buyers prefer the new book."

He put the book on the pile.

"Have you got anything else?"

A. put his black bag on the floor of the shop, unzipped it and handed the bookseller some paperbacks.

"This is a bit more like it. I could use these. But again, you're not talking much money."

"I can't split them. If you don't want all then there's a place that I can take them."

The bookseller sighed again.

"Well, if you feel like that. Really, you haven't got much here."

A. began to put the books back into plastic carrier bags.

"Well, I could give you a price for all of them but it would be low. I'd have to carry some of these for a long while. Really, it's not good business for me. I'd rather not have the hardbacks. The paperbacks would probably sell but the hardbacks would be taking up space."

"How much?"

Pause.

"Fifteen pounds."

A. nodded, went to his knees and unloaded the contents of the bags on to the floor by a gas heater. The man handed him three five-pound notes. As A. stepped out of the shop, sun broke through clouds. A. stood for a couple of moments on the wet pavement, eyes closed, face turned to the unseen sun.

(66)

A. was in Burlington Gardens, looking through a curved glass display window. On wooden shelves were selections of leather-bound diaries and wine-list holders, gold-plated pen holders and bottles of ink, necks with ribbon bows.

When A. opened the door, a bell jangled. The shop

assistant didn't look at him, continued to read a fashion magazine with Italian text. A. went to a rack in the corner with a stand of circular, brass-plated seals. Each seal had different initials. A. picked one with two initials and a separate handle with a screwed end and took them to the counter where the woman wrapped them. He bought some handmade paper and envelopes for them, two metres of red ribbon and sealing wax in black, pink and red, one stick of each. He paid with two notes and received three coins change.

He left the shop and walked through the arcade towards Regent Street.

(67)

"Fuck."

A bead of red wax sat on the back of A.'s index finger like a drop of blood. Brushing it off showed a subcutaneous scar underneath.

The table in the lobby was covered by folded paper, printouts, sheets of paper dotted with wax and short lengths of ribbon tied in bows. The hot end of a cheap lighter had left a mark on the table top. A. slid a sheet over the mark then dipped his index finger into a cup of water.

"Man sits down, smiles, rewind, man sits down, smiles, rewind, man sits down, smiles, rewind. The editing is such a head-fuck. I hate it. Last night, I dreamed I was in the world's biggest ever editing suite. Seriously. I'm dreaming it. There's no escape."

Mack was sitting in his office with the door open. He was talking into a telephone.

"Yeah. Yeah. If only."

A. looked at his finger then put it back in the water. With his other hand, he picked up a scrap of paper. The wax had melted the ribbon, which had shrivelled and curled where the wax had come into contact with it. A. dropped it into a waste basket. He started to scratch wax out of the seal with a pin.

"Could you tell Mack I've scanned these and emailed the files to him?"

The blonde girl from reception with the crop top was at the table. She put down a collection of photographs. The uppermost was of a painting showing a woman's open legs, hand at her vagina.

"Thanks."

Once the blonde girl was at her desk, A. laid a sheet of paper over the photographs and then another sheet of paper over the burn he had just revealed.

"How are you getting on?"

Mack was standing at his door looking at the table. He was frowning.

"The wax burns the ribbon. The wax sticks to the seal. The paper's wrong for your printer." A. rubbed his finger over a word and left a smudge.

"Don't worry about the printer. We have a better one. We can get the brochures professionally printed. That was a test."

Mack walked over and picked up an envelope.

"We could save by folding over the brochures and sealing them rather than using envelopes and sealing wax."

"We don't want to look cheap."

"That won't be a problem," said Mack

Mack examined a piece of ribbon.

"Why don't you take this stuff and see if there is some way of using ribbon without burning it? Leave me the paper. I'll print out more brochures. I'll experiment with printers."

"I'll call tomorrow."

"I won't be able to do anything tomorrow because I'm editing. Actually," Mack looked at the ceiling. "Call me on Monday."

"On Monday."

"I'll cover this. How much was it?" Mack took out his wallet.

A. told him the amount and took the money. Mack went back to his office. A. cleared the table, putting items in his bag. He left the sheet over the mark on the table.

(68)

"You don't know what you're doing to me. You don't understand anything."

The man was staring across the desk at a woman.

"The records show you didn't attend your interview here scheduled for three forty-five on Thursday, the third of October. We don't have any choice but to suspend your payments. You can appeal and the appeal will be considered by processing centre. I can get you a form, if you like."

"You're cutting me apart. You want to finish me off," said the man.

He was gripping the sides of his seat.

The security guard was standing at the front desk watching him.

"I'm afraid that the decision to suspend your claim has already gone through. It goes through automatically. It's the system."

The woman had her hands clasped in front of her.

"Yes, but who's running the system?"

Pause.

"I don't understand, sir. The system runs itself."

"No, people run it. You talk to each other through your computers. I know what you're saying to each other about me. The man said that the trial wouldn't affect my payments."

Pause.

"The suspension isn't related to your trial, sir. The benefits system and the judicial system are separate. If you are seeking work and able to start any job you may be offered up to the point of your-- Up to the end of any proceedings, then you are entitled to claim JSA."

"They've been asking me questions."

Pause.

"Did you hear me? They've been asking me questions."

"Yes, sir."

"They were asking me about all this. Then the man said the trial won't affect my payments. He said it to me."

Pause.

"Would you like an appeal form?"

"Give me my money."

"Sir."

THE NAKED SPUR

The security guard approached the man.

"I need my money."

"I think you better leave, sir. It'll give you a chance to cool down," said the guard.

"Give me my money!"

The man lunged across the desk. The woman uttered a squeak and flinched. A set of trays broke apart on the floor, scattering papers. The man's chair toppled backwards. The guard manhandled the man away from the desk. He was joined by a second guard. They guided the man away, one on either side of him, holding his arms.

"Don't kill me!"

His eyes were bulging. The sinews in his neck stood out. He bucked and wriggled between the guards.

"OH MY GOD DON'T KILL ME DON'T KILL ME PLEASE OH MY GOD!"

He kicked over a plastic pot plant as the group passed A. A spray of clay pebbles emerged from the pot and spilled across the floor. The men went to a side exit. The swing doors shut behind them. The man's screaming became progressively more muffled.

A. looked down. The men's feet had crushed some of the pebbles into the beige carpet tiles.

The woman who was standing at a filing cabinet. A female colleague was talking to her. The woman had her arms wrapped around herself. The consoling woman had a hand on her shoulder. The first woman was shaking her head in reply to a question. A male member of staff righted the plastic plant and brushed the pebbles aside with a foot. A woman joined him with a piece of paper and a sheet of card. She brushed the pebbles on to the card with the paper and poured them back into the pot.

The consoling woman helped the first woman to collect items from the floor. Some minutes later, two police officers arrived and walked through the office and out of the side exit. They brought out the man in handcuffs. His shoulders had sagged. He was crying. Snot covered his upper lip. One of the policemen brushed the pot plant and it fell again. The plant came loose from the pot and its metal stand was visible below a disc of brown fibrous matter.

(69)

The voice was saying: "In the past several days, you have attempted to communicate with us. We have researched the option you stated and found that it is not possible electronically to comply in the manner you requested. However, we remain open and ready to talk to you about the options you have mentioned. It is important that we do this without anyone else getting hurt. Call us at the same number you used before to obtain the eight-hundred number you have requested. If you would feel more comfortable, a private PO Box number or another secure method can be provided. You indicated that this is about more than violence. We are waiting to hear from you."

(70)

The cinema was closed. The foyer was unswept and

THE NAKED SPUR

filled with boxes. The shutters over the confectionary kiosk were down. Some letters on the display outside had fallen off. In the yard by the cinema bar, stalls were being set out. A woman was putting out dishes on blue fabric. A man was lifting crates of records out of an estate car. Another was tying a mirror to a stall frame. An awning was being fixed over a stall of books. On the ground was a polished copper coal scuttle, a sea chest, an angle-poise lamp.

"…me?"

A. turned his face from the window. A woman was standing next to him.

"Excuse me? Our customer-service agent is ready to see you now, sir."

A. followed her to an office where a man with a name badge on his white shirt was sitting at a desk. He gestured to the seat opposite.

"I believe you wish to extend your overdraft."

A. said he did.

"Has there been any change in your circumstances?"

A. said not.

The man's fingers hovered over the computer keyboard.

"It's just, you don't seem to be receiving your wages into that account any longer. There haven't been any deposits since the—" he scanned the screen, "—the thirtieth of August. Since then there have only been withdrawals."

A. adjusted his tie.

"As part of our care package, we like to match our service to the need and circumstances of our customers.

To do that, we need up-to-date information about your financial and work situation."

A. said that he was working freelance on a new pay structure and would not be getting paid until Christmas.

The pen wavered over the form.

"And you're still at the law firm?"

A. agreed he was.

"If there's nothing else you'd like to tell us…"

A. told him there was not.

The man filled in several boxes on the form and A. signed it.

After he left the bank, A. went to a bench and sat down. A child sucking a lollipop stopped.

"You all right, mister? You're white as a sheet."

The boy sucked a bit more. After a time he took out his lollipop.

"You ain't gonna die, are you, mister?"

"No."

The boy put the lollipop back in his mouth and walked away.

(71)

"—Tarot Card Killer, after a killing spree that has lasted twenty-two days and left ten people dead and three wounded. The men were arrested in a motorway rest area off Interstate 70 near Myersville, Maryland. Police say a firearm was recovered at the scene. The vehicle matched the description of a blue saloon car given by the police two days ago. Police say inquiries are ongoing and the investigation is not at an end."

THE NAKED SPUR

(72)

A chaffinch hopped along the path. Grass had overgrown the edges of the path. Bush boughs drooped with wetness. A.'s face was a trace on the glass. He stepped back from the door and switched on the television. He sat on a settee next to the ginger cat, flicking between channels. The cat froze, watching A.

A news programme had an image of the entrance to an underground station with grills pulled closed. Shot of people in a rain-lashed street reading a board. Shot of a white board written over with "Station closed due to flooding. No Northern line trains till further notice." This picture was replaced by that of a dimly-lit underground platform next not to train tracks but a canal of black, glassy water. A man spoke into a microphone.

The cat walked to A. and put one paw on his thigh, its eyes locked on A.'s face.

Animated graphics of a plan of the London underground system. A water table was indicated, then a chart of daily rainfall.

The cat climbed on to A.'s lap, its muscles tense.

Image of a queue of people under umbrellas at a bus stop. Image of a bus driver being interviewed.

A. brought a hand to the cat's face. It sniffed the hand.

"Hey, Archie," said A. "It's been a long time."

A. stroked the cat sitting on his lap.

(73)

"Georgette's had this idea for an article to coincide with the opening. She thinks she can get it into a woman's weekly magazine. It's not necessarily the type of market we're targeting but we need coverage and we need punters."

"Tell me about it."

A. was hunched over the telephone, handset jammed between head and shoulder, hands in his armpits. The telephone box smelled of urine and cigarette ash.

"She follows the commissioning process from start to finish. The article will have a human-interest angle. There'll be a series of photographs of the different stages involved. Essentially, it's a photo-story. So, first stage, woman reading Naked Spur brochure. Second, woman in classy lingerie being photographed by girlfriend. It'll be all friendly and non-sexual. Maybe there'll be some glasses of wine around, maybe a third friend, everyone relaxed. Third stage, woman puts Polaroid into envelope. Maybe a shot of the outlet. Next is the canvas being delivered. We'll make sure we get a good view of the wrapping and the wax seals. The last shot is the woman holding the completed painting next to her. So, we follow one example from start to finish. Georgette will write about how the woman feels, get her perspective, the consumer experience and so on. It'll almost be a product test. Then, at the end, is a byline giving details of the outlet."

Droplets were being blown across the glass. Between the park gates, a woman was struggling with an umbrella. As her companion helped her, the umbrella turned inside out and left the woman's hands. It bounced a few metres and wedged under a parked car.

"Sounds good."

THE NAKED SPUR

"Like I say, it's not the hip set but it's business and it's what the service will do. So, you'd be okay about doing this painting for the story?"

"Yes."

Wind was rattling the door.

"I'm ready for work. Let me know."

"Great. We're a little way off. We need to pin down the outlet then arrange the article for the launch. Like I say, Georgette is fairly confident that she can get this piece accepted. It's got a great consumer and human-interest angle to it."

"Any idea when the launch might be?"

"Well, we're kicking around some ideas. We were thinking of the first of December, maybe last week of November. That way we time it to get commissions for Christmas. That's not so far away. The launch itself will be pretty quick to arrange. You'll see."

"I'm ready to start."

The woman had fixed her umbrella and was walking with her companion to the waterfront.

"Just give me the word."

(74)

The man with the moustache turned the camera over in his hands. He detached the lens and looked inside the camera body. He replaced the lens and altered the aperture setting. He opened the back and blew into it. He pressed the shutter release several times, winding on the film-advance lever each time.

"No strap?"

A. shook his head.

"Other lenses? Zoom?"

A. shook his head.

"Flash unit?"

Another shake of the head.

The man chewed his lip.

"Hold on," he said and went to a back room, taking the camera, leaving A. alone in the shop.

A. wandered to the telescopes on tripods. He looked through an eyepiece. Holborn was dim, traffic half obscured by fog. A. jerked away from the telescope. At the window was a tramp. His hair was matted and his skin dark and lined. There was dry blood at one temple.

Sound of a person clearing their throat. There was a bald man at the counter. He was holding A.'s camera.

"Fifty."

"Fifty?"

The bald man waggled the camera.

"Fifty."

A. took the camera, put it in his bag and walked out into the fog. On High Holborn, there was a one-pound coin lying on the pavement. A. picked it up. On Great Russell Street there was chestnut vendor outside the British Museum. A. bought a bag of chestnuts with the coin. He carried them to Southampton Row and ate them, sitting on the step of a disused bank doorway. A woman muffled in a pink scarf glanced at him as she went south. He threw the shells to a pigeon. Each peck sent a curved husk piece spinning on the pavement. A. stood up and brushed his clothes.

He went down Kingsway to Aldwych. The fog muffled traffic sound. On the pavement next to the London

THE NAKED SPUR

School of Economics, two young women were talking with American accents. The draymen were delivering to "The Mitre" off Fleet Street. A. walked down to the Thames. The south bank was hidden. Barges were plying the river, shapes moved. On one a figure stood at the bow of a barge propelled by a tug. The tug sounded its horn.

A. began to shiver. He found some steps and huddled in his jacket. Figures descended the steps, becoming more solid then dissolving as they descended to the river path. A.'s head was down. He heard footsteps. Oxfords, brogues, white trainers, black leather shoes, workman's boots, black leather shoes, black leather shoes. His eyes closed. Later, when footsteps paused, he opened them. A figure, indistinct in the fog, was below him on the stairs. The figure was stationary, twisted round to observe him. A. unfolded his arms and raised his head. After a moment, the figure walked away.

(75)

"Seriously, you'll think I'm pulling a fast one on you but I swear…"

Mack laughed. It sounded as though he was shaking his head.

"I put my key in the lock and the thing snapped. It snapped right there in my hand. Apparently that happens a fair bit with vintage Porsches. Metal fatigue. Christ, well as long as it's only the keys not the drive shaft. Anyway, locksmiths would charge me half the value of the car to come out and change the locks on a Sunday night. No, sorry, man. Tuesday – no, Wednesday at the soonest. Jinxed, I tell you. But we're getting there."

(76)

Standing on Creek Road looking through the window of a second-hand clothes and costume-hire shop was Elizabeth. She was wearing a beret and an overcoat. She was leaning towards the glass. When the traffic lights had changed to red and A. had made his way through the crush of people, the pavement was empty and the shop closed.

(77)

The woman in spectacles placed a printout on the desk.

"This is your job-search restart interview. It will take place on Tuesday the twenty-sixth of November at ten minutes past eleven. It's with Andy Chang. When you arrive go to the desk and hand in this letter. You must arrive ten minutes early, that's eleven o'clock sharp. Bring this letter and a CV. Do you have a CV? If you don't, Andy can help you write one. Okay. So, this letter, a copy of your CV—make sure it's up to date—and any other documents relating to your claim. If you have letters from employers regarding your applications, bring those too. We need evidence that you've been actively seeking employment for the period of your claim. If you can't provide evidence then your claim may be affected. If we have reason to believe that you are not actively seeking work then your claim may be affected. If you can't attend this interview because of sickness, family crisis or court appearance, then you must let us know in advance. In that case, your interview will be rescheduled. If you have a job interview then you should go to that. Again, let us know that you won't be attending the interview here and we'll reschedule it. If you are late or fail to attend the interview then your payments may be affected and your claim suspended. This interview is mandatory. Because it's on your usual signing day, Andy will sign you during the interview. You won't have to come in again later that day to sign. Do you understand? Do you have any questions? Please sign here. This is to confirm you've received the invitation letter for the job search restart interview. Okay. If you'd like to take a seat over there, one of my colleagues will call you over to sign as usual."

(78)

"I can't make Tuesday," said A. "Something's come up."

"I'm glad you phoned. I can't do Tuesday either. I have to go to Helsinki to do this pitch. It's a bitch. Anyway, Dahlia said she's done some work on the brochure. She's tinkered with the wording. I think you'll like it. She'd changed the typeface too. It's called… I don't remember. You'd know it. You appreciate those points. She's pleased with it. But don't phone her. She's a bit stressed at work. I think her boss is getting her to work overtime. Whatever. I'll tell you what, how about you phone me when I get back from Helsinki on Thursday and we'll set up a meeting for all three of us?

"How's the painting?"

"Coming on."

"Okay. I've got to go. Someone's just come in. Sorry

about Tuesday but it sounds like you have stuff going on too. Catch you Thursday."

"Thursday."

(79)

A. reached into the bag and withdrew a tube of paint. The label read "Artist's Gouache". He upended the bag over the bed, then spread the articles over the cover. Two tubes of gouache paint, plywood wedges, pencils, pencil shavings, an eraser, a till receipt rolled into a ball. He stared down.

A. moved the contents of a shelf, then heaped every item on the bookcases on the bed. He picked up armfuls of paper from the armchair, unfolded newspapers, shook them over the bed. A couple of pens fell on to the pile. He removed the armchair's cushions. He tipped out cardboard boxes, opened drawers, shifted the bed away from the wall. On his hands and knees, he swept the narrow gap beneath the bed with a ruler, then the space below the chest of drawers.

From a bag of rubbish, A. retrieved a capless tube of titanium-white oil paint. The tube was wrinkled and curled. From the nozzle, A. wiped off the dusty tip of the extruded paint. He squeezed it on to the saucer. He put the tube on the floor and crushed it under a boot. He added to the dab on the saucer. The slenderest brush was inserted in the nozzle and probed until nothing further was extracted.

He tossed the tube back into the rubbish.

THE NAKED SPUR

(80)

"Good morning."

"Good morning."

"As you'll know by now, this is your mandatory job search restart interview. That means it's compulsory. Everyone gets one of these at this stage in their claim, so there's nothing to worry about. We're not after you in particular for any reason. This meeting is just so we can find out what you've been doing for work and see if we can help by revising your jobseeker's agreement. Perhaps we might need to widen your specified job types in order to give you a better chance of finding work. Now, I see you've got down here proofreading, paralegal administration and general clerical. Have you had any luck in those areas?"

"No."

"No interviews?"

"No."

"Okay. Have you considered secretarial work?"

"I've never done that."

"What's your typing speed?"

"Low."

"Can you touch type?"

"No."

"Have you ever done audio typing?"

"No."

"Have you ever operated a switchboard?"

"No."

"Have you ever worked on reception?"

"No."

"Okay. Well, we can add secretarial to the list anyway. They'll ask you these questions if you get to interview stage. Now, I see you don't have a mobile telephone number listed on your personal screen. Do you have a mobile phone?"

"No."

"And you don't have access to the Internet at home?"

"No."

"It says on the computer that you don't have a car. So, you're looking for work near public transport. Now, at the moment it says you are limiting your search to places within forty-five minutes radius of where you live. I think we should extend that to travel time of up to ninety minutes from where you live. How does that sound?"

"Okay."

"It says on your jobseeker's agreement that you check the papers, visit and telephone places and write letters to employers. Is that correct?"

"Yes."

"And it says that you will contact two employers a week. I think because you're not having any success that perhaps you should try three per week from now on. How does that sound?"

"Okay."

"You realise that because you've agreed to these conditions as part of your agreement that if you don't comply with any aspect then your claim may be affected and payments suspended or stopped? I've updated your agreement and it's printing now. Now, you're quite happy with that? I'll ask you to sign both copies. One is for you, the other we keep. Okay. Now, if you'd like to sign your form as usual. Thank you."

(81)

By the parking-ticket machine were a couple of coins. A. picked them up.

He entered the yard and went to the skip. The attendant was looking under the engine of a car with another man. A. climbed the movable set of stairs and jumped inside the skip. There was a cooker, a microwave oven, a toaster, rolls of carpet, a snapped wicker carpet beater. A cardboard box contained CDs. A. picked out the least damaged and put them in his bag. A scattering of cutlery included a silver-plated cake slice and bone-handled carving knife. A box full of smashed ornamental glass contained a couple of intact ceramic horses. He spread a bag of clothes on the rubbish and searched the garments. In the pocket of a tweed jacket riddled with moth-holes he found a ten-shilling note.

A. climbed out and walked to the station.

A coin-and-stamp seller on St Martin's Lane bought the ten-shilling note. In Camden Market, A. sold the other items to the owners of a junk stall and a second-hand-record dealer.

(82)

"Yeah. The thing is, next week isn't so good. I'm producing this advert and it's a mother-fucking monster that's eating all my time. It's eating my life. We're going into post-production next week. I just can't do next week but we can sort this out on the phone. There isn't so much to talk about. Now I'm working with Georgette, things are moving much faster. She's a natural PR person so she can see all the angles I miss. Dahlia's kind of taking a back seat now. She talked to me and she's had problems at work. Nothing serious but it stresses her out. She's fine about Georgette handling the marketing side. To be honest, once Dahlia went cold on the photography side, all she was doing was tinkering with the brochure and if we're going in with Heliotrope X, the company will deal with that. It's got staff that handle brochures and promo material full time. And the idea of Dahlia taking Polaroids was a fun idea but it would have been a nightmare in practice. It's worked out for the best. The shop will be the point of contact for clients, so there's no need for Dahlia to go round bars with a box of slides. This new approach kind of takes a bit of the mystery and secrecy out of it but it'll be better business. You'll see. People will feel more secure about commissioning through the shop than handing over money and Polaroids to some girl they met in a bar when they were drunk. Things will get done quicker. The shop's open regular hours. It doesn't go off sick or go on holiday or have a quiet night at the cinema or get drunk and have a hangover the next day. You won't have to call up Dahlia and ask her, did you do this, did you do that, can you get me that money, did you put the photographs in the post. I think the responsibility was getting to her. The idea that your livelihood was dependent on the Naked Spur was worrying her. She wants to do the right thing. She didn't want to let you down, that's why she didn't say anything earlier. I kind of got it out of her. So, Dahlia's kind of jumped ship. But at least you know how things stand. So, you see, there wasn't the need for us to get together with Dahlia. That was a reason I was putting it off, so I could talk things through with her. We can go full speed ahead with the meeting with Heliotrope X. Just me and Georgette. I can't see a problem."

(83)

A. climbed into the skip. Tiles crackled under his boots. He stepped over to bags of wallpaper strips and plastic sacks of rubble. He hefted sacks from a corner to reveal a chair. The back was loose. When a leg came away in A.'s hands, he tossed it to one side. A tall lamp leaned in a corner. A. moved away the rubble and lifted the lamp. The plug had been cut from the textile-wound cable. He lifted it over the side and put it on the pavement. A couple of girls in crop tops and miniskirts waiting at the bus stop watched him. They were eating kebabs. The glitter on their cheeks sparkled in the streetlamp light.

By some paint tubs filled with rancid water, A. found a steel toast rack and a box with a broken clasp. He brushed plaster dust off the box. Inside was a set of silver-plated fish cutlery. A. did not try to extract a plastic chair with a cracked back. Under a mattress with springs poking through the cloth were the smashed remains of a ceramic basin. A. raised objects out of the dark to look at them in orange light. A hardware-store bag filled with food wrappers and empty drinks cans. Decorator's brushes solid with emulsion.

A car with tinted windows, pulsing bass and ultraviolet lights underneath ran a red light at the deserted junction between Blackheath Hill and Greenwich South Street. A mini-cab waited outside the off-licence until a man emerged with two bottles of beer and climbed into the car.

A. cut his hands trying to free a brass curtain rod attached to a velvet curtain. Half-cleared, the rod proved to be bent. There were pipe fittings coated with layers of gloss paint, which A. dropped back on to the debris. He split some black plastic sacks. Garden waste. Household refuse. Clothes. Lengths of old wiring, strands of wallpaper attached. A bag of books A. carried out of the skip. As he climbed out, a point of iron ripped a 'V' in his jeans.

A. carried the bag to an unlit alley where he put it next to an abandoned washing machine. He went back to the skip and slipped the cutlery case inside his shirt and carried the lamp and toast rack to the house, where he put them in the garden. Then he returned to the junction and collected the books, gripping the tear in the plastic sack with his fists. He clutched the bag to his body ascending the stairs. A. looked at his watch. It read ten minutes past two in the morning.

(84)

"So these are your acquisitions."

Ibrahim watched A. wiping the lamp with a dishcloth. A. was sitting on the doorstep of the garden door.

"I saw them this morning and I thought that somebody had broken into a house and had stolen these and hidden them in our garden. Then I thought, no, they're not worth anything. Who would steal these? But then I wondered how they got there. Ah, so they're yours?"

"Yes."

A. began to attach a plug to the lamp cable.

"And now I guess you're going to sell them, right?"

"Yes, at the second-hand market in Greenwich."

"Good thinking. People throw out stuff like this and only on the corner there's someone selling exactly the same sort of stuff, sometimes not as good, for money. You wouldn't believe it. There's money in it and I'm glad some of it's going your way. By the way, Elsa's driving up to the supermarket this afternoon. Do you want anything?"

"No, thank you."

"If you're trying to save money, I think you're right. They're not so cheap at that supermarket but they do things you can't get on Trafalgar Road. But you live a simple life. You are a man of simple tastes. I've noticed that about you. I'm pretty much the same actually. I think it's a male thing. Or maybe not. I don't know." Ibrahim laughed and said, "Elsa says I've been reading too much Updike. She says he's a misogynist. Maybe she's right but it doesn't make him not worth reading, don't you think?"

That afternoon, A. carried the objects to West Greenwich and got ten pounds each for the lamp and the cutlery set and two-pound coins for the toast rack. The first bookshop he went to refused the paperbacks that A. took out of his rucksack. A second dealer selected a pile and paid him ten pounds for them. A. took the remainder to a charity shop and walked back to the house where Elsa was unpacking her bags of shopping.

(85)

"Here's the pitch.

"Heliotrope X stock Naked Spur brochures and act as a contact point for customers. They will be the exclusive outlet for this service. They will take thirty percent of transactions as commission and they will handle the banking aspect. The brochures will be designed in co-operation with the company's publicity department and checked by the company's solicitors. The Naked Spur service will be included in their promotional literature. Brochures could be given to customers with their purchases in their bags. They could do mailouts. We'd have to talk about that. The Naked Spur would be on their website. The prices we'd have to work with them on. They would have final say but they'd listen to us.

"I talked it through with Georgette. She thinks they could go with this. We're meeting with the manager next Thursday. It's in the diary. It's happening.

"Hang in there. This is going to happen. This is going to be big.

"Now, what I need from you is—"

(86)

A. put a bag on the lobby table and Mack took out the paintings. One was of a slender female torso with a pendant. The second was of a woman lying on her back on carpet. Her brassiere was pulled down to reveal tops

THE NAKED SPUR

of her nipple. At the bottom of the picture were the ends of two chair legs.

Out of his black bag, A. took a roll of brown paper, string, a bar of red sealing wax, the brass seal and a lighter. He cut a strip of paper and a short length of string. He folded the paper to make a join and laid the string over it. He sat down and screwed the brass seal to its handle. He looked at the orientation of the script on the seal and put it directly in front of him. He moved a cup of water close. The blonde girl from reception, who was carrying a stack of computer discs through the lobby, stopped to watch.

A. held the bar of wax at one end and melted the other over the lighter flame, the flame set on high. The wax dripped off the inverted end over where the paper join and the string met. When a coin-size drop of molten wax had collected, A. dropped the bar hot end first into the water, picked up the seal and pressed it into the molten wax. He kept it pressed for five seconds then lifted it, holding the paper to the table. The seal came up from the wax cleanly, leaving its mark clear and the seal wax free. The join and the string were connected by the blob of wax. A. blew on the wax and handed the paper to Mack, who nodded.

"Got it."

(87)

There was a coin in the chute. A. retracted the piece of rigid plastic binding, crimped it and reinserted it into the machine. A member of staff was moving through the concourse towards him. The coin clattered in the drawer. A. flicked open the drawer, retrieved the coin and pocketed it with the binding, walking to the exit.

A train pulled up at the platform and A. boarded it. When the train terminated at Bank, A. spent a few seconds scanning the platform tiles after the passengers had dispersed. There was a one-way ticket on a seat. A. discarded it and headed to the ticket hall.

He found a couple of coins at the foot of the escalator. The ticket barriers were busy. A man inserted a ticket in a barrier. When the flaps opened to allow him to pass, A. pushed up behind and followed him through.

"Hey!"

A. had moved into the crowd. The trays in the ticket vending machines were coinless. By the photo booth, A. found an unused phone card still in its plastic wrapping. The payphones yielded a couple of coins.

Out of the station and up Prince's Street, there was a newspaper vendor facing the Bank of England on the corner with Gresham Street. A. stepped on to the road and studied the kerb. There was a coin which had been depressed into the asphalt. A. couldn't dislodge it. The newspaper vendor laughed.

He worked his way up to Moorgate station, getting nothing from the returned-coin slots of payphones. The ticket machines in Moorgate had sixty pence in coins. The payphone in the Barbican he went to had nothing.

A stamp dispenser in Liverpool Street had a book of first-class stamps in its slot. More of the public telephones here were card operated. The snack-dispensing machines on Liverpool Street station were coinless or out of order. He jumped the barrier and took a train to

THE NAKED SPUR

East London, changing back for a central-bound train at the first stop.

In a pub on Brewer Street, A. paid for a tomato juice with a counterfeit pound coin and a Bermudan fifty-pence coin. There were coins in the cigarette machine but he couldn't work them loose. Whenever the barmaid came to the cash till, she looked over at him. He had his body pressed against the machine, concealing the hand that held the plastic loop. He found a seat at the back of the pub. From the gap between the seats and backs of benches there he got a cigarette lighter and a couple of bronze coins. The condom machine in the toilets snagged his loop and he couldn't free it. With his pocket knife he cut himself a new length from the spare he had in his pocket.

Someone had set up the payphones on Oxford Street. Each coin slot had a coin in it. The coin-feed buttons had been glued closed. Coins inserted in the narrow slot could not drop into the machine nor be extracted with fingers. In a telephone box, A. got out his knife. He took chewing gum out of his mouth and bit a tiny part from the ball. The small piece of gum he pressed on to the tip of his knife. He then slipped the tip into the coin slot and drew out the recessed coin which adhered to the gum. He collected three pounds and twenty pence from machines on the north pavement of Oxford Street and over five pounds from the south side.

He walked down Duke Street, St. James. He stopped outside a window. In the display were a selection of large hardback folios in cellophane wrappers. The sign read "Simms Reed Rare Bookshop". A. went to Green

Park. Entrances to the underground station were taped over, police standing by. On steps down to the station, two men in blue underground staff uniforms were talking.

"—one under."

They laughed, hands in pockets.

A. walked up New Bond Street, passed fashion boutiques, jewellers and restaurants. He walked down Cork Street. Men in suits hurried by art galleries. A taxi idled outside a framers.

Bloomsbury Square, Russell Square, Cavendish Square, Manchester Square, Portman Square and back again. In a pub on Tottenham Court Road, A. sprang a condom dispenser in the toilet. The slot filled with coins which rolled across the tiles when he opened the flap. One rolled under the door of an occupied cubicle. The lock of the door turned and A. stopped collecting coins from the floor and left the pub.

It was twilight.

When he checked the payphones of Oxford Street, he found the coin slots had been emptied before he got there.

He walked through Chinatown. In windows clouded with condensation, browned ducks turned on rotisseries. Pedestrians spilled from the pavements into the roads, mingling with rickshaws and taxis.

In "Pitcher & Piano" on William IV Street, A. found a ten-pound note under a table. He used it to pay for a drink and persuaded the barmaid that she had given him the wrong change and that he had given her a twenty. While she was talking to the manager, they

THE NAKED SPUR

looked at him. A. walked out, leaving his glass half full.

In Charing Cross station, a drunk scattered a pocketful of change by a ticket booth. A. stepped on a coin and stood still, checking his watch against the station clock. The drunk retrieved his coins and stood looking at A. A. looked at his watch. The drunk went to the desk and paid for a ticket. A. bent to tie his bootlace and slipped the coin between his fingers as he did so.

At Greenwich station, A.'s last piece of binding snagged in the parking-ticket machine and he walked home.

(88)

A. emptied the turpentine bottle into the jar and washed his brushes. He dried them and placed them handle down in a jar on the bookshelf. In the painting, a woman was bending over on a bed, face concealed. A. put the magazine into a box, arched his back and sat on the bed.

He rubbed his eyes.

There was a painting on the armchair. The head of the painted figure had been defaced with a slash of white paint.

A. looked at it, hands held between his knees.

He went to his jacket hanging from the door and got his pocket knife, unfolded the blade and went to the armchair. Grasping the stretcher with a hand, he cut down. The knife skated over the figure's torso. When the knife went through the linen it made a popping sound. A. cut a wedge out of the centre of the canvas. The swatch came free, loose thread tugging at the remainder. The figure's midriff was on the flap of linen in A.'s fist. He looked at it then dropped it on the floor.

(89)

The cigarette machine on the stairs dumped coins in the returned-coins chute. A. couldn't get the flap open. A man descended the stairs and paused under the sign marked "Gents". He looked at A., A. looked back. The man entered the toilets and A. thumped the machine. Coins clinked dully. The binding did not move when A. pulled it.

A. took out his knife and worked it at the side of the coin guard. The guard held. The knife jumped out of the crack, left a looping scratch on the machine fascia and sank into A.'s hand. The white comma in his skin began to fill with blood.

Wadding his hand with tissues, A. folded his knife and left via the fire exit that had been chocked open. A girl in an apron was smoking in the alley. She glanced at A.'s hand then looked away.

In Soho market, A. got another length of binding from a bundle of packing material.

An obstruction had been placed in the returned-coins chute of a chocolate dispenser on one of the underground platforms. A. dislodged it with binding and coins fell to the tray. A. took the coins and found a folded travel card among them.

He emptied the coin slots of Oxford Street payphones and walked north.

On Euston Road, he took a bag from the steps outside a block of flats. On the ramp of an underground car park, he emptied the bag. It contained children's clothes. A. left them scattered on the oil-marked concrete.

Euston station was full of hustlers. A. saw an emaciated black man in a porkpie hat dipping the payphones. In the ticket foyer, all the ticket machines were in use, queues winding out to the concourse. There were a couple of coins kicked under baskets of crisp packets at a convenience store but it was crowded. A security guard leaned on a column, chewing a toothpick.

A. dropped the wad of tissue into a bin in Tavistock Square. The cut was dry. The rain had stopped.

At a sandwich bar near Strand, A. picked puffs of lint and a twenty-pence coin from the seat-upholstery gap. When the girl at the counter bent over the dish-washing machine, A. left through a cloud of steam without paying for his coffee.

He caught a train out of Charing Cross station. A one-pound coin had lodged between two parts of a radiator cover. It was wedged firm. Trying to pry it out, A. broke off the knife's tip. The train drew into a station. He alighted on the Kent-bound platform of Westcombe Park. He went to the opposite platform and waited.

He was the only person there. The payphone had been jammed. A. retrieved the coin lodged in the slot using a match. The ticket-vending machine was broken.

He read all the posters and timetables and sat on a bench. It was getting dark.

In Silvertown was a pair of tall chimneys. They were concrete. Each had a red light at its tip. The lights flashed at almost the same interval. They were slightly out of unison. As A. watched, the flashing of the two diverged further until they flashed alternately. As minutes passed, the flashing began to converge gradually. Eventually, they blinked in synchronicity before slipping out of phase.

A train approached the platform, casting light on the banks beside the tracks as it travelled.

On a seat in the carriage was a wallet. Inside was a photograph of smiling girl wearing sunglasses. A. took out the banknotes, pulled his shirt sleeves over his hands and wiped the wallet all over with the material before jamming the wallet behind a seat.

In East Greenwich, A. found a black girl wearing a silver puffa jacket and chewing juicy-fruit flavour gum who gave him a blowjob for the notes he had found in the wallet. Afterwards he asked her how old she was. She paused. "Eighteen," she said with a smile.

When he got home, Elsa was talking on the telephone, television on mute. The ginger cat in the hallway blinked. Upstairs, Ibrahim was in the bathroom brushing his teeth, shirt unbuttoned. He waved at A. A. waved back.

(90)

"My God! What happened to your face? Are you all right? What happened?"

A. paused on the staircase. Elsa was standing at the kitchen doorway. There was a grater in her hand.

"I fell over."

"What is it? Is it A.?"

THE NAKED SPUR

Ibrahim emerged from the living room, holding a copy of The New Yorker. A game show was on the television in the background.

"Oh boy! Wow. You're going to have a black eye tomorrow."

"Hold on," Elsa disappeared into the kitchen. The freezer door opened and closed. "Have this." She handed him a bag of frozen peas. A. placed it over his cheek.

With his door shut, A. emptied his pockets of coins. The collection made a depression in the duvet. He went to the bathroom and put a piece of plastic binding from his jacket into the wicker bin, pushing it deep into tissue-paper flowers and cotton swabs. He paused to look at his face in the shaving mirror, not removing the bag. He left, switching the light off after him.

(91)

"They like it. They're going with it. The manager we talked to was fascinated by the whole Naked Spur spiel. We were playing up the business aspect but even so, she liked the canvases and the slides with the viewer that we showed her. So, she's going to her boss, the owner of Heliotrope X, and they're going to chew it over and get back to us.

"The best thing is for us to go ahead with the launch of The Naked Spur as a separate project. They'll watch how it goes. Georgette can write about the launch party for a magazine and add a couple of your pics to the spread. Once we have some client response, Heliotrope X will decide on whether to take it up. I think they want to see how it will operate in practice before they commit.

"It was a masterstroke to wrap your canvases in brown paper with string and wax seals. She was really taken with the presentation aspect and the fact the artist is anonymous. Georgette knows the industry and she could speak this woman's language. I think they know each other already or they've met or something.

"Georgette completely agrees with me about the launch. It should be classy, stressing exclusivity. If we can get some faces in, then there'll be photographers around.

"Georgette's handling more of the launch preparations, or she knows someone, an events organiser. I've got a shoot soon so I have to put in more groundwork for that. But Georgette can find a venue then we can think about what we need. Each venue has its own lighting and furniture for hire. When we know where the launch will be, we'll see what sort of offer the venue can make and what we'll need to hire from other companies. We can work on the size of the banners when we have the dimensions of the venue.

"I know we talked about a December launch in time to catch Christmas commissions but that's not going to happen. I don't think that's a bad thing. It might work to our advantage. We want the launch to be perfect. Heliotrope X won't take up The Naked Spur if we fuck up the launch. This delay just gives us a chance to prepare better.

"Georgette suggested a launch in February. I don't know how you feel about that. We were looking at February the fourteenth, Valentine's Day. We would use the romance angle to get people interested. Make a play of it in the press release.

"Listen, I know it's a drag it's taken this long, but it looks like we're making progress. From your perspective it looks pretty slow, but it isn't. Trust me."

(92)

A. woke and stared at the ceiling. He went to the kitchen and made breakfast. The clock read twenty-three minutes past eleven. All the rooms were silent apart from the bubbles in the fish tank. A single fish swam back and forth.

A. went to his room. The sheet from the radiator was folded over a stack of canvases under one window. A depleted tube of black paint lay next to the brush jar. The brush bristles were short and dark. The painting saucer resting on a window sill was furred with dust.

A. undressed and climbed under the bedcovers, resting his head on the pillow purple-yellow cheek upwards.

Some light fell under the closed roller blinds. Trains were arriving and departing. Children shouted. Liquid moved in the radiator. It was getting dark.

A. slept.

(93)

Dear Policeman: I am God.

(94)

A. was naked, staring into the shaving mirror. He pivoted the mirror to the magnifying side and squinted at the reflection. He used his fingers to pull open his mouth to reveal his teeth. With the index finger of his right hand, he pressed a canine, fingers of the left hand holding apart the lips. He ran a fingernail over the gum of the upper jaw. He released his lips and watched the lips settle back into position. The mirror steamed over and his reflection disappeared.

A. climbed into the bath and turned off the taps. He lay back, eyes open. From between the blind slats, light shone in bars over the ceiling. Through the open window sounds came. Children's voices, a ball bounced. A male voice speaking Amharic into a mobile phone. Staccato of high heels. The whir and hiss of bicycle wheels.

A. sat up and reached for a small plastic box on the bathtub side. He slid a paper-covered blade out of the razor dispenser. He unfolded the waxed paper and rested the blade between the tips of thumb and index finger of the right hand. Slight pressure flexed the blade.

– ⊠ – ⊠ – ⊠ – ⊠ –

The wrapper was wet and formless in the fingers of his left hand. He let it fall to the floor.

A. brought the razorblade close to his face, looking at the flat side. Then, holding it in the fingers of his right hand he passed the edge over the interior of his left forearm. A thread of red materialised on the skin, fattening, making a bloody drop at its lowest end. The drop did not fall. A. looked at his blood. Then he repeated the act. This parallel line swelled and swooped to the crook of the elbow where it ran a red cable into the bathwater. The water turned pink then opaque. Outside, a wood

THE NAKED SPUR

pigeon was calling. Sound of far-off traffic.

Putting the razorblade next to the taps, A. lifted himself out of the wine-dark water. As he did so, his left hand slipped. He toppled to the floor, a foot kicking over a frosted-glass jar of tangerine-colour bath salts. He lay there.

When the front door banged shut, A. got to his feet. Where he had lain was a curve of red. His left side was covered in bloody water. He pulled the plug in the tub. He took a towel from the rail and pressed it between his left arm and torso. Reaching for another, he slipped.

"Is that you?" Elsa called.

With the second towel, A. smeared blood over the bamboo flooring.

"You can't come up."

"What? What did you say?"

The water had drained from the tub. A. sprayed away the pinkness with the shower head.

"You can't come up. It's a surprise."

He rubbed around the plug hole with a swatch of toilet paper. He put it with the razorblade in the bin, covering them with tissue paper and cotton buds. He brushed dry crystals back into the jar and tipped wet ones, along with the razorblade's paper wrapper, into the toilet bowl. He wiped the floor with damp toilet paper, then flushed the toilet.

"Can I come up yet?"

"In a minute."

He left the bathroom and stuffed the bloody towels into the rubbish sack in his room. He picked up a framed painting of a man in a suit and left it on the landing. He left the door open and climbed into bed.

"Can I come up?"

"Yes."

Elsa appeared at the top of the stairs. She stopped.

"Is this for me?"

"Yes."

"Thank you. It's lovely."

She held the painting.

"How thoughtful of you. Have you done anything today?"

"I was cleaning the bathroom, but I didn't finish it. I got tired."

"It could do with a good clean."

Elsa was at his door looking at him. On the laminate floor between them was a smear of blood.

"I had to throw away your towels. I spilled bleach on them. Sorry."

"I was going to buy new ones anyway. Never mind. You're okay?"

"Yes."

"You're sure? You look a bit pale."

"I'm okay."

"Thank you for the painting. Is there anything I can do for you? Can I get you anything?"

"Could you close the door? I'm a bit sleepy."

"Okay. Sleep tight."

She closed the door. From the station platform came the sound of footsteps. A. lay still.

(95)

The ATM winked a light and ejected the card. A. took it

THE NAKED SPUR

and dropped it through a street grating outside St Alfege Church. He wove through the stationary vehicles. He passed the bookmakers, the bakers, the sandwich-makers, the restaurant, the fish-and-chip shop, the teashop, the clothes shop, the fast-food chain restaurant, the Mexican-theme bar and turned up Creek Road. He crossed the road outside a ruined pub, dodging traffic.

He walked west to Creek Bridge.

The tarmac on the bridge was patched, in places worn to metal. A. faced north over Deptford Creek, feet straddling the gap at the bridge's shallow apex. As lorries drove over, the two halves juddered, the line of light between his boots expanding and contracting.

Behind him, a load of gravel was disgorged into the yard, coughing grit into the air. In front of A., Deptford Creek wound to the Thames. To his left were brick-faced flats with balconies overlooking the river. The Creek was at low tide. A khaki stream meandered between banks of brown, ridged mud. Boat carcases lay in the banks, holding water.

A. reached into his pocket and brought out his knife. The handle was wood, flat, tipped with brass at both ends. He opened the blade. It was worn narrow, notched and spotted with primer. The tip was missing. He held the pocket-knife in a palm then threw it into the Creek. He turned his face away before it landed.

(96)

All the lights downstairs were out except for the globe in the kitchen ceiling. Ibrahim was leaning on the edge of the sink. His face was rough with stubble. He was gazing into the dark glass. The cigarette in his fingers was half ash.

"Oh, hi, A.," said Ibrahim.

The ash tip fell into the sink and hissed.

"I was just--"

He drifted off, eyes unfocused.

"I was just, you know, having a smoke."

A. nodded and took a carton of milk from the refrigerator.

"I'm finding it a little difficult to adjust. My sleep patterns—"

Ibrahim cleared his throat. He stared blankly at the window.

"Now it's dark."

Silence.

"Night always used to be my time. I worked. I read."

He brought the cigarette to his lips. The end burned orange.

"Yeah."

Silence.

"Funny."

Smoky breath.

"Yeah."

Silence.

"I always was a night bird but without my routine--"

Cough. Pause.

"It's difficult. I need some kip. I thought having a smoke might help but, you know, it doesn't help so much."

Pause.

"It used to help."

THE NAKED SPUR

Pause.

"I don't know any more."

Ibrahim studied his cigarette. A. poured milk into a glass. Ibrahim turned his head at the sound. His eyes were bloodshot.

"Yeah, maybe less smoke, more milk."

A. proffered him the glass. Ibrahim shook his head slightly, smiling.

"It's too late for that."

He searched for the ashtray and stubbed out his cigarette. A. paused in the hallway.

"Goodnight, Ib."

"Goodnight, A. Sleep well."

"You too, Ib."

The only light on downstairs was the kitchen one, which cast a strut of light over the rush mat by the front door. Framed by the doorway, in a rectangle of light, Ibrahim stood at the sink, staring into the dark night.

(97)

The gallery was crowded. There was smoke in the air. On the gallery walls were rectangular panels of strong colours, not more than two colours on each painting. By the reception desk, a man was handing out drinks. Wineglasses were regimented on a white cloth before him, one third of them filled with white wine, one third with orange juice, one third with water. A. picked up a glass of orange juice and an invitation card from the desk. There was a stack of large exhibition catalogues with plain-card covers and spiral binding. A man handed over a ten-pound note and a five-pound note and the drinks man gave him a catalogue.

By a panel of bright green and Prussian blue, Nelson Nicobar was talking to a man in a suit. The man was nodding. A girl in a patterned dress carrying a catalogue and a photocopied price list wandered over and took the suited man's arm. The man did not divert his attention from Nicobar, who was gesturing with a glass of wine to the far corner of the room.

A short man with a quiff approached the trio and said something. He and Nicobar shook hands. Nicobar made a comment and the group laughed. The short man passed Nicobar a catalogue and a pen. Nicobar asked him a question and leaned forward to catch his reply, then he wrote in the catalogue and signed it. Once he had returned the catalogue back to the man, the woman handed Nicobar her catalogue. Nicobar used the same pen to sign his name. Then he passed the pen to the short man and said something that made them all laugh.

Surrounded by a cluster of people was Agnetha Gold with a small child in her arms. One of the figures was a slight man in designer-label clothes with a loud laugh.

In the centre of the gallery was Damien Cole wearing a linen suit and a T-shirt. He was with two women, one elderly. The younger one was pregnant. He smiled and nodded in A.'s direction. Barry Janus joined them. He adjusted a belt hidden by the swell of his belly. There was paint on his knuckles. A slender girl with heavy mascara and wearing a red dress followed him, a couple of catalogues held against her chest.

A. stepped away.

THE NAKED SPUR

The painting before A. was red on yellow. A grid of red lines covered part of the painting. At the grid edge it had disintegrated into spars and crosses across the surface of the panel, breaking apart across a plain yellow ground. A. moved a pace closer. Between the regular squares of red, yellow paint had wrinkled. The spotlights showed gentle undulations. Contractions had buckled the skin. Where lines had been separated and the underpaint was unobstructed the yellow paint was smoother. Here and there it flowed like water over a pebbled bed, in places thick like lava. The effects were subtle. Close viewing showed seething movement. Graphic firmness gave way to organic textures on close scrutiny.

A. broke away from the painting and went to where Hartley was. He was in a throng of people. A middle-aged man was holding a catalogue steady for him to sign the title page. A couple pressed close together watching Hartley. Loud conversation mixed with laughter. Sound of a mobile telephone ringing. A camera flashed. A. pushed between the figures to reach Hartley.

Hartley smiled at A.

"What do you think?" Hartley asked A.

"It's just right. It's there," A said.

Someone's hand was on Hartley's sleeve. "Adam, Adam." A. leaned towards Hartley and looked him in the eyes.

"Adam, you're the painter."

A. turned into the crowd. The crowd turned into A. Figures came between A. and Hartley. A. made his way to the door and stepped into the night street. He had walked to the first turn in the street when he looked to his hand. He was holding an empty wineglass. He set it on the pavement close to a wall and walked away.

(98)

"I'll hold."

A. was watching a man in green overalls and a workman's jacket. He was scraping ice from the cobblestones between the gateposts of Greenwich Park. A.'s breath fogged the windowpane.

"Hello."

"Hello."

"You called before. Sorry about that. The courier fucked up our delivery. I had to speak to the executive marketing officer of this Finnish bank. The work met the deadline but the disc went to the wrong office. Listen, I haven't had much time for your project since we spoke."

"The launch."

"The thing is I've been tied up with this head-fuck animation and, ah, I haven't had a moment free. Georgette's been picked up by this publishing company in Geneva so she's not actually in the country at the moment."

"What about the Valentine's Day launch?"

There was no answer. Crows in the sky. The man outside straightened and flexed his shoulders.

"Mack?"

"Nothing's been done."

The man bent over his snow shovel.

"It's not going to happen."

THE NAKED SPUR

Pause. A voice was talking in the background at the other end of the line.

"I know this is a big deal for you, but you need someone who can work on this full time. I can't make any promises because I know I can't keep them. Georgette knows some PR agents who could work with you on the launch. I can call her. They can help you set up the project and once it's going Heliotrope X will take over. It's their project now really. They'll take care of the practicalities and publicity. All you have to do is paint. I am sorry for you. Really. Listen, I have to go. There's someone on the other line."

"I understand."

He hung up the telephone and left the box.

When A. passed the man, the man asked him for a light. A. apologised and walked into the white park.

(99)

L. Cornelissen & Son was at 105 Great Russell Street. The name was written in cream and red on the green frontage. On the window were the words "PARIS" and "VIENNA" and decals of medals with the dates "1867", "1873" and "1878". Below a decal of a heraldic device was "Est. 1855". The footplate was of polished brass. Inside, the floorboards were bare. Lamps with plain circular shades hung from the ceiling. The woodwork of the shelves and drawers is dark. On the immediate left upon entering the shop were short shelves of books on art technique and materials. There were sketchbooks of different makes. Sizes and number of pages varied. Pages were of cartridge paper, coloured paper, Ingres paper (white, cream or a selection of tints), watercolour paper of many thicknesses and finishes (rough, not and hot-pressed, in increasing order of smoothness) and handmade papers. Bindings were signature, perforated and ring-bound. Covers were paper, cloth, plastic-coated, card and combinations. Some had cloth spines, ties or ribbon page markers. Suggested uses were sketching, pastel, watercolour and line-and-wash work. Around the corner were racks of art periodicals and postcards of views of the shop. Further along the left wall was an alcove of shelves with sketchpads. Like the sketchbooks, these had many different paper types. Beyond this were shelves dedicated to oil painting. At waist height were rows of paintbrushes with bristles of acrylic, nylon and hog, ox, goat, badger, mink, sable, squirrel, wolf and mongoose hair, handles cream, dark green, brown, blue, varnished and bare wood, each stamped with the maker's name, range and model number. There were brights, fans, filberts, fitches, flats, hakes, liners, mops, riggers, rounds, domed sashes, pointed sashes, signwriters, spotters and swordliners, some long-handled, some with angled heads. Above these were shelves of oil paints in tubes, jars and tins. Brands represented were Winsor & Newton, Daler Rowney, Lucas, Lefranc, Spectrum, Rembrandt and Michael Harding. Next were shelves of lustre powders, silver, bronze and red-bronze. Above these were labelled jars of pigment. Flake white (lead carbonate), titanium white, zinc white, alizarin crimson, coral red, cadmium red, cadmium red deep, cadmium vermilion, cadmium brown, lead red (minium), potters pink, quinacridone magenta, quina-

THE NAKED SPUR

cridone red, quinacridone scarlet, vermilion (imitation), madder root pieces, rose madder, vermilion deep genuine, cadmium yellow lemon, cadmium yellow light, cadmium yellow middle, cadmium yellow deep, cadmium yellow orange, chrome yellow light, chrome yellow middle, chrome yellow orange, cobalt yellow (aureolin), Indian yellow imitation, tartrazine yellow, lemon yellow barium, Naples yellow dark, Naples yellow light, gamboge, lead tin yellow, litharge, orpiment, realgar, cadmium green, chromium oxide, cobalt green deep, cobalt green light, cobalt turquoise (Rinman's green), permanent green, phthalo (monastrel) green, phthalo turquoise, viridian green, terre verte, green earth light, malachite, synthetic malachite, verdigris, Antwerp blue, cerulean blue, cobalt blue, manganese blue, oriental blue, phthalo (monastrel) blue, Prussian blue, ultramarine blue dark, ultramarine blue light, ultramarine blue limewash, azurite, blue verditer, Egyptian blue, lapis lazuli, smalt, indigo blue genuine, indigo blue synthetic, alizarin violet, cobalt violet dark, cobalt violet light, manganese violet, ultramarine violet, caput mortam, Indian red, mars red, mars violet, mars yellow, golden ochre, red ochre, yellow ochre, Pozzuoli red, burnt sienna, raw sienna, translucent orange oxide, translucent red oxide, translucent yellow oxide, burnt umber, raw umber, raw umber greenish, Vandyke brown, Venetian red, burnt green earth, graphite, heavy French black, ivory black, ivory black genuine, lamp black, mars black (iron oxide), spinel black, vine black French, carbon black mogul. On the top shelf were jars of casein (lactic), ammonium carbonate, carrageen moss fine shred, isinglass fine cut (South America), isinglass sturgeon (salianski), parchment clippings, pearl glue, rabbit skin glue, carboxyl methyl cellulose, gesso di Bologna, french chalk, gypsum, precipitate chalk, marble dust, Fuller's earth, plaster of paris, alumina hydrate light, fumed silica, pumice powder, rottenstone pink, rottenstone grey, gum ammoniam, gum arabic Kordofan number one, gum arabic Nigerian number three, gum benzoic, gum copal (Manila), gum elemi, gum mastic, gum sandarac powder, gum sandarac lumps, gum tragacanth pharmaceutical, gum tragacanth industrial, gum damar (origin Indonesia), colophony, dragons blood, dragons blood pieces, ketone resin, powdered rosin fine, shellac button (India), shellac clear de-waxed, shellac lemon (India), shellac orange (India), beeswax bleached pellets, beeswax natural pellets, carnauba wax (grey), carnauba wax (yellow), Japan wax, microcrystalline wax, paraffin wax, bole red, tallow, Vandyke crystals, asphaltum powder, lime putty, crocus powder, chloramine T. Then came solvents, oils, painting media and varnishes: rectified spirit of turpentine, pure gum turpentine, white spirit, larch Venice turpentine, Canada balsam, Strasbourg turpentine, oil of spike, English distilled turpentine, lemon oil, sansodor solvent, quick-drying petroleum, cold-pressed linseed oil, refined linseed oil, stand linseed oil, drying linseed oil, bleached linseed oil, sun-bleached linseed oil, thickened linseed oil, safflower oil, poppy oil, drying poppy oil, walnut oil, black Claude Yvel, Roberson's oil painting medium, Maroger medium, parris marble medium, glaze medium, siccative, impasto medium, Liquin original, Liquin impasto, Liquin fine detail, Liquin light gel, Eliza Turck's Florentine medium, JG Vibert painting medium, colourless painting medium, Flemish siccative, Flemish medium, Duroziez Harlem drying medium, Venetian medium, crystal medium, brown constrai dryer, copal dryer, solution of beeswax in white spirit, Megilp, Mussini Painting Medium Number One, Mussini Painting Medium Number Two, Mussini Painting Medium Three, tempera gel, Malgel drying retarder, drying accelerator, translucent gel, rapid medium, damar varnish, picture mastic varnish, picture varnish (matt), picture varnish (gloss), amber varnish, ceronis picture varnish, copal picture varnish, vernis a retoucher. There were cans of aerosol varnishes. Wooden racks held thick bars of oil pastel. There were bags of gesso powder and tubs and tins of primer. On the shelves furthest the back walls were printmaking materials. In a case were etching needles, roulettes, burnishers, scrapers, double-draw scrapers, burins, mezzotint rockers, awls, gouges and sharpening stones. There were engraver's leather sandbags, glass mullers, pestles and mortars, leather dabbers, rolls of scrim, etching-press blankets, discs of wax, tapers, aquatint resin, tins of Rhind's etching varnish and copperplate oil, jars of nitric and sulphuric acid, lithographic crayons, crayon holders, pin vices, zinc plates and tins, tubs and tubes of ink in different colours for intaglio and lithographic printing. There were glossy slabs of lithographic stone. On the shelves and in cupboards samples of rollers with polyurethane rollers black, translucent green and clear rested on their backs. There were wooden-handled knives and spatulas. These continued along the back wall. There were linoleum tiles and lino knives, craft knives, scalpel handles and blades, scissors and tubes of ink for linocut and woodcut printing (oil- and water-based). High on the back wall were silkscreen meshes on sturdy frames and below were tubs of silkscreen ink and extender. At the back in an alcove were shelves with stretched canvases at the top, each standing on its side. Prices were written on the plastic covers in marker pen. On a freestanding set of drawers and shelves were inks, Indian, Chinese, ox gall, sepia and coloured. There were sets for Chinese calligraphy, including brushes, disc of ink, china bowl and muller in a cloth-covered box. There were quills, bamboo pens, nib holders and little drawers full of nibs, as well as sticks of sealing wax red and black, with and without wicks. There were watercolour paintings in tubes and wrapped cubes, boxes containing tubes and dry blocks, jars of watercolour medium, natural sponges, ceramic palettes, steel dishes with clips, steel clips, spray tubes, brush holders, jars, bottles, rulers, set squares, drawing pins, rolls of tape, boxes of daylight bulbs, table easels, mahl sticks and palettes, one piece and folding, oval, rectangular and shaped. From the ceiling hung a folding canvas-seated stool. Lower were a series of thin, wide drawers with slots cut into foam inside them. Inserted in the slots were rows of pastels. The pastels were thick at the middle, tapering to the ends, Sennelier paper bands ringing them, dusty cigars in every colour. In the corner were some easels. There were folios at the back of the right wall, in card and plastic plain and patterned, with rigid spines, ring binders, zips and ribbon ties. There were racks of loose paper sheets. There were racks of gouache in tubes and acrylic paint in tubes and jars. A display of palette knives stood on a shallow shelf, to an ovoid palette eye hooks had been affixed and from each hung the knives. To its right was a wire stand of inks and rising above was an array of brushes hanging from hooks. On the right wall, facing the left wall with the brushes, oil paint and pigment jars, were trays of paper in large sheets for watercolour, printmaking, drawing, pastel and craft. There was Ingres paper, rice paper, mulberry paper, blotting paper, tracing paper, tissue paper, Japanese paper, coloured paper, card of different kinds, archival mounting card. Below this were racks of pencils, graphite sticks, coloured pencils, water-soluble pencils, chinagraph pencils, charcoals sticks, chalks, erasers and pencil sharpeners and holders. The cash till was close to the window against the right-hand wall, next to a descending staircase. Around it were drawers going to above head height, each numbered. Here there was specialist decorating paraphernalia and materials for leafing gold and silver, skins, beaters, grounds, blades, awls and punches, jars and tins of Vulpex, laponite, greygate, paraloid resin, paraloid resin solution, ketone resin, acetone and xylene. There was a glass case with fans of brushes and hooks with brown paper bags hanging from them. Near the ceiling were the words "L. CORNELISSEN & SON ARTIST'S COLOURMEN EST. 1855" and a clock and a barometer. Around the cash till counter were cases with arrays of pencils and palette knives. On the counter was an artist's perspective frame.

In the window were a series of wooden artist's mannequins posed sequentially jumping, a ball-jointed hand and an articulated model horse.

(100)

It was snowing. It fell heavily and clung to the leaves and the overhead wires. It was starting to collect on the railway tracks. In the yard, two Vietnamese girls played gloveless, flakes catching in their dark hair. They threw handfuls of snow into the air. A train arrived at the London-bound platform. Figures left shelters to board the train. One of the girls gripped the chain-link fence beside the platform and shook it. Lines of snow were dislodged and caught in the wind which broke them into pieces, lifted the particles high and dispersed them. The train pulled out of the station. A gust stirred snow from the leylandii.

The girls were gone.